"Here are the areas of significant damage. The most serious of them is this one here," he said, pointing to the base of the starboard warp nacelle pylon, where it met the main hull of the engineering section. He reached over and pressed a button, and the image switched to a closer view of that area. "The blow we took there had enough force to send the whole structure vibrating, riddling it with microfractures."

Kirk frowned as he looked from the schematic to Scott. "But we will be able to make the necessary repairs, yes?"

Scott involuntarily grimaced as he said, "To a degree, yes, sir."

"To what 'degree'?" the captain asked.

"Any repairs our crew would be able to make would only be temporary ones, at best. We just don't have the equipment or matériel to do more than that on our own."

"So, these six weeks of repair you describe," said Kirk, frustration coloring his tone, "they would only be so that we could get back to Federation space, in order to get more repairs."

"I'm afraid so, sir. And, I'm afraid there's more."

Kirk pressed his fingertips to his temple. "Do I want to know?" he asked.

The engineer wished he could answer "no," but of course the captain needed to know the full extent of their situation. "Because of the nature of the temporary repairs, we'd be limited to the low end of the warp scale. The higher our velocity, the greater the risk to the ship."

"How long would it then take to get to the nearest Starfleet facility?" the captain asked.

"We would be_____ti-mately ten weeks.'

"Four months

STAR TREK®

THE ORIGINAL SERIES

THE SHOCKS OF ADVERSITY

William Leisner

Based upon *Star Trek*
created by Gene Roddenberry

POCKET BOOKS
New York • London • Toronto • Sydney
New Delhi • Wezonvu

Pocket Books
A Division of Simon & Schuster, Inc.
1230 Avenue of the Americas
New York, NY 10020

This book is a work of fiction. Names, characters, places, and incidents either are products of the author's imagination or are used fictitiously. Any resemblance to actual events or locales or persons, living or dead, is entirely coincidental.

First Pocket Books paperback edition June 2013

POCKET and colophon are registered trademarks of Simon & Schuster, Inc.

For information about special discounts for bulk purchases, please contact Simon & Schuster Special Sales at 1-866-506-1949 or business@simonandschuster.com.

The Simon & Schuster Speakers Bureau can bring authors to your live event. For more information or to book an event, contact the Simon & Schuster Speakers Bureau at 1-866-248-3049 or visit our website at www.simonspeakers.com.

Manufactured in the United States of America

10 9 8 7 6 5 4 3 2 1

ISBN 978-1-4767-2240-5
ISBN 978-1-4767-2242-9 (ebook)

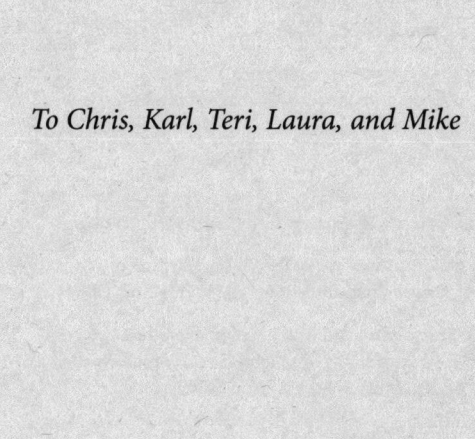

To Chris, Karl, Teri, Laura, and Mike

"Be courteous to all, but intimate with few, and let those few be well tried before you give them your confidence. True friendship is a plant of slow growth, and must undergo and withstand the shocks of adversity before it is entitled to the appellation."

—George Washington

One

The deck fell out from under James Kirk's feet, and for a moment he was left suspended weightless in midair.

In the next instant, the ship's artificial gravity field reasserted itself, and he hit the gymnasium floor with a loud *whoomph*. Despite the padding that covered the deck underneath him, his head struck hard enough to send a barrage of shooting stars streaming across his field of vision. *Well, I asked for that*, he silently reprimanded himself.

"Captain!" As the shooting stars began to clear away, he saw Lieutenant Joseph D'Abruzzo bent over him, wearing a look of worry on his young face. "Are you all right, sir?"

"Oh, just fine," Kirk replied, trying to sound as though he hadn't just had the wind forced out of him. "Why do you ask?"

He raised his right hand up toward D'Abruzzo, who grasped Kirk's hand and helped pull him back up onto his stocking feet. "I am sorry, sir. I didn't mean to throw you that hard, really."

"Don't apologize, Mister D'Abruzzo," Kirk told the younger man. He adjusted the shoulders of his bright orange judo *gi*, which matched the one worn by the lieutenant. "I invited you to be my sparring partner specifically because I knew you would challenge me." D'Abruzzo had been the captain of the Starfleet Academy martial arts team, and had been instrumental in leading them to the United Earth Intercollegiate Championship in his graduating year. "The last thing I want is for you to hold anything back. Come on," he said, stepping to the opposite side of the mat and standing on the short white line that marked his starting position. D'Abruzzo took his place on the opposite mark, then the two men bowed before advancing to meet at the center of the mat.

Five seconds later, Kirk was flat on the deck again. *Well, maybe holding back isn't the* last *thing I want him to do*, he considered silently.

"Well, at least you didn't go airborne that time."

Kirk raised his head and turned it in the direction of where Leonard McCoy stood watching. Bones was leaning against the wall by the gymnasium doors, his eyes bright with mischievous amusement as he grinned like a madman. Kirk slowly pushed himself back up to his feet, this time ignoring D'Abruzzo's extended hand. "Don't you have some other, better things to do, Doctor?"

"Other things, sure," McCoy answered. "Better things? I have to say this is at the top of that list."

"You know, Bones," Kirk said, as he rotated his right shoulder, trying to work some of the low ache away, "for someone who is so insistent about his patients' getting regular exercise, it seems to me that the only reason you ever visit the gym is to mock others."

"I'll have you know that I practice my own daily calisthenics routine every morning before breakfast," McCoy told him. "You're more than welcome to join me if you like. Very low impact, probably more appropriate for you."

Giving McCoy the tightest of smiles, Kirk turned back to D'Abruzzo. "Again?" The lieutenant, who had been watching the exchange between captain and chief surgeon with the reaction-free face of a cadet undergoing inspection, nodded and moved into position again.

The deck lurched under Kirk's feet again, but this time, D'Abruzzo had nothing to do with it—he was also thrown off balance, along with McCoy and everyone else in the gymnasium, by what the captain assumed was a sudden and unexpected failure of the ship's inertial dampers. "What the hell?" McCoy blurted, pushing himself away from the nearby bulkhead he'd been tossed against.

Once the ship and Kirk had both regained their steady bearing, the captain crossed to the closest wall-mounted companel and punched the transmit toggle. "Kirk to bridge. What's happening up there?"

Commander Spock's cool, unflappable voice answered him from the speaker grille: *"The Enterprise just dropped out of warp, Captain, and encountered some unanticipated subspace turbulence during the transition to normal space."*

"Another of the Nystrom Anomaly's surprises?" Kirk asked.

"It would appear so, sir."

"I'll be right there. Kirk out." He closed the open circuit, and then turned back to where D'Abruzzo stood and waited. "I'm afraid we'll need to cut this session short, Lieutenant."

"Yes, sir," D'Abruzzo said as he bent forward in the traditional low bow. Kirk returned it before heading to the locker area, tugging at the knotted cloth belt around his waist and freeing it. He shrugged the *gi* off and turned to toss it into the clothing reclamator by the doorway, noticing only then that McCoy had been following right behind him.

"You know, Jim," the doctor said, handing Kirk a towel, "you really ought to lighten up a bit on D'Abruzzo."

"What?" Kirk asked as he accepted the proffered piece of terrycloth, and proceeded to rub it over his sweat-slicked chest and sore, aching shoulders.

"Just . . . go a little easy on him."

Kirk stopped and stared at McCoy, stunned. "Me, go easy on *him*?" he said. "Did you not see what he did to me out there?"

"Yes, I saw what he did," McCoy agreed. "And I saw the look you gave him when he did."

"What look?"

"The look that said, 'Keep tossing your commanding officer around like an old rag doll, and don't be surprised to find yourself reassigned to waste extraction for the rest of this mission.'"

"But at least I didn't say it aloud," Kirk joked, and tossed the towel back to McCoy. "You have to give me credit for that." The captain turned and opened the locker where he had stashed his uniform and boots before the start of his workout, and began to dress.

"No, you weren't that plain," McCoy said. "But the way you kept addressing him as 'Lieutenant' and 'Mister D'Abruzzo,' making sure he didn't forget his place in the chain of command."

Kirk paused, shirt in his hands, looking at McCoy. "You're not saying I was purposely trying to intimidate him, are you, Bones?"

"Not intentionally, no, Jim," McCoy allowed. "But you are the captain; that alone is pretty intimidating to most of these kids. Then you put D'Abruzzo in the position you did, where he really had no choice but to hold back on you."

"Oh, no, he wasn't holding back." His abused muscles complained as Kirk put his arms through the sleeves of his green, wraparound uniform tunic.

"Okay. If that's what you want to believe," McCoy told him, in such a way that Kirk had to seriously consider the possibility that he was not kidding. "My point is," he continued, "you've got to keep in mind who and what you are to your crew. These have an effect on people"—reaching out, McCoy plucked at the rows of golden braids that circled his wrist—"even when you're not wearing them."

Kirk considered McCoy silently for a moment. Ironic that such counsel should come from the one man aboard on whom his rank seemed to have the least effect. "You're right. Thank you, Bones."

McCoy nodded, and left Kirk alone in the locker room with his own thoughts. While Bones had certainly meant well, he hardly needed to remind Kirk how set apart he was from the rest of the crew. A starship captain was first and foremost a leader, one who had to require obedience from his crew and make difficult, if not impossible, choices on a regular basis. It was not the sort of environment that allowed a captain to form many close friendships. McCoy was an exception, due to his decidedly non-Starfleet personality. And Spock, too, of course . . . though as much as he valued the Vulcan's friendship, it could never be compared to the one he'd shared with Gary Mitchell. The two had been inseparable for much of their early careers, and when Kirk was given his first command, he brought his closest friend aboard as a bridge officer. And when Gary had been transformed during the *Enterprise*'s encounter with the galactic barrier, it was Kirk who had to kill him.

The captain gave his head a quick shake, dispelling those old memories, then finished pulling on his boots and left the gymnasium. He strode down the corridor, passing by crew members in groups of two and three. Kirk gave them all only the curtest of nods in acknowledgment as he moved on to the turbolift, and then rode to the bridge alone.

The Nystrom Anomaly appeared on the bridge's main viewscreen as little more than a luminous oval smudge against the starscape beyond. Even with the *Enterprise*'s state-of-the-art sensors and computerized color image enhancers, the picture they generated revealed little more scientific data than had been collected by *Friendship 1*, the first-generation warp probe that had discovered the stellar object eighty-nine years earlier.

At first, the only remarkable thing about those original images was that the ancient pre-Federation probe had still been operational and able to capture and transmit them back to Earth. At first glance, the unnamed stellar object had been identified as a small planetary nebula, consisting of a shell of hydrogen and other stellar gases ejected by a star transforming from a red giant into a white dwarf. But Doctor Loretta Nystrom, a junior researcher assigned to the long-running mission, noted that over the course of *Friendship*'s long-distance flyby, the nebula displayed no evidence of either expanding outward or contracting back in on itself. Instead, it appeared that it was an almost completely stable accretion disk, holding static at five billion kilometers in diameter.

Naturally, this data was deemed unreliable because of suspected signal degradation over the vast distances and because the probe was by then in its twelfth decade of operation. The data from *Friendship 1* had cut off only months later, and it was assumed that the probe had finally failed and was lost. However, when subsequent Federation deep-space probes were dispatched to follow up on those initial surveys, they confirmed the earlier readings, and also discovered additional inexplicable peculiarities.

Over the decades, the Nystrom Anomaly had remained one of the more curious mysteries within the Federation's astronomic community. Some had theorized that the Nystrom Anomaly was composed of an undiscovered form of dark matter, or that it was an exotic extradimensional construct. Others posited that it did not exist at all and was a mere sensor shadow. It was these debates that had led to the *Enterprise* crew's current assignment: to serve as the anomaly's first live observers and to uncover the answers to these long-standing questions. Thus far, though, the answers had remained elusive.

Spock studied the image of the anomaly from his present position in the bridge's command chair, while Ensign Pavel Chekov manned the science station. Unable to glean any meaningful information from the indistinct visual representation, the first officer found himself turning to look at the young human officer, hunched over the hooded viewer. Spock felt the illogical urge to ask for a report, though he knew with certainty that any new findings would be promptly relayed to him. All the same, the Vulcan was finding the viewscreen less worthy of observation than the shifts and twitches of Chekov's back and shoulders as he continued his silent examination.

From behind him, Spock heard the turbolift doors slide open. Determining with a ninety-nine point thirty-nine percent certainty that this was Captain Kirk come to relieve him, Spock vacated the captain's chair. "Captain," he said in greeting, and as Kirk stepped down into the command well, Spock moved to relieve Chekov from his temporary post.

"Spock," Kirk returned the acknowledgment. "Report."

"We are approximately three billion kilometers from the Nystrom Anomaly," Spock said as he took his first survey of the science station's readings. "Unfortunately, the information being gathered by our sensors is woefully lacking."

"So, we can't chalk the mystery up to poor quality equipment on the old probes," Kirk noted as he assumed his place in the captain's chair. Turning his full attention to the viewscreen, he asked, "Is this the best resolution we can manage?"

"Yes, sir," Chekov said as he slipped into the navigator's seat, next to Lieutenant Hikaru Sulu at the helm. "Whatever the anomaly is, it's almost impervious to all our scans. It's like they used to say about Vladivostok: there is no there there."

"What about that subspace turbulence we hit earlier?" Kirk asked. "That was something new."

"Yes, sir," Sulu reported, without turning his attention from his console. "We're still encountering a good deal of subspace distortion, but I'm compensating."

"Well done, Mister Sulu; I don't feel a thing," Kirk praised the helmsman with a smile. The captain then turned to his first officer. "Shouldn't the old probes have detected subspace distortions in the vicinity, even at their ranges? For that matter, shouldn't we have?"

"One would have expected so, sir," Spock answered, looking up from his console. "The pattern of the subspace distortion we are currently encountering would appear to indicate that the Nystrom Anomaly is bending local space-time and subspace, as stars and other high-mass objects do. And yet, there is not a concomitant gravitational effect."

"Curiouser and curiouser," Kirk said thoughtfully as he turned back to the enigmatic object showing in the forward viewscreen. "Mister Sulu, how bad are these subspace distortions?"

"Not very, sir," Sulu replied. "Just a bit unpredictable."

Kirk nodded and asked, "Current speed of approach?"

"One-quarter impulse."

"Let's strap in and take her up to half impulse."

"Aye, sir," Sulu said as he keyed the commands into his console. "Half impulse."

The deck began to shudder perceptibly as the ship accelerated through a series of subspace resonance waves that should not have been present. As Spock analyzed the subspace readings that were now being relayed to his station at a steady rate, the beginnings of a hypothesis began to take shape. As the science officer continued to collate data and extrapolate the possible conclusions to be drawn, his focus was drawn away by the captain, who had moved from his seat over to the red rail that separated the raised stations from the center of the bridge. "Spock . . . is it just me . . . or is the center of the anomaly getting brighter?"

Spock turned and looked at the main viewer. His left eyebrow lifted above the right, and he told the captain, "You would appear to be correct." He turned back to his monitors and referred to the older readings, comparing them to the current ones. "Peak luminosity in that specific area of the anomaly has increased fifteen point eight percent since we began our approach."

"But what we are looking at here is a computer-generated and -enhanced visual interpretation of our stellar sensor array," Kirk said.

"You are correct, sir," Spock answered. "The sensor array's subroutines are programmed to compensate for subjective distance and make any corrections necessary for the accuracy of scientific study. Likewise, such variations in areas of luminosity should not be affected by proximity."

Turning back to the main viewer with a thoughtful expression on his face, Kirk observed, "This is the same way the probes studied the Nystrom Anomaly. What if we were to look at this just in the visible light spectrum?"

Spock, knowing that the captain's remark was not an invitation to speculation, reached for his console controls and deactivated the sensor display protocols. When he turned back, the difference was minor, but still marked. The bulk of the anomaly now appeared as a translucent field surrounding a single, large light-emitting source at its center.

"A star," Kirk said. "A star system, surrounded by . . . something."

The science officer shook his head. "We are not picking up any gravimetric readings, or other associated readings which would be expected in a star system. It could simply be an illusion."

Kirk shrugged. "What is the old Vulcan saying, Spock? 'The evidence of the eyes is often immune to logic.'"

Spock, impressed by the captain's knowledge, let one corner of his mouth bend upward slightly. "Yes. Or, as the human aphorism has it, 'Seeing is believing.'"

Kirk smiled and asked, "And if what we are seeing here is a star system whose gravitational field is being restrained by some sort of shield? We need to take a much closer look." The captain turned to Sulu, ordering, "Helm, full impulse. Bring us right up to the edge of the anomaly."

The journey in was a rough one, or at least it was rougher than Sulu would have liked. He prided himself on his abilities as a starship pilot, and he considered every slightest bit of turbulence as a shortcoming on his part. He winced silently as the ship momentarily lurched, its impulse engines reacting to an unanticipated subspace energy wave. But he made the needed compensations on the fly, bringing the *Enterprise* quickly back to an even keel. It was a challenge, to say the least, to guide a starship into a system that did not follow any of the established rules. He had been able to smooth their ride to a large degree by determining—from the small amount of sensor readings they were able to gather from the Nystrom Anomaly—that the star at its center was likely a type M1 subdwarf and plotting his helm corrections accordingly. It was very much how he imagined his long-ago ancestors had navigated their way across the Pacific Ocean, guided only by the North Star, a small degree of meteorological information, and pure intuition.

As the *Enterprise* drew closer to the perceived edge of the phenomenon, the anomaly began to resolve itself on the ship's main viewscreen, from a fuzzy and indistinct haze of light into what looked like a shimmering field of trillions of sparkling gemstones. However, the forward sensors detected only visible light, even as those gems steadily grew into gigantic onyx-hued crystalline asteroids refracting the light from what was now unmistakably a star at the heart of the anomaly. "Captain, I'm not able to get an accurate reading on our distance," Sulu said, as the proximity alerts remained unsettlingly quiet. If his eyes were to be trusted, the largest of the objects were at least triple the size of the *Enterprise*.

"Full stop, Mister Sulu," the captain ordered. For a moment, no one on the bridge spoke a word, all silently taking in the display.

It was Lieutenant Uhura, turned forward in her seat at the communications station, who finally broke the silence. "It's beautiful."

"And fascinating," Spock added, looking from his readouts to the viewscreen. "Sensor scans are still not returning any readings. It would appear that the field is absorbing all the energies directed toward it, from our sensors as well as the majority of the stellar emissions."

"Except for visible light," Kirk noted.

"Yes," Spock said. "Extremely curious." After years of serving with the Vulcan science officer, Sulu was able to detect the tiniest hint of annoyance underneath his otherwise emotionless tone. "And none of our standard analytical protocols are yielding any information about the nature or composition of the objects."

"Could we beam one aboard," the captain suggested, "for more hands-on testing?"

But Spock replied, "Impossible. The transporter would be unable to get a coordinate lock without effectual targeting scanners."

"Tractor beam?" Kirk asked, and when Spock did not immediately shoot down that idea, the captain said, "Mister Sulu, try pulling in one of the smaller ones."

"Aye, sir." The helmsman had to manually target the tractor emitters, but still managed to accurately project a beam and make contact with one of the strange crystals. But it had no effect whatsoever on its trajectory. "It looks like they absorb gravitons, too."

Kirk rubbed his chin as he considered that, then said, "Well, let's try approaching this the old-fashioned way, then." He turned back to his command chair and hit a button on the armrest. "Kirk to engineering."

The distinctive brogue of the chief engineer replied over the companel speaker. *"Scott here, Captain."*

"Correct me if I'm mistaken, Scotty," Kirk said, resuming his seat, "but don't we have an old-style grappler assembly in ship's stores?"

"Aye, that we do."

"Is it in good working order?"

"Sir!" Scotty sounded genuinely indignant. *"You're not suggesting that I would let any piece of equipment aboard my ship fall into disrepair, are you?"*

"Heaven forfend, Scotty," Kirk answered, successfully keeping the smile he wore from his voice. "How long to get it set up for use in the cargo loading bay?"

"An hour, sir," Scotty said, then added, *"May I ask why, sir?"*

"Of course, Scotty," Kirk told him. "We're going fishing."

The longer Scotty prodded at the inner workings of the old grappler assembly, the more he worried that his quadrupled estimate would not be time enough.

He lay flat on his stomach on the deck of the large bay in the aft section of the ship, aiming a light into the open panel on the side of the bulky gray apparatus. With his other hand, he poked at the outdated circuitry with a probe. To one side lay one of the loading bay's tractor beam emitters, which was used for the ingress and egress of supply pallets through the exterior cargo hatch, which was situated a deck below the shuttle hangar at the ship's stern. The power supply and control cable from the tractor emitter was now plugged into the older contraption, but it was stubbornly refusing to activate for some reason. Or, as Scotty now realized, for a whole myriad of reasons.

"Ach," the engineer grunted through his teeth, between which he clenched a microlaser refuser. He swapped that tool for the one in his hand, and then reached back into the machine's guts to fix another failed connection. If he didn't know better, he would have suspected this ancient piece of machinery might actually have been salvaged off the pre-Federation *Enterprise*. Grapplers like this one were part of the standard equipment on nearly all space vessels of that era, and up through the early part of the current century. But as tractor beam technology improved and became more sophisticated, the older devices had fallen out of use. Scotty himself had not actually seen an operational grappler since his first Academy training cruise, and had been surprised to discover this one during an inventory conducted shortly after his assignment to this ship. As best he could determine, it had been added to the *Enterprise*'s stores when she was initially launched, at the insistence of Captain April's executive officer, but had sat unused the entire time since.

Finally, Scotty completed his diagnostic. As he was bolting the cover panel back onto the grappler's side, the doors to the bay slid open, admitting Captain Kirk. "How's it coming, Scotty?"

"All set, sir," Scott said as he pushed himself up and latched the lid of his tool kit shut. He stood, taking his tools in one hand and with the other grabbing one of the handles of the antigrav unit clamped to the disconnected tractor beam emitter. Kirk took the other, and together they moved out of the loading bay into the small control room forward of it, opposite the space doors. Once sealed inside, Scotty seated himself at the primary control panel, set before the transparent aluminum bulkhead that looked out onto the wide, empty deck. "I'll be honest with you, sir," Scotty said as he ran a final check of his handiwork. "I've never been much of a fisherman, and I've never used this type of reel." It had taken a bit of jury-rigging and creative computer programming to coordinate the cargo bay's tractor control with the grappler, and the engineer could only hope it would work in practice the way he thought it would in theory.

"Fishing is a sport of patience, Scotty," Kirk answered with one of his easy smiles. Scott nodded back, appreciative of the captain's sentiment, but hoping he wouldn't let him down.

Satisfied with what he saw on his board, Scott then pressed a sequence of controls, beginning the depressurization process. Warning alarms sounded as the atmosphere was evacuated, and once the air had been cycled out and the alarms had fallen silent, Scotty keyed in another command. Looking up from the console through the transparency as the large exterior hatch slid open, he got his first glimpse at what lay beyond the ship.

The *Enterprise* had reoriented itself so that, from their vantage at the ship's stern, Scott and Kirk could look directly into the vast field of crystalline shards, tumbling slowly in their orbits. As they moved, their black surfaces reflected back an oddly muted yet stunning prism of colors, like an oil slick on the surface of a shallow puddle. "Oh, my, but that is a pretty sight," Scotty said in an awed whisper. It seemed unbelievable that they were all but invisible to sensors yet so beautiful to the naked eye.

"The viewscreen did not do this justice," Kirk told him, sounding equally awed by the sight. "It just goes to prove, there really is no substitute for sending people out here, seeing things like this up close, close enough to touch." Then the captain tore his eyes away and turned to Scott. "So . . . let's touch one."

"Aye, sir," Scott said as he turned his attention to the targeting panel before him. "At least the fishing pond is well stocked." The grappler had been built in the day when its operator would more often than not have to rely on visual targeting, so Scott was able to pick out a reasonably sized, slow-moving asteroid from the field, track its trajectory, and as it reached the center of his field of vision, hit the launch trigger.

Trailing a carbon-fiber tether, the large duranium claw flew out the open hatch and made impact. The four-meter-long, pencil-shaped sliver began to tumble away, but not before the grappler head engaged and secured itself, finding purchase in a small fissure or micrometeor pockmark. Scotty slapped the control that stopped any more line from reeling out and gritted his teeth as the mass the grappler had attached itself to pulled the cable taut. The cable held, though, and after a moment it slackened again, the asteroid's kinetic energy spent. "Nicely done, Mister Scott," Kirk said, impressed.

Scott shrugged modestly and pressed another control on the panel to start slowly reeling the line back into the ship. The crystal was drawn closer, meter by meter, bringing it gently toward the open bay doors. Scotty fired one of the miniature positioning jets that formed a ring around the base of the grappler's claw head, adjusting the captured object's angle of approach, in order to bring it in cleanly through the open hatch. He misjudged only slightly, and triggered the opposite thruster to compensate.

That one, however, only sputtered feebly before failing. "Damn," he said, just as all of the control readings from the grappler's remote assembly went dead.

"What is it?" Kirk asked.

"I don't know, sir," Scotty said as he hit more controls and found them all unresponsive. "I don't know if it was the impact or the age of the blasted machine, but I can't work the remote maneuvering system."

"Is the crystal interfering with your command transmissions?" Kirk posited. The reason wasn't especially important at the moment; the immediate concern was that they had a large asteroid coming at them that could no longer be controlled. The ship's shields were of no use against the energy-absorbing object, and it was on a path to hit lengthwise against the outer edge of the open hatch, doing serious damage.

The engineer's first thought was to cut it loose, but inertia would only make that a futile act. As the options raced through Scotty's head, none struck him as particularly good. But one was the most likely to accomplish the task at hand. "Captain, ye may want to get down," he said, and then boosted the speed of the grappler tether retrieval to maximum. The straining of the intake reel could be heard through the transparent bulkhead as the line went tight again, and the crystal was pulled around, so that it was coming at the *Enterprise* straight on, like an oversized harpoon.

"Scotty, what . . . ?"

Watching the velocity of the incoming object as it increased, Scott ignored the second thoughts shouting to be heard from the back of his mind. The long and disturbingly pointed crystal shard had now been pulled into a straight trajectory into the open bay, and Scotty stopped the spinning reel. The asteroid stopped accelerating, but it was still coming at them at close to thirty meters per second.

"Down!" Scotty shouted, as he slammed the button to rapidly repressurize the loading bay, and at the same time tackled the captain, knocking him flat onto the deck. On the opposite side of the bulkhead, air vents opened wide, filling the bay with gas, much of which quickly blew out the open doors into space. The jet of oxygen offered enough resistance to slow the incoming asteroid fractionally, but it still struck the loading bay deck with a mighty crash, bounced, and hit the transparent bulkhead with enough force to crack it. Air started hissing out of the control room, and Scotty disentangled himself from the captain in order to reach up and get the space doors closed. Within seconds they were sealed, and Scotty peered out the still largely intact observation window to see their prize broken into roughly a dozen sharp-edged pieces, none longer than one meter, scattered across the deck. Scott let out a long, noisy breath of relief.

Then, from the deck beside him, he heard the captain groan and then say, "You know, I'm getting a little tired of having my officers knock me to the floor today. . . ."

Two

Spock sighted his target down the barrel of his phaser rifle and fired.

The beam struck the precise center of the crystal fragment held in an elevated brace at the far end of the laboratory, at first having no apparent effect on the sample. After 8.8 seconds at a constant sustained setting, however, visible fractures began to form and grow. After 20 seconds, it broke into pieces, not in an explosive blast as would have been anticipated, but simply splitting and falling away. The thin chips that separated from the large sample sounded like chimes as they landed on the deck.

Spock lifted his forefinger from the firing stud and turned to Kirk, who was standing behind him. "As you can see, the amount of directed energy these crystals are able to absorb is not unlimited," Spock observed.

"Still, that's a lot of phaser fire you had to pour into it," Kirk said, walking down to the other end of the improvised firing range and squatting down to examine the broken pieces. "Any theories on where all that energy is going?"

"It appears that it is being shifted into a dimension of subspace," Spock said. "There are molecular similarities to dilithium, though it does not have the same effect on subspace."

Kirk asked, "Can we get through to the other side of the field without it posing a risk to the ship?"

Spock shook his head. "The energy displacement effect is not a risk factor. We do still need to take into account the physical damage the crystals can inflict."

"And even if we were to try using the ship's phasers to blast a path through the field," Kirk said, standing up again, his palm outstretched, holding a small pile of crystal chips, "we'd just end up with that many more pieces of this nystromite to worry about."

"Yes, sir," Spock answered, not bothering to protest the captain's use of the term "nystromite." The other scientists on his team had coined it during their initial experimentations, even before they had determined its actual molecular makeup and could formulate a more apt scientific designation. But now that the name was being used by the captain, there was little chance of a new one being accepted into common usage.

The captain clenched his fist around the chips and began pacing the laboratory in a characteristic demonstration of frustration. "Mister Spock, we have only scratched the surface here of one of the

Federation's longest enduring scientific mysteries. I'm not keen on the idea of abandoning it so easily."

"Nor am I suggesting we do so, sir," Spock assured him. "The focus of my study has been the ways that nystromite absorbs energy, and while resistant to most, there is one form of energy to which it is still susceptible."

Kirk turned back to Spock. "What is it?"

Spock answered by holding his open palm out to Kirk. After a moment, the captain poured the small pieces from his hand into Spock's. In turn, the science officer selected the largest of the pieces, turned, and threw it across the lab. He hit the large target sample directly, but this time sent it and its brace falling over. "Kinetic energy, sir."

"Kinetic energy," Pavel Chekov muttered under his breath, only just loud enough for Sulu to hear.

Sulu looked back at him and shrugged. "Hey, if it works, it works."

"I know, but still . . ." Chekov said, and gestured to the viewscreen. "We've been reduced to literally throwing rocks."

That rock—a large, common nickel-iron asteroid located among the nystromite crystals that dominated the field before them—was being directed by the *Enterprise*'s tractor beam off its natural path and into the thick of the field. Smaller crystals were knocked aside as it penetrated deeper, leaving a clear path behind.

"Disengage tractor," Spock ordered.

"Tractor beam disengaged," Chekov confirmed as he depressed the cutoff button and stifled a sigh. The science team's research with nystromite had allowed them to make minor refinements to the sensors. The readings were still indistinct—more like sensor shadows than genuine reports of objects in space—but clear enough that Chekov could see that the cleared path was far too narrow for the *Enterprise* to follow. They would need to repeat this exercise with a rock as big as or bigger than the *Enterprise* itself, assuming an object of that mass wouldn't overtax and burn out the tractor beam emitters. Chekov found it hard to comprehend why Spock had even bothered with such an obviously futile effort.

"Mister Chekov," the captain said, "arm one photon torpedo, maximum yield and dispersal pattern."

Then, the Russian understood. "Photon torpedo ready," he said after quickly keying in the program, and silently apologized to Spock for ever doubting him.

"Fire."

The torpedo launched from its firing tube and followed the cleared path all the way to the surface of the asteroid, where it detonated. The resulting blast lit up the forward viewscreen, and once the computer activated the protective polarizing light filters, they were greeted by the sight of an open tunnel leading inside the Nystrom Anomaly. It seemed as if every station encircling the center well had suddenly been reactivated, as a flood of new sensor data began to stream into the computer banks to be processed and analyzed. Chekov was shocked to realize just how quiet the bridge had been until then.

"So it *is* an M1 subdwarf in there!" Sulu declared as he read the new information being fed to their astronavigation console, with not a small amount of pride for having predicted the star's presence earlier.

"Indeed," Spock confirmed from the science station. "Along with at least six planets and eight planetoids. The fourth planet may be Class-M."

"*May* be, Spock?" Kirk asked.

Spock seemed to hesitate before elaborating. "It appears that the Nystrom system beyond this field is not entirely free of nystromite," he reported. "It is in particulate form, and is having the effect of degrading our sensor resolution."

"Would this particulate nystromite pose a danger to the ship?" Kirk asked. "Can we take the *Enterprise* into the system? Take a closer look at that planet?"

Spock's mouth pressed into a thin line. "Since

the particulate nystromite is in combination with the more common varieties of space dust, I believe that our navigational deflectors will be reliably effective within this environment. I do need to caution, however, that our studies of this new substance are still very preliminary. There is no way to guarantee—"

Spock was cut off by Uhura saying, "Captain?"

The captain turned, asking, "Lieutenant, what is it?"

"I'm not entirely certain, given what Mister Spock was just saying," she said as she pressed her Feinberg receiver to her ear, "but I believe I'm picking up subspace radio signals from the fourth planet."

"What?" Kirk stood up from his chair and stepped up to where the communications officer sat.

"The signal is faint, and there's a lot of interference," she said, "but it has all the earmarks of intelligent communication."

"Sentient life, in here," Kirk said, and the glint in his eye was enough that he didn't even have to speak the next order. Chekov turned back to his panel and had already entered the necessary commands by the time Kirk called out, "Mister Chekov, plot a course through the field and to the fourth planet."

"Course plotted and laid in, sir," he answered immediately.

Sulu smiled sidewise at him. "About time," the helmsman whispered as he engaged the impulse engines and the *Enterprise* headed in.

Nystrom IV did turn out to be a Class-M planet, and although Uhura did not pick up any further radio transmissions, what they did find, once the *Enterprise* achieved orbit, was readings of an artificial power source on the surface. However, although scans were infinitely clearer at this closer range, there was still enough particulate nystromite in the planet's atmosphere to call into question any of those readings, including the negative readings they'd found for any advanced life-forms.

"If you can't even get a decent sensor scan through that stuff," McCoy growled as he followed Kirk and Spock on their way to the transporter room, "why in hell would you trust that blasted machine to get your atoms through in working order?"

"Doctor, I am continually astonished by your ignorance of even the most basic operational principles of transporter technology," Spock said without turning back or breaking his stride. "The same annular confinement beam used to clear the transporter target coordinates of any matter which may interfere with the rematerialization process—"

"And I'm continually astonished by your refusal to allow anything in this universe to astonish you.

You really have no idea if the transporter will work in this system."

"Bones," Kirk interceded in his best calming manner, "I've already said you don't need to come along."

"For which I thank you," McCoy said, sounding anything but grateful. "But now we're talking about you, and the rest of the landing party."

Kirk stopped just short of the transporter room doors, turned, and put his hands out on McCoy's shoulders. "Bones. If I didn't have both Spock and Scotty telling me that this would be safe—safer than piloting a shuttlecraft through a nystromite-heavy atmosphere—I wouldn't be doing it. Now," he said, clapping his palms on the doctor's upper arms, "stop being such a mother hen."

"Fine," McCoy said unhappily, and then added, as Kirk turned away and rejoined Spock, "Good luck."

The captain smiled back over his shoulder as he entered the transporter room, where the rest of the landing party had already gathered. Two members of the ship's science section, Lieutenant Jean O'Reilly and Ensign David Frank, were joined by two security officers, Lieutenants Jameel Farah and Joseph D'Abruzzo. Kirk nodded a greeting to the group, and noted that D'Abruzzo had very quickly broken off eye contact with him. *I should listen to McCoy*, Kirk told himself.

Which really was not a thought he wanted to have just as he was climbing up on the transporter pad. He brusquely dismissed it as the rest of the party assumed their positions, then looked over to Lieutenant Kyle, who was standing behind the transporter control console. "Energize."

The familiar sensation of the transporter enveloped him, and once it had faded, the captain found himself standing on the bank of a small creek, on the edge of a forest. Once he ascertained that the rest of the party members were present and accounted for, he pulled out his communicator. "Kirk to *Enterprise*." He winced as he was answered by a blast of static, and started adjusting the two knobs below the speaker. "*Enterprise*, do you read me?"

After several seconds of fiddling with the settings, Uhura's voice cut through the background noise: "*. . . ing to compensate, sir. Are you reading now, Captain?*"

"Yes, Lieutenant, I have you now." The interference was still heavy, but that had been anticipated. "Landing party is down and safe. We'll check in again within fifteen minutes."

"*Acknowledged, sir,*" the lieutenant answered, and Kirk flipped the communicator shut. He paused a moment to take in their surroundings and to appreciate the natural beauty of this planet. To find a world with such a vibrant biosphere in orbit of a subdwarf star was remarkable, to say the least. The expressions on the faces of O'Reilly and Frank, as they surveyed the area with their tricorders, indicated that it was even more remarkable than Kirk knew.

He stepped over to where Spock stood studying his own portable scanner. "Any negative effects from the atmospheric nystromite on the tricorders?" he asked.

"Yes, but it appears minimal," Spock answered, turning in a slow semicircle while his attention remained glued to his readout screen. "I believe my recalibrations will allow us to collect reliably accurate data." The science officer looked up then, and pointed in roughly the same direction that the stream beside them was flowing, into the thick of the woods. "The power source is five hundred seventy-two meters in that direction," he said.

"All right." Kirk nodded to the party's two security officers. "Farah, you take point. D'Abruzzo, you'll bring up the rear." Farah nodded as he double-checked his phaser's power level, and then, holding it at the ready, started into the woods. Spock and the two science officers followed, the trilling of their tricorders joining together in a strange but not unpleasant electronic harmony. They remained close to the stream, but as they worked their way deeper into the forest, the trees became larger and the bank narrower. Progress slowed as they had to start winding their way around the thick-trunked trees and up the gentle slope away from the waterway.

At one point, Kirk's foot landed awkwardly on a root, sending him stumbling and nearly pitching forward onto his face. Just as he regained his balance, D'Abruzzo was there behind him, one hand grabbing onto his right arm. "Steady there, sir," he said.

"Thank you, Lieutenant," Kirk said. "Nice of you to help keep me upright for a change."

"Aye, sir." D'Abruzzo looked abashed as he pulled his hand away and took a step back from Kirk.

Do I really intimidate the boy that much? Kirk asked himself. D'Abruzzo certainly appeared to be more nervous now, caught under his captain's scrutiny, than he had minutes before, on the lookout for any surprise threats as they explored this alien world. "Lieutenant . . . Joseph. May I call you Joseph? Or do you prefer Joe?"

"Whichever you like, Captain."

Kirk struggled to hold back a sigh. "I believe that I owe you an apology," he said, as they started following the rest of the team.

"Sir?" D'Abruzzo answered as he moved to keep up with him.

"In the gymnasium yesterday," Kirk said, taking occasional glances over his shoulder to ensure the security officer was keeping up and listening. "I get the impression that you were somewhat uncomfortable being matched up with your commanding officer."

D'Abruzzo hesitated before saying, "Perhaps somewhat, yes, sir."

"And that's my fault," Kirk told him. "It really wasn't all that long ago that I was in your place, a young junior officer intent on doing whatever I had to to impress my superiors." Briefly, he reflected on the sense of respect and awe with which his younger self had regarded Captain Bannock during his time aboard the *Republic*, and Captain Garrovick on the *Farragut.* "Sometimes, I suppose I forget that I'm the one being looked up to in that way now. But I want you to know that, on the judo mat, I absolutely want and expect that you consider me your equal."

D'Abruzzo did not answer immediately, and when he did, what he said was, "Permission to speak freely, sir?"

Kirk looked back over his shoulder again. "Of course."

"Well, sir, it's just . . ." D'Abruzzo hesitated again, then blurted out, "On the judo mat, we're not. Equals. You're pretty badly outmatched, to be honest."

Before Kirk could find it in himself to answer that charge, Farah called back from the head of the column, "Captain!"

"What is it?" Kirk asked as he and Spock moved up to where Farah had stopped at the edge of a small clearing. The ground was covered with what looked like bootprints of differing shapes and patterns, clearly made in the very recent past. At the center of the roughly circular patch of bare soil was a pile of charred wood and ashes. "Spock?"

The Vulcan consulted his tricorder and reported, "My readings indicate that this fire was extinguished no less than thirty-six hours ago."

"And what about signs of higher life-forms?" Kirk asked.

Spock shook his head. "Still detecting none."

"Then where are the people who built this fire now?" Kirk asked, looking past Spock and beyond the tree line at the clearing's edge. The *Enterprise* had first arrived at the Nystrom system a little less than thirty-six hours earlier. While it was by no means unthinkable that these beings could have left the planet and system without attracting the *Enterprise*'s notice, it seemed far more likely to the captain that they were still here on the planet.

Kirk's question was answered by the whine of a weapon discharge from off to his left. A bolt of energy streaked past the edge of his peripheral vision, striking a nearby tree trunk. Tiny sharp bits of scorched bark peppered both him and Spock. "Take cover!"

The *Enterprise* party quickly fell back the way

they had come, into the relative safety of the woods. Kirk, with Spock close at his heel, vaulted over a large fallen tree and pulled himself low to the ground behind it. The barrage of shots continued, though all of them flew wide and high. *They're just shooting blind*, Kirk decided. They likely hadn't even seen the landing party, but had merely detected movement around the old campsite and were trying to scare them away.

Not that their intentions would make any difference if one of those shots found its target.

Kirk, with his back against the tree's moss-covered bark, pulled out his communicator and flipped the grille open with a snap of his wrist. "Kirk to *Enterprise*: we need an emergency beam-out, now!"

The only answer he got back was static.

Talk to me.

Uhura sat hunched over her station console, one hand cupped over the receiver she had inserted in her left ear, and the forefinger of her right hand plugged into the other. She listened intently to the signals being fed through the communications array, which most people would interpret as nothing more than meaningless noise. A part of her brain told her that those people would be absolutely correct in that conclusion.

The communications officer had been unable

to tease any further information out of the brief signal they had intercepted when they had initially breached the nystromite field. Uhura had been scanning continually since then for any similar signal patterns that might signify a form of communication. To her frustration, though, she'd so far come up with nothing.

So absorbed was she in listening for alien messages that she failed to hear Sulu move up behind her and speak her name. It wasn't until he lightly tapped her shoulder that she responded, gasping and nearly throwing herself out of her seat. She spun around toward the helmsman, who had stepped back away from her, the back of his thighs pressed to the red railing at the edge of the bridge's upper level, and his hands held palms out in what was meant to be a calming gesture. "Sorry, Uhura, sorry," he said. "I didn't mean to startle you like that."

"No, it's all right, sir," Uhura said as she quickly recomposed herself. With the captain and Mister Spock down on the planet, Sulu had the conn of the *Enterprise*, and she made sure to afford him the deference that entailed. "I'm sorry I didn't hear you."

Sulu dismissed the apology with a shake of his head and took a step closer to her again. "Have you picked up something interesting?"

"No," she said with a frustrated sigh, plucking out the earpiece. "I'm not picking up anything."

Uhura dropped the device onto her console and then rubbed her eyes. "I don't know, maybe I really didn't hear what I thought I heard when we broke through the asteroid field." She hated to think that she could have made such a mistake or, worse, that her mistake might have led them on some kind of wild snipe hunt. But it wasn't something she could dismiss as an impossibility, either.

Sulu considered her with a thoughtful expression, then said, "Well, to me, it seems just as likely that whatever you heard wasn't intended to be heard by anyone outside of this anomaly. And once whoever it was realized that we were here, they went silent."

Uhura's eyes widened as she considered that scenario, and what it meant to the ship. "Do you really think that?"

"I think it's something we have to consider as a possibility. And if there are others in this system keeping their eyes on us, then it's to our advantage that we did get your warning right off the bat." Sulu gave her a smile of encouragement and said, "Keep listening, and let me know if you hear anything more."

"Aye, sir," Uhura said, smiling back at him. He turned and continued to walk the circuit of the upper bridge stations as she picked up her earpiece again. *He's going to make an excellent commanding officer someday*, Uhura thought, replacing the receiver in her ear.

The earpiece was still full of static, but Uhura immediately detected a difference in its tonal quality. She removed it and checked the settings, thinking at first that she'd knocked something out of adjustment when she'd tossed it down earlier. Everything appeared to be normal, but when she put the device to her ear again, there was still the same unexplained change in the signal.

Acting on a hunch, Uhura switched the active channel on her board and tried to hail the planet's surface. "*Enterprise* to Captain Kirk." She received no reply. "*Enterprise* to landing party, come in."

Sulu, now standing at the engineering station where he had been talking with Ensign Strassman, turned back around toward her. "What is it, Uhura?" he asked.

Before she could answer, the ship was rocked by a surprise collision.

"*Enterprise!*" Kirk put the communicator directly to his lips, trying to make himself heard to the communications officer while at the same time hoping not to draw the attention of whoever it was still shooting at them. "*Enterprise*, come in!" The captain tried manipulating the device's settings as he repeated his message, but to no avail. With a frustrated sigh, he snapped the communicator shut and looked over to where Spock had taken cover, flat on his stomach behind the thick trunk of another ancient tree. With only a look passing between them, his first officer clearly understood that the landing party was all on their own.

Kirk slipped the communicator back into place at the small of his back, and then drew his phaser. Slowly, the captain lifted himself off the forest floor, turned over onto his knees, and peered over the top of his log to try to assess their situation. The rapid-fire volley of shots ended as suddenly as it had started, and a stillness descended over the forest, broken only by the faint buzz of flying insects. Kirk slowed his breathing as he listened, and after only a few seconds, he heard approaching footfalls, and then indistinct voices.

He looked around for the other members of the landing party. Ensign Frank was off to his right, past Spock. To his left, Kirk spotted a glimpse of a red uniform shirt, belonging to either D'Abruzzo or Farah, standing out plainly against the browns and greens of his surroundings. Kirk winced, and wondered why Starfleet opted to put their security personnel in such a highly visible color. O'Reilly and the second security officer were out of Kirk's sight, and he hoped out of sight of the aliens who were now making their way toward the clearing.

There were two of them, both humanoid, standing just over a meter and a half tall, wearing gray armor-plated uniforms and carrying what looked like phaser rifles. Both wore helmets of the same dull gray material, with translucent visors covering their faces. Through the face plates, they appeared to be reptilian, or perhaps amphibian, with greenish complexions and large, outward-bulging eyes.

They stopped as they entered the clearing and immediately took notice of the dead campfire. "See? They were here," the first of the pair said.

"This fire has been dead for three *dohs*," the second one said as she—both aliens had higher-pitched voices that made Kirk automatically identify them as female—lowered herself onto her haunches and sifted her gloved hand through the cold ashes. "It was probably just some animal you heard; the Taarpi are long gone."

"It was no animal. It was voices."

Kirk held himself perfectly still as he watched and waited to see what these two would do next. They didn't seem to be carrying tricorders or any similar scanning devices, which gave him some hope that they still might be able to escape notice and avoid any sort of confrontation. Whoever these "Taarpi" were, the captain was sure he did not want his landing party mistaken for them.

The alien soldier who had been studying the dead fire now stood and began to pace in a slow circle around the clearing. Even through the visor, Kirk got the distinct impression that not much was escaping the notice of those large eyes. "Oh, *pyurb*," she said, as something on the ground caught her attention and she squatted down again.

"What?" her partner said, moving to look over her shoulder.

"This," she answered, pointing to something Kirk could not see.

"That's no animal track."

"No, it sure isn't." The soldier stood again and peered out into the woods beyond the clearing. Kirk saw that she was looking in the direction of the red-shirted security officer who had drawn his attention earlier, and he had to resist the urge to pivot his head and look that way also. Instead, he kept his gaze fixed on the soldier, who tilted her head as she studied whatever it was that had caught her eye. Hopefully, with any luck, she would decide she was looking at a brightly colored flowering plant or something equally innocuous.

That hope was proved futile when she raised her rifle in a smooth fluid motion and sighted down its barrel. Kirk had no choice now. He raised himself on the balls of his feet, just enough to swing his arm over the top of the log, and fired a shot at the alien. Her weapon discharged into the dirt as she pitched forward and crashed to the ground, stunned.

The second soldier reacted immediately, bringing her weapon to bear at the same instant Kirk revealed himself. Her free hand went to the side of her helmet, touching a button there, which emitted a clear electronic chime. "Code 1-2! Co—" she barked, before she was felled by a shot from the far left side of the clearing. A second later, D'Abruzzo came leaping across the clearing, making a beeline for Kirk. "Captain, we have to—"

"—get out of here, yes," Kirk finished in unison with him. Whoever was listening on the other side of the soldier's comm link surely wouldn't waste any time once they realized both their advance scouts had gone silent. The rest of the landing party members had broken cover and were moving in together again. "This way," he said to them, just as the first shots began firing in the distance. "Spock, keep trying to raise the ship."

The landing party started winding their way through the thick forest growth while behind them the clomp of heavy boots joined the sounds of energy weapons fire. Kirk led them up a gentle slope away from the stream to slightly higher ground. He hoped that a fight against these aliens was not inevitable, but if it was, he needed to put his people in the most defensible position possible.

"No response from the *Enterprise*," Spock said, running up parallel with the captain and keeping pace with him. He hadn't even broken a sweat yet, damn his Vulcan stamina.

"I was afraid of that," Kirk said, ducking under a low-hanging branch as he ran. "We may be forced to hold out here on our own until the cavalry arrives." *If it arrives*, he thought.

"In that case, I suggest changing our course," Spock said, pointing in a direction nearly perpendicular to the way they were moving. "There is a relatively large stone outcropping this way which should offer a better degree of protection."

The captain simply nodded, and Spock moved ahead of him, zigzagging over the uneven sloped ground with the ease of a mountain goat, or whatever the analogous animal native to Vulcan's mountainous regions. Kirk stopped and turned back to make sure the rest of the party were still together, and directed them to move ahead of him, following after Spock. D'Abruzzo was bringing up the rear, and after all the others had passed ahead of him, he stopped short. "You first, Captain," the security officer said when Kirk tried to gesture him on.

"Lieutenant, we don't have the time for—"

Kirk's reprimand was cut off when a phased energy beam streaked up at them from the bottom of the slope and struck D'Abruzzo in the arm. The lieutenant yelped and staggered in pain, but maintained enough presence of mind to raise his other hand and fire back at his assailant. Kirk started firing his phaser as well, while at the same time, he wrapped his other arm around D'Abruzzo's waist and pulled him in the direction of the outcropping.

Somehow the captain got himself and D'Abruzzo

to the relative safety of a large line of limestone-like rock jutting up from the hillside, where the other members of the landing party were giving them covering fire. D'Abruzzo all but crumpled to the ground once they stopped running, and Kirk motioned to O'Reilly to come to his side and administer what emergency first aid she could. The captain then moved up to where Spock was pressed against the outcropping, phaser in hand. "I'd say this is yet another sign of higher life-forms on this world, wouldn't you, Spock?"

"I will assume you don't actually require an answer to that, Captain," Spock replied. "Is the lieutenant seriously injured?"

"Seriously enough," Kirk said. "If we don't get him to sickbay quickly . . ." *Of all the times to decide to leave McCoy on the ship . . .*

Every system on the bridge threatened to fail at once, with the exception of the emergency alert klaxons, which sounded their steady warnings. "Report!" Sulu had to shout to be heard above the noise.

Chekov studied his console with anger and confusion. "I'm not sure," he answered. "I think we were just struck by a nystromite asteroid."

"What?" Sulu moved up behind him and looked at the sensor readouts over Chekov's shoulder.

"Something bigger than particulate matter, you mean?"

"It sure didn't feel like particulate matter," Chekov quipped.

"Ensign," Sulu said, reminding him with that single word that he couldn't address the temporary commander of the ship in the same way he did his colleague at the astrogation console.

"Yes, sir, a larger-sized asteroid," Chekov said, at the same time checking the sensor readouts before him, trying to spot the nystromite mass in the mess of indistinct and nearly incoherent readings.

"Damage reports coming in from Decks Six and Seven," reported Lieutenant Rogers at the science station. "Whatever hit us had to be close to the size of a shuttlecraft."

"How did we not see something the size of a shuttlecraft coming at us?" Sulu asked in a tone of disbelief.

Chekov wished he had an answer for him. The refinements Spock had programmed into the sensor computers should have allowed them to pick up something as large as that, even if they hadn't been looking for it this far into the system. But even now, as he was actively searching, Chekov wasn't seeing anything coming up on their scans. He redirected the external sensor arrays and intensified his scan of the area near the point of impact, and saw nothing.

From behind him, Chekov heard Uhura say,

"Lieutenant, there's something interfering with our communications that may be interfering with sensors, as well."

"Intentionally?" Sulu asked Uhura, just as the ship was rocked again. He didn't wait for the communications officer's answer, and instead addressed the relief helmsman. "Mister Stevenson, evasive pattern alpha!"

"Impact on the engineering hull, starboard," Rogers informed the bridge as Stevenson complied with Sulu's order. Meanwhile, Chekov switched the focus of his scans in response to Rogers's report, and this time discovered something he hadn't expected to see.

"Mister Sulu!" he shouted, and without prompting, put what he had found up on the main viewscreen. "Look!"

The entire bridge crew turned forward and looked at the view from the external visual pickup, located in the rear of the saucer section just below the impulse engines. From its vantage point at the top of the *Enterprise*'s saucer section the engineering section extended away, with the two nacelle pylons branching outward from the center of the hull in a V. Space beyond was black and starless, due to the field surrounding the system. There was still no indication of any asteroids, nystromite or otherwise. But there was, just off to the starboard side of the ship, a very small, very dim flare flashing briefly before disappearing. "What was that?" Sulu asked, moving forward again to stand to Chekov's side at the end of the console.

"It looked like the output of a fusion rocket," Chekov said. "And it looks like it's mounted to a shuttle-sized mass of nystromite."

"So the nystromite can be used as a weapon," Sulu said, just as the ship was struck again.

And then again.

Kirk threw his arm across the top of the stone formation, fired two quick phaser blasts, and then ducked back behind the barrier as the aliens returned fire. Large chunks of stone were blasted free, raining down on Kirk's back. He could not help but wince as they cut through his shirt and bit into his skin.

The captain paused and listened to the whine of energy beams flying overhead. Spock crawled over to where he was crouched. "Our situation is becoming untenable, Captain."

Kirk shook his head, even though he knew his unerringly logical friend was correct. They were outnumbered, and the stone formation behind which they had taken refuge was being steadily chipped away by superior firepower. Unless the *Enterprise* came to their rescue soon—and with each passing second, the hope they would do so became dimmer and dimmer—he'd have to give the team the order to break cover and retreat. Where they might hope to retreat to was a question there wasn't any good answer to.

Another hailstorm of stone shrapnel rained down on him and Spock. When Kirk felt it safe to open his eyes again, he found himself looking in the direction of Joe D'Abruzzo, lying unconscious just a few meters back. They'd been forced to tie a tourniquet around his wounded arm—the most primitive and brutal form of medical treatment Kirk could think of—but he had already lost a tremendous amount of blood before that. If he was lucky, he'd only lose his arm. If he wasn't lucky . . .

Kirk turned to Spock again, and after exchanging a look with him, came to a decision. "Hold your fire!" he called out, primarily to his own team, but loud enough to be heard by the alien squadron. "Hold your fire!"

The other members of the landing party dropped behind the outcropping and stayed down below its top edge. The firing from below continued, but its intensity had fallen off perceptibly. Then . . .

"Cease fire." The alien voice spoke in a tone of complete authority, and he was instantly obeyed. "Are you surrendering yourselves, Taarpi?" the voice called out again.

"Yes," Kirk said, not bothering to correct his misidentification.

"Show yourself, then."

Kirk handed his phaser to Spock, and then raised both his empty hands, palms out, over the edge of the stone barricade. When the alien weapons remained silent, he slowly raised his head, and his upper body, into view of the aliens on the other side. Looking down toward the bottom of the slope, he counted nine or so soldiers, all in identical armored uniforms, and all armed. All aimed at him from tactical vantage points behind trees and other pieces of cover, with the exception of one, apparently their leader, who stood out in the open. The reflections on their helmet visors obscured their faces, but once Kirk had fully revealed himself, their body language betrayed surprise. Whatever a Taarpi was, Kirk clearly didn't bear a very close resemblance to one. "Who and what are you?" the alien leader demanded.

"My name is James T. Kirk. I am the captain of the *Starship Enterprise*, representing the United Federation of Planets. We apologize for trespassing on this world. We are explorers; we meant you no harm."

"United Federation of Planets?" the leader repeated.

Kirk nodded. "Yes. We are a union of over a hundred worlds, located about one hundred light-years away."

"Really?" Though Kirk still could not make out

the alien's facial expression, his voice conveyed what sounded like absolute shock, bordering on fascination.

Kirk decided to press this advantage. "One of my men is seriously injured, and in dire need of medical attention. Can you help him?"

"I'm a physician!" One of the other alien soldiers abandoned his cover and moved forward.

The leader quickly moved to intercept him. "Deeshal!" he admonished, as he put out an arm to hold him back.

"You've already accepted their surrender," the one named Deeshal argued. "We're obligated to offer care to them now, Commander."

"I didn't know what they were when I accepted," the leader countered. "We don't know anything about these people. Plus we have our own casualties to take care of."

"Our worst casualty suffered nothing more than a concussion, because they're using nonlethal weapons," Deeshal said, refusing to back down. "Knowing that about them is by itself enough for me to trust them."

The two men considered one another wordlessly for several seconds before the alien commander finally dropped his restraining hand and gestured for the doctor to go on ahead. Deeshal came running up the incline, pulling off his helmet as he did. The captain was somewhat surprised to see that he was not of the same amphibian species they had encountered in the clearing. Rather, Deeshal somewhat resembled a Caitian, though with a longer muzzle and a thick mane of pale yellow fur circling his face. "Where is your injured soldier?" he asked as he reached Kirk.

The captain gestured to where D'Abruzzo lay on the ground, with O'Reilly and Frank kneeling beside him wearing expressions of helplessness. The medic quickly moved to his side and knelt as well. "What is his familiar name?" he asked as he pulled a small handheld device from a pouch on his belt.

"Joe," Frank answered.

"Hello, Joe. My name is Deeshal," he said in a soft, soothing tone as he began to move his scanner over D'Abruzzo's torso and shoulder. As he watched the physician go about his examination, Kirk was taken by his bedside manner, and how humane—how human—his behavior was. It was a marked contrast from being chased and shot at, to say the least.

And as if to remind him that the danger had not yet passed, Spock and Farah suddenly raised their phasers, aiming behind Kirk. He spun, and saw that the alien leader had moved about three paces closer while his back had been turned. *Stupid*, he berated himself. "We didn't say anything about anyone other than your doctor coming up here."

The alien leader, now frozen in his tracks, said, "Of course. I have no intention of violating our truce, Captain James T. Kirk." He held his rifle out to his side, pointed to the sky, and with his free hand, he detached the faceplate from his helmet, revealing himself to also be a leonine alien like Deeshal. "My name, by the way, is Laspas, Commander, of the Goeg Domain Defense Corps. I do regret mistaking you for the criminals we've been tracking, and the injury to your soldier, as well."

The man's apology sounded sincere to Kirk's ears. "I appreciate that, Commander Laspas," he acknowleged, and then decided to take a step forward himself, further closing the gap between the two of them. "And I do hope that now the Federation and the Goeg Domain will be able to move beyond this misunderstanding to a more positive interaction."

Laspas's lips pulled back in a wide smile. "I would be very happy if that were to be," he replied. Kirk returned the smile, his hope for a positive outcome to this mission rebounding.

That hope was dampened when he noticed Spock and the alien doctor, wearing a dour expression, coming his way. "How is he?" Kirk asked them both.

"He is in very poor condition." Deeshal's head tipped as he spoke, his jaw touching his chest. "But I've done what I can for now, and I believe I should be able to forestall any serious permanent damage."

"Forestall it for how long?" Kirk asked.

The doctor put his hands out in a gesture of

helplessness. "I can't say. There are some similarities between our species, but also far too many differences. I don't have enough knowledge of your species."

"Your ship . . ." Kirk turned back toward Laspas, who continued, "I assume you have medical facilities aboard. Is it nearby?"

The captain was momentarily taken aback by the question. Were their captors really considering letting them go? "It's in orbit," he answered. *Or, it's supposed to be,* he added silently to himself. At this point, he could only hope that if these soldiers did permit them to go, they would still have a way to leave.

"Then you have a shuttlecraft?" Laspas asked.

"No. We—" He cut himself off before getting sidetracked into an explanation of the transporter, and instead asked, "May I try contacting our ship?"

Laspas nodded. "You may."

Even though Laspas was no longer brandishing his weapon at him, Kirk made sure to move slowly as he reached for his communicator and flipped the grille into its open position. "Kirk to *Enterprise. Enterprise,* come in."

This time, through the wash of electronic interference, he faintly heard what he thought was Uhura's voice, and underneath that, the unmistakable sound of the Red Alert klaxons. "Uhura! What's happening up there?" If Uhura answered, her reply was lost in the background noise. "Dammit!"

Kirk turned and looked back at Spock, who also now had his communicator out. He was attempting to adjust the device's settings, but having no luck. "There appears to have been a marked increase in interference from the nystromite, Captain," he said. "I am having difficulty counteracting it."

"'Nystromite'?" Laspas asked.

"The crystalline substance that envelops this system," Kirk explained. "Keep trying, Spock."

"And you say the levels have suddenly increased?"

Spock gave the alien leader an appraising look. "That would seem to be the case, yes."

An oddly triumphant expression came across Laspas's face as he reached up and touched the side of his helmet. "*814*: status codes 1-7 and 1-25. Directive 1-42, execute."

Kirk was nearly knocked off his feet then, as the ground began to vibrate violently. A near-deafening rumble rolled over and through their hillside, and when Kirk turned to look up over the top of the ridge above them, he saw a large, heavily armored gray-green space vessel lifting off and up into the pale blue sky. It measured about seventy meters long, with an angular, almost boxy shape, and two arching wings extended out from either side, supporting heavy warp nacelles. It was clearly not intended primarily as an atmospheric craft, and lacked any of the elegant curves of the *Enterprise*, yet it ascended with a smooth grace and confidence Kirk found he could admire. "Your ship?" Kirk shouted over the roaring engines at the alien leader, as it rose higher into the sky.

The other captain nodded proudly. "The Goeg Domain Starvessel Class III/*814*. Finest ship in the fleet."

Kirk grinned. "That's a coincidence. My ship is the finest ship in our fleet as well."

"Well," Laspas said, giving Kirk a simpatico smile in return. "Imagine that."

Even without the flood of reports being routed to the bridge, Sulu knew the *Enterprise* was damaged, and badly. He could sense the way the impulse engines were struggling to push them away from danger, sending unattuned vibrations up along the deck plates, through the seat of the command chair, and all the way up his spine. *When Captain Kirk gets back, he's going to have my hide.*

"*Engineering to bridge,*" Scott's voice cut through his private moment of gallows humor. "*How much longer are ye planning to let this poor girl get knocked around like this? I'm trying my best to keep everything running down here, but you're not making it easy.*"

"It's not me, Scotty, I swear," Sulu answered him. "How bad is it?"

"It's not good," he answered. *"Warp engines are off line, and impulse power is under seventy percent. I've got damage control teams all over the ship—"*

"Sir!" Chekov shouted. "There's another ship incoming from the planet surface!"

Sulu felt his stomach tighten into a knot. "An actual ship, or another of these asteroids?" he asked.

"A ship," Chekov confirmed, "with real weapons systems, running hot."

Sulu realized there was no more putting off his next order. "Helm, break orbit."

Stevenson pivoted in her chair, looking back at him in alarm. "But, the captain—"

"We can't do the landing party any good without a working ship," Sulu said, cutting her off sharply. "Set a course toward the third planet, full impulse." Stevenson turned reluctantly back to her console and executed his command. The ship was still handling sluggishly, and once the other ship was close enough to be seen on the viewscreen, it became clear that they weren't going to be able to outrun them.

"Ready all phaser banks and photon torpedo launchers," he ordered.

As the rest of the bridge braced for possible battle, Lieutenant Rogers pulled his face away from the science station's hooded viewer and reported, "Sir, I think . . . it looks like the asteroids . . . are retreating."

There's a sentence you'll never hear uttered anywhere other than the bridge of the Starship Enterprise, Sulu told himself. "Retreating?" He turned to look the science officer's way.

"They're showing us their tails, sir, see?" he answered, pointing to the overhead display above his station. Sulu looked up, and just as the lieutenant said, the engines that they'd only caught quick glimpses of before were now shining clear and bright.

"The alien vessel is going after them," Chekov reported. Sure enough, when Sulu turned to the main viewscreen again, he saw the vessel veer off. Whipping his head to the right again, he watched the other vessel launch pulses of energy at the asteroid-mounted engines, which then exploded in huge blossoms of light that quickly disappeared into the black invisibility of their nystromite masses.

Sulu suppressed the urge to cheer, but he knew he couldn't assume that the enemy of their enemy was truly their friend. His caution proved justified as the alien ship swung around in a wide arc and came back toward the *Enterprise*. "Stand ready, weapons," Sulu told Chekov in a low voice.

Then Uhura announced, "We are being hailed, Mister Sulu."

Sulu let the breath he had been holding out in a long hissing exhale, then answered, "Put them through."

On the screen, the image of the planet was replaced by that of a leonine alien on the bridge of the other ship. *"NCC-1701. My name is Satrav, Second Commander of the Goeg Domain Defense Corps Starvessel Class III/814. You are saved now."*

"Thank you," Sulu said, though there was something in the way he said this that made the hair on the back of his neck stand on end. "Your help is appreciated."

"I should imagine it is," Satrav said, curling his lips up in a smile, flashing a mouthful of sharp-looking teeth. *"Welcome to the Goeg Domain."*

Three

"Of all the times for Jim to decide not to drag me along on one of these damned landing parties . . ." McCoy muttered under his breath as he, Nurse Christine Chapel, and orderly Morgan Gannon hustled down the ship's corridors from sickbay to the main transporter room.

"I could swear I heard you tell the captain you didn't want to beam down to the planet with the team," Chapel said.

The doctor shot her a mock-angry look and said, "Nurse, don't ruin a perfectly good rant by bringing up facts." Had he known at the time that someone in the landing party would end up seriously injured . . . well, then, he would have argued that much harder with Jim to call his excursion off. McCoy wished now he had sucked it up and beamed down with them to ensure the landing party was properly cared for. Now, they had to rely on some alien doctor who had never seen a human being before. McCoy had been in that position himself, having to treat a patient of a species he had no actual knowledge of, too many times before. Although he always managed to maintain a confident front, inside McCoy felt like a first-year medical student who'd napped through his classes. It was a nightmarish situation to be caught in, and he could only hope this Goeg doctor had the smarts and skills to help a human patient.

They reached the transporter room, and McCoy nodded to the young woman manning the station. She nodded back in response while at the same time pulling down the trio of control sliders, activating the device. Two pillars of energized particles appeared on the platform, forming a semicircle around a third form lying stretched out flat at its center. As the figures solidified, McCoy looked from the injured security officer to the alien doctor and noticed the look of disorientation on his feline face. Once the transporter cycle was complete, he nearly swooned, before Spock stepped up from his spot on the transporter pad to steady him. "Doctor Deeshal, I presume?" McCoy said.

The alien jerked himself upright again and blinked a couple of times at McCoy before answering, "Yes. Sorry. This transporter of yours . . ." He shook his head and forced himself to focus. "You're Doctor McCoy, then?"

"That's me." Under other circumstances, McCoy might have commiserated with the new arrival about the experience of being transported. But he brushed right by Deeshal as he stepped up onto the transporter stage, tricorder open and active, and knelt down to examine D'Abruzzo.

"He's lost much of his blood," Doctor Deeshal reported unnecessarily. "Your people were able to stanch the hemorrhaging, and I provided an injection of an oxygenation enhancer, in hopes of preventing any serious deterioration of the brain or other major organs."

McCoy noted a high concentration of triox compound—or at least a close variant—in D'Abruzzo's system. McCoy was heartened to learn that the gap between Goeg and human medicine wasn't all that wide after all. "That may well have saved him," he said. D'Abruzzo was in rough shape, but he was still treatable. That certainly wouldn't have been the case, though, had Deeshal not ensured the little blood he had left was carrying a greater supply of oxygen to his brain, and keeping it viable.

McCoy then gingerly peeled away the emergency bandage from D'Abruzzo's arm and examined the wound. There was little more he could actually tell from a simple visual examination that he hadn't already determined from the tricorder scan. But it was too easy to let the cold computerized readout of his devices act as a divider between him and his patients. That direct physical connection, McCoy believed, was vital. He looked at the burnt skin and muscle, and did not like what he saw. "Dammit. Okay, let's get him to surgery." Gannon unfolded the antigrav litter he had been carrying, and together with Chapel they lifted D'Abruzzo up from the platform. "I only hope we can save his arm."

"Is there a question whether you can?" Deeshal asked, as the medics headed to the transporter room doors.

"Well, of course there is," McCoy snapped at him. "You don't just blast a hole in a person's body and expect it's gonna heal on its own!" He knew Deeshal didn't deserve that level of vitriol from him, particularly given the fact that he'd probably saved D'Abruzzo's life. But by the same token, it was his people who had injured him in the first place.

Deeshal stepped down from the transporter dais, and would have chased after McCoy if Spock hadn't reached out to restrain him. "But you are able to regenerate the tissue that's been destroyed, aren't you?" the Goeg doctor shouted after McCoy.

McCoy stopped, stepping back just before the doors slid shut behind him. "Can *you* regenerate lost muscle tissue?" he asked, one eyebrow cocked at him.

"I've treated many similar injuries before," Deeshal said.

McCoy considered him for an extra moment, then said, "Well, then, come on, Doctor. Don't just stand there and leave our patient waiting!"

Deeshal hesitated only a moment before snapping to and following after McCoy to sickbay.

Laspas stared at the space where his doctor had been standing a moment before, then turned to Kirk with a look that was equal parts astonishment and suspicion. "And when the energy is reconverted back to matter aboard your ship . . . it's a perfect reconstruction of their bodies?"

"Absolutely," Kirk told him. "Right down to the last hair on his head."

"That must serve as quite a tactical weapon," the Goeg said. Suspicion now appeared to overwhelm his astonishment.

"It does have its military applications," Kirk allowed. "But Starfleet is primarily a peaceful organization."

"A very well armed peaceful organization," Laspas noted.

"We do not kill or injure unnecessarily," Kirk told him, "but unfortunately, we do sometimes encounter things out there that require a stronger response."

"Yes, we've often found the same thing," Laspas said.

Kirk held his gaze steady. "You mean the Taarpi."

"Yes, like the Taarpi, plus others in our history," Laspas said, turning and looking back toward his squad. "But the Goeg have always found that the best way to defeat an adversary is to turn them into an ally." The soldiers had been given the order to stand down earlier, and most had removed their helmets while taking advantage of the rest period. The Domain team, Kirk saw, was a mixed group of at least five different alien species.

"The Federation is based on the same philosophy," Kirk told Laspas. He understood now why Laspas had been so surprised to hear about the Federation; the Goeg Domain was apparently a like organization, a collection of many races from many worlds, united in a common cause.

Laspas turned back to Kirk. "Then perhaps, despite the way this encounter began, we could together turn it into something positive."

A wide smile slowly stretched across Kirk's face. "Nothing would please me more," he said, just as his communicator chirped for attention. "Excuse me," he told Laspas as he pulled the device out and answered, "Kirk here."

"I have a preliminary ship's status report, sir," Spock said without preamble.

"Yes, go ahead, Spock."

"The ship has taken extensive damage and is currently incapable of warp speed," he said. "Mister Scott suggests we will need to remain in orbit for at least twelve hours while he and his team assess the full extent of the repair work necessary."

Kirk silently cursed himself for not having been aboard during the assault on his ship. "Acknowledged," he answered Spock through his tightly clenched jaw. Intellectually, of course, the captain knew there was likely little he could have done to prevent the unconventional attack by the Taarpi, but still he found himself second-guessing every choice he'd made that had led up to it.

"*Also,*" Spock continued, "*Nurse Chapel has informed me that Lieutenant D'Abruzzo is now in surgery, and is expected to recover.*"

That news, at least, provided some small relief to his heavy conscience. "And his arm? Is McCoy able to save it?"

"*Doctor Deeshal is currently assisting Doctor McCoy in that very endeavor.*"

Kirk turned to Laspas at Spock's mention of his doctor, eyebrows raised. The other ship commander was clearly pleased to hear of the cooperative effort between the two physicians. "Good news, Mister Spock. Keep me updated. Kirk out. Well," he then said to Laspas as he folded his communicator closed, "it seems our ships' doctors have already turned this meeting into something positive."

"Yes, and I'm heartened to know a truly tragic result to our misunderstanding has been averted," Laspas said, sounding genuinely relieved and grateful. "Cover your ears."

"What?" Kirk asked, just as a massive sonic boom rattled the ground and sent every tree in the forest shaking wildly. Overhead, through the gaps in the canopy of leaves, Kirk saw Laspas's ship returning, making its way back to their landing site. The Domain squadron began to pull their equipment together, replace their helmets, and prepare to move out.

"Our patrol of this system is scheduled to continue for another day," Laspas told Kirk, after flashing some sort of hand signal to his men standing downslope. "I think all the Taarpi *pyurbs* are gone now, but in case there are more still lying in wait in orbit, your ship will have some cover while you complete your repairs. And I suspect Deeshal will want to continue assisting your doctor."

Laspas punctuated that last comment with a soft, weary-sounding sigh and a shake of his thick mane, giving Kirk the impression that the Goeg physician was probably just as bullheaded as his human counterpart. "His help is very much appreciated," Kirk said. He only hoped that McCoy wasn't subjecting Deeshal to the full brunt of his personality, and undoing all of the goodwill being generated here. "As a show of our appreciation, I would like to invite you aboard my ship. In my culture, it is traditional to share a meal in order to celebrate a new friendship."

Laspas laughed. "We have that very same

tradition, although it is always the host who invites the guests."

"If you insist," Kirk said with a slight bow. The captain felt the kind of anticipation and excitement that made first contacts such a rewarding part of a Starfleet officer's duties. "I should get back to my ship for now . . ."

"And I have my duties to attend to as well," Laspas commiserated. "But I will have preparations made. I look forward to receiving you, and learning more about your people and your Federation."

"No more so than I do learning about you and yours," Kirk replied.

The first thing to strike Spock as he, Kirk, and McCoy beamed aboard the Goeg ship was how cramped its interior was. The vessel itself was little larger than Starfleet's old *Daedalus* class, and the main entry airlock where they had been instructed to board stood in marked contrast to the transporter room they had just left behind.

The second thing to strike him was the fact that the small space was made even smaller by the number of armed security guards pointing their weapons at them.

"Oh, hell," Spock heard McCoy, standing beside him, hiss under his breath, "I knew this all was going too well."

"Code zero! Zero!" Commander Laspas, followed by another, older-looking Goeg with a gray-streaked mane of hair circling his head, pushed their way forward from behind the guards. Laspas grabbed the arm of an amphibianoid guard, whose species Spock had learned was called Abesians. "These are the humans, for Erhokor's sake!" the Goeg commander said as he forced the guard to lower his pistol.

Spock pointedly ignored the snicker from McCoy, as the rest of the guards lowered their weapons and Laspas turned his attention to his guests. "Don't be alarmed," he told them. "Your matter transporter triggered a defensive response. Welcome aboard, James Kirk."

"Thank you," Kirk answered. His tone was even, but Spock could detect the minor degree of adrenaline-stoked stress just underneath. "May I present my first officer, Commander Spock, and my chief medical officer, Lieutenant Commander Leonard McCoy."

"Leonard McCoy, yes," Laspas said. "Deeshal spoke well of you."

"Well, thank you," McCoy answered. "He strikes me as a fine man and an excellent doctor as well."

Laspas then gestured to the older Goeg with him. "And I introduce my executive officer, Satrav, and . . . Chief."

Another alien stepped forward from behind the

guards, this one of yet another race they had not encountered on the planet. Her skin was ashen gray in hue, with small black eyes, ears situated at the top of her skull, and a cleft upper lip that revealed a pair of broad incisor teeth. "And this is my head engineer, Senior Chief N'Mi."

With the introductions disposed of, Laspas led the group out of the entry chamber and into the narrow corridors of the ship. They had to walk in single file in order to allow Domain crew members to pass in the opposite direction. Their footfalls on the metallic deckplates echoed against the bare, featureless bulkheads. Spock was again reminded of the *Daedalus*-class ship he had once toured at the Starfleet Museum, a relic of the Earth-Romulan War built with little concern for aesthetics or amenities, but with the single purpose of combat.

They followed their hosts down the equally narrow steps of a gangway and into a small private dining hall, dominated by a metallic table loaded with platters of a variety of unfamiliar foodstuffs. "Well, now, come!" Laspas said, smiling broadly and gesturing to the empty chairs surrounding the table. "We discovered this cache of supplies the Taarpi had left behind on the planet. What better way to celebrate our new allies than in sharing the spoils of our shared battle?"

They all were seated, with Laspas at one end of the rectangular table, Kirk opposite him, and Spock and McCoy sitting side by side at the captain's right, across from the other Domain officers. The two Goeg immediately began grabbing at platters and loading their own plates, with Chief N'Mi showing deference to them before doing the same. Kirk and McCoy exchanged a look across the table, and then the captain shrugged and reached out for a bowl of what appeared to be orange bean pods. "When in Rome . . ." McCoy muttered as he also stretched his arm out for one of the platters.

"Pardon?" Laspas asked him through a mouthful of food.

"It's an old Earth expression," Kirk explained. "It means, basically, when you're in a strange land, you should follow the customs of the natives."

"Oh," said N'Mi, the first word she had uttered in their presence. "We've offended you." Spock noticed her attention focused on the empty plate before him, which he had not yet made the effort to fill.

"Not at all," Spock assured her, as he accepted the bowl Kirk now passed to him. "Merely an observation of different social norms."

"One of many, I'm sure," Satrav said, just before sinking his teeth into what appeared to be the roasted leg of a small game animal and ripping flesh from the bone.

"And yet, at the same time, so similar," Laspas said, while sucking on a stripped leg bone of his own. "It's simply remarkable: a whole new civilization, a whole other Domain on the far side of the Keempo Expanse, run by a new race: humans!"

"Well, first, I need to make it clear that humans do not run the Federation," Kirk said, after quickly swallowing his food. "Ours is a democratic union made up of nearly two hundred different representative species."

Satrav smiled tightly. "And yet, you and your senior officers are all humans."

McCoy nearly choked, holding back a laugh. "Sorry," he said, covering his mouth.

"Is something wrong?" Laspas asked, concerned.

Rather than answering, McCoy turned to Spock expectantly. The first officer glared a moment longer at the doctor, then said to Laspas and the others, "I must correct your misperception that we three are all humans. I am of a different race, called Vulcan."

All three of the Domain officers looked stunned. "You are?" N'Mi asked.

"What? You didn't notice those points on the sides of his head?" McCoy asked.

Laspas tilted his head as he considered Spock and his ears. "I'd assumed it was merely a minor genetic variation."

"And you are the officer second in command of your ship?" N'Mi asked.

"I am," Spock told the chief, who appeared to be astonished by this revelation.

"It seems I'd misjudged you," Laspas interjected. "Based on the encounter with your landing party, and before understanding Mister Spock's nature, I assumed your crew was all human."

"No," Kirk said. "Granted, the majority is human, but in addition to Mister Spock, we also have several other races represented: a Caitian, a Triexian, an Efrosian . . ."

"But they're exceptions?" Satrav asked.

"Well . . . yes, unfortunately," Kirk allowed. "Starfleet started out as a human organization, before the Federation was formed just over a hundred years ago. Even though the space fleets of all our member worlds were brought together under the Federation Starfleet umbrella at that time, the process of integration has been a slow one."

Spock added, "My own father is a high-ranking Federation diplomat, who has spent his career strengthening the ties between Vulcan and the other member worlds, and even he was opposed to my joining Starfleet."

"How interesting," Laspas said, leaning forward on his elbows. "The Domain and the Defense Corps have always believed our greatest strength has come from bringing as many different and diverse peoples together as possible in working toward the common good. Take the Liruq," he said, gesturing to N'Mi. "For years, we were at war with them. A stupid, bloody, and pointless war that cost tens of millions of lives, including N'Mi's own family. But Lir was eventually brought into the Domain, and that young war orphan has grown up to be the highest ranking Liruq in all of the Defense Corps."

"A most noteworthy distinction," Spock said, nodding his head to the chief, who had her own chin modestly tucked to her chest.

"Indeed it is," Kirk agreed. "And I believe that people like Spock—and I assume, like Chief N'Mi as well—can serve as examples and as inspiration to others of their kind."

"But being the only one of your kind on a ship that's commanded by a human," N'Mi said, looking to Spock, "with an overwhelmingly human crew . . . don't you find that makes it difficult to command the respect due to you?"

"On occasion," he answered.

"What?" McCoy blurted.

Spock slowly turned to face the doctor, just as an expression of embarrassment came across his face. The Vulcan held his gaze for a second or two longer than necessary before saying, "I believe you remember Lieutenant Stiles, Doctor." Seventeen months earlier, while the *Enterprise* was engaged alternately in the pursuit of, and evasion from, a Romulan bird-of-prey, the former *Enterprise* navigator had accused Spock of being an enemy collaborator due to his nonhuman heritage. "However, on the rare occasion when I've had to deal with illogical, prejudicially-based attitudes," Spock continued, turning back to N'Mi, "I have always managed to negate the biases of those individuals, and prove myself worthy of their regard."

"I suppose there are always such difficulties where beings from different worlds come in contact," Laspas said.

"But the rewards for working through those difficulties are, I believe, more than worth the effort," Kirk said.

"Hear, hear," McCoy immediately interjected, though he avoided looking at either Spock or Kirk as he spoke.

Before the captain could continue, he was interrupted by the whistling signal from his communicator. "I beg your pardon," Kirk said to Laspas as he stood up and moved away from the table to answer. "Kirk here," he said once he had pulled the device out and opened it.

"*Scott here, Captain,*" Kirk heard the distinctive burr of the chief engineer from his communicator. "*I apologize for interrupting your meal . . .*"

"But I'm sure you wouldn't do so if it wasn't something serious."

"*Aye, and it is serious, sir,*" Scott said. "*We're not going to have a functional warp drive for at least six weeks, sir.*"

"Six weeks?" The captain turned his face briefly toward Spock, awash with emotion. "That is not acceptable, Mister Scott."

"Believe me, sir, I don't want to accept it, either. But the pylon supporting the starboard warp nacelle took critical damage during the Taarpi's attack. If we were to attempt to go to warp in our current state, the nacelle would be sheared right off." Were that to happen, the uncontrolled warp field collapse would rip the *Enterprise's* hull to pieces.

Kirk drew a deep breath and let it out slowly. "Scotty . . . when you say six weeks . . ."

"I mean six weeks, sir," Scott affirmed. *"If we were at a starbase, with a dedicated crew of specialists working round-the-clock shifts, we might be back in shape in two, two and a half weeks. But we're talking about multiple EVAs to work on the exterior of the ship, of the kind we're really not equipped for. Out here, left to our own devices with no other support . . ."*

Kirk's face turned ashen as Scott trailed off, and Spock understood the reason for the physiological response. Even in the best of circumstances, extravehicular activity carried extreme risks. And although every person aboard the *Enterprise* had undergone Starfleet's required micro-*g* training and its basic engineering courses, only a very limited number of crew members could reasonably be expected to perform such critical exterior repairs with any level of proficiency. In Spock's judgment, Scott's estimate of six weeks, rather than being overstated as was often the chief engineer's wont, may have in fact been overly optimistic.

"Understood, Mister Scott," Kirk finally said. "When we return to the ship, Mister Spock and I will stop by engineering to go over the details. Kirk out." The communicator's hinged antenna clacked shut, and for several seconds, Kirk stood stock-still and silent, his eyes unfocused and unseeing, lost deep in thought.

That silence filled the dining hall as all eyes fixed on Kirk. Finally, McCoy broke the wordless lull with a low, concerned "Captain?"

That was all it took to spur Kirk, causing him to rein back his emotional reaction to Scott's report. "I'm sorry, Commander Laspas." Kirk gestured to Spock and McCoy. They both stood, and the Domain officers did so as well. "I appreciate your having invited us here this evening, but we really need to get back to our ship."

"I understand," Laspas said. "Is there anything we can do to help? Perhaps N'Mi or her staff could assist in some way?"

"Begging the commander's pardon," Satrav interrupted, "but we have our mission. We cannot spend weeks in this system for these aliens." He then turned to Kirk and added, "I don't wish to seem unsympathetic . . ."

"You don't need to apologize," Kirk told him. "And while I appreciate the offer, I wouldn't wish to strain our new friendship. You have your duties, just as we have ours." Kirk then put on one of his characteristic smiles, though Spock could clearly see how forced it was. "We're a resourceful lot. I'm sure we'll manage to work these matters out."

They left the dining hall, and from there a waiting guard led them back the way they had come. "If I may, Captain," Spock asked as they followed behind their escort, "how certain are you that we can successfully effect these repairs in our current situation?"

Kirk gave him a glum look. "Let's just say, I wish I were more certain."

"Damn," McCoy said, "I was afraid you'd say that."

Lieutenant Commander Montgomery Scott plugged the last of his data cards into the slot on the bridge engineering station and called up the damage assessment overview. On the monitor screen overhead, a green wire-frame diagram of the *Enterprise*'s exterior appeared, with five of the component polygons highlighted in red, like the angry wounds they were. Scott stood up from his seat and turned to Kirk and Spock, who had been standing behind him. "Here are the areas of significant damage.

The most serious of them is this one here," he said, pointing to the base of the starboard warp nacelle pylon, where it met the main hull of the engineering section. He reached over and pressed a button, and the image switched to a closer view of that area. "The blow we took there had enough force to send the whole structure vibrating, riddling it with microfractures."

Kirk frowned as he looked from the schematic to Scott. "But we will be able to make the necessary repairs, yes?"

Scott involuntarily grimaced as he said, "To a degree, yes, sir."

"To what 'degree'?" the captain asked.

"Any repairs our crew would be able to make would only be temporary ones, at best. We just don't have the equipment or matériel to do more than that on our own."

"So, these six weeks of repair you describe," said Kirk, frustration coloring his tone, "they would only be so that we could get back to Federation space, in order to get more repairs."

"I'm afraid so, sir. And, I'm afraid there's more."

Kirk pressed his fingertips to his temple. "Do I want to know?" he asked.

The engineer wished he could answer "no," but of course the captain needed to know the full extent of their situation. "Because of the nature of the temporary repairs, we'd be limited to the low end of the warp scale. The higher our velocity, the greater the risk to the ship."

"How long would it then take to get to the nearest Starfleet facility?" the captain asked.

"We would be able to reach Starbase 43 in approximately ten weeks."

"Four months lost," the captain fumed. "Plus however long we need to be in drydock." For several seconds, no one on the bridge said anything. The *Enterprise* had only recently passed the halfway point of their five-year mission, and no one liked the idea of being out of commission for any more of their diminishing time than necessary.

Then Spock asked, "What will you require in order to meet your six-week repair estimate, Mister Scott?"

"I'd like to have every crew member aboard with the appropriate engineering cross-training to give me three shifts a week," Scott told him. "Also, I think we need to change the protocol for environmental suit use."

Spock said, "You wish to have all the environmental suits in use at once, with none kept in reserve in case of emergency." Scotty nodded; the first officer, naturally, had anticipated his request. "I would recommend against this, Captain. Should a situation arise where one of those emergency suits is needed . . ."

"With all due respect, sir," Scott interrupted,

"we're in an unexplored and dangerous part of space, with our closest help nearly a hundred light-years away. I don't think we can afford to be that cautious."

To the engineer's surprise, Spock did not automatically contradict him or dismiss his argument as illogical or emotionally charged. Scott had actually been hoping the first officer would propose a better plan, or otherwise offer hope that the situation was not as dire as he'd believed. Scotty looked from Spock to Kirk, and judging from the expression on the captain's face, he also had been disappointed that the Vulcan didn't have a better solution.

Lieutenant Uhura broke into the discussion. "Captain? The commander of the Goeg ship is hailing us."

Seemingly grateful for the temporary distraction, Kirk told Uhura, "Put him on the main viewscreen," and stepped down into the command well in front of the astrogation console. The forward viewer switched to a close-up image of the alien captain's lion-like face. "Commander Laspas."

Laspas dipped his muzzle slightly. *"Captain Kirk, has there been any change in your engineer's repair estimates?"* he asked.

"Unfortunately not. Why do you ask?"

"Because, if you still require the services of a repair facility, there is one nearby."

Scott perked up at hearing that, as did everyone else on the bridge. "There is?" Kirk asked, a bright note of cautious optimism in his voice.

"*Yes,*" Laspas said. "*At Wezonvu, twenty-two light-years from here.*"

And the hope that had risen up in Scotty's chest just as quickly crashed. "Unfortunately, without an operational warp drive, twenty-two light-years is still an impossible distance for my ship," Kirk told the other commander, visibly deflated.

"*Yes, understood, but . . . what if we were to help?*"

Kirk took a step closer to the viewer. "What do you mean?"

"*N'Mi,*" Laspas said, turning to his side to address his subordinate, just off camera. "*Explain.*"

Chief N'Mi stepped forward into view, blinking rapidly as she said, "*Captain Kirk. I've studied your vessel's exterior and have taken note of the damage done. Am I correct in assuming that it's the damage to your nacelle support structure that has crippled your ship, and that the matter/antimatter reactor is still operational?*"

Kirk turned to Scotty, who took a step forward and answered, "Aye, the warp core is running just fine."

"*Then I suggest that, if we were to reroute the warp plasma generated by your more powerful reactor to our spacewarp generators, we could create* a sufficient subspace drive field to encompass both ships, and achieve a warp velocity high enough to get your vessel to Wezonvu in ten days."

"Rerouting our warp plasma to your ship?" Scotty asked. "Then you're talking about hard-docking both of our ships together, linking the two warp systems into one, and keeping them linked for the entire journey?"

The other engineer nodded. "Yes, precisely."

Scotty realized that Kirk, as well as the rest of the bridge crew, were looking his way in expectation. "What even makes you think our systems would be compatible enough to pull off such a thing?" he asked N'Mi.

"To be honest, I have no idea if they are or they aren't."

"But, if there is a chance it could work," Laspas said, "it would be worth investigating, wouldn't it?"

As Scotty considered the feasibility of N'Mi's idea, he began to feel the bubble of hope rise in his chest again. "Well, it would be a challenge, that's for certain," he said. But, simply getting the Enterprise out of this system and away from the threat of further nystromite damage, whether accidental or malicious, would definitely make it worth the effort.

If the captain was as encouraged by the Domain crew's offer of help as Scotty was, he hid it quite well. "Perhaps if you were to send a set of your ship's full schematics for my chief engineer to review, so we can decide on the feasibility of such a plan."

"*Of course,*" Laspas said. "*And if you would do the same for Chief N'Mi. Let us know what you conclude as soon as you can, though; we're scheduled to leave the system in two hours.*"

The Goeg signed off, and once he did, Scotty moved up to Kirk's side. "Sir? Are you not keen on the lass's idea?"

The captain put up a hand to slow him down. "Let's not put the cart before the horse, Scotty. Go back to engineering, look over the schematics for the other ship, and bring me your report in an hour."

"Aye, sir," Scotty said and headed for the turbolift, already considering the dozens of potential obstacles to the proposed undertaking, and formulating possible solutions to each of them.

Once Scotty had exited, Kirk turned and walked back to where Spock was still standing at the engineering station. "What's your take on Laspas's offer?"

"I believe your hesitation is warranted, sir. We would need to cede much of our control over the *Enterprise* to an unknown entity. While their offer of help does appear to be altruistic, we do not know what ulterior motives they may have."

As usual, his first officer had summed up his concerns succinctly. And he was far from happy about it. "But, is it fair to assume that they do have ulterior motives? Couldn't their altruistic offer of help be just that, nothing more?"

"It could be," Spock answered. "But just as we cannot assume they harbor any ill intent toward us, it would be irresponsible to assume that they are being absolutely guileless."

Kirk shook his head. He knew Spock was right, that turning over control of his ship would be a risk. Hell, even turning the ship over to an ally was a potential risk, as their experience with Doctor Richard Daystrom and his M5 computer just a few months earlier had demonstrated.

And yet . . . "If the shoe were on the other foot, Spock . . . if we were to discover an unknown alien ship that had been attacked by Klingons along the Neutral Zone, wouldn't we offer to help them however we could?"

"Yes," Spock allowed, "but while there do appear to be parallels and similarities between the Goeg Domain and the Federation, it does not follow logically that they would behave the same way as the Federation would."

"Isn't that a bit arrogant, though, Spock?" Kirk challenged. "For us to assume that we're the only truly noble and selfless ones in this galaxy?"

"I make no such assumption, Captain," Spock

answered. "Commander Laspas may indeed be totally genuine in his offer of help. But even taking our limited interactions thus far into account, there is no way of knowing."

"So, logic says to distrust them?"

Spock hesitated an oddly long moment before making his reply. "Logic is dependent on facts. The concept of trust only comes into play where there are uncertainties."

Kirk gave him a bemused smile. "We're Starfleet officers, Spock. We deal with uncertainties every single day."

"Yes, sir," Spock answered. "And those prior experiences inform the things we choose to trust in moments of uncertainty." Spock's eyes fixed on Kirk's as he added, "Such as one's own judgment, or the judgment of one's closest associates."

Kirk gave his friend a smile. "And I appreciate your trust, Spock. You have the conn," he said as he turned to the turbolift, slowing just long enough to take another look at the graphic of his damaged ship above the engineering station.

I hope that trust can be justified, he thought as he left the bridge.

"Thanks for the hospitality, Nurse," Crewperson Chao told Christine Chapel as the two walked together out of the recovery ward, heading for the medical section's main doors. "I hope we don't do it again anytime soon."

"Likewise," Chapel said with a small laugh. "But remember, if you have any discomfort or any other problems, you come back, whether you want to or not." Kaylee Chao had been in a warp monitoring station during the Taarpi attack, and had been hit by an electroplasma discharge, suffering second-degree burns across her chest and abdomen. She was the last of the injured crew members to be discharged, with the exception of one. As Chapel bade her farewell and the corridor doors slid shut, the nurse turned back into the ward to check on her sole remaining patient.

Joe D'Abruzzo was asleep, as he had been since coming out of surgery. His entire torso was wrapped in a metallic-hued electrosensor bandage, binding his left arm to his side, from shoulder to wrist, immobilizing it. The bandage provided microelectric stimulation to the damaged muscle and nerves. With the rest of the patients gone, Chapel pulled a chair over to the lieutenant's bedside and sat silently with him.

"Christine?"

Her head jerked up as she heard her name and felt the touch on her shoulder. She twisted in her seat, and was mortified to discover it was Captain Kirk who had caught her napping on duty. "Sir, I'm sorry," Chapel said as she got to her feet. "I only closed my eyes for a second, and . . ."

"At ease, at ease," the captain whispered, favoring her with an indulgent grin. "I know full well how hard you work yourself. Is McCoy around, or has he gone off duty?"

"He's off duty now, yes, sir."

"Oh, well." Kirk's smile faded then as he gestured with his chin to the man in the biobed. "How is he doing?"

Quickly composing herself, Chapel said, "He's recovering well. Far better than could have been expected. Doctor Deeshal saved his life."

"Don't let your boss hear you giving all the credit to someone else," the captain teased.

Chapel smiled at the captain's joke, but told him, "Actually, those were Doctor McCoy's exact words."

Kirk shook his head slowly back and forth. "Saved by a Goeg, after nearly being killed by them. Which is the more representative act?"

"I'm sorry, sir?" Chapel asked.

"No, nothing," he told her. "Just thinking out loud."

"Oh," Chapel said. She studied the captain's face as he looked at D'Abruzzo, taking note of his furrowed brow and his mouth drawn tight in thought. "Though if you wanted my opinion . . ."

Kirk looked up as she trailed off. "Yes?"

Seeing the captain was genuinely interested in her thoughts, she answered, "From the way Deeshal described the melee down on the planet, that was sparked by a knee-jerk reaction, with no real thought or real intention behind it. But his choice to help Lieutenant D'Abruzzo, to come aboard and to spend the time he did in surgery to save his life and try to save his arm . . . there was a purposeful effort behind that. That seems to be the truer measure of a person to me."

Kirk considered her words for a long moment, then said, "Thank you, Christine," before turning to go.

"You're welcome, sir," she said, and then asked, "Did you want me to tell Doctor McCoy you were looking for him?"

Kirk flashed a broad smile over his shoulder. "That won't be necessary. I think I got what I came here looking for."

Main engineering was abuzz with activity, with Scott and his staff exchanging high-level engineering lingo at a clipped and rapid-fire pace. As Kirk entered, he saw one group standing before the main diagnostic schematic along the wall, pointing out and arguing over simulations of system interactions, while others manned the row of computer stations that ran down the length of the room, running a variety of analyses. Scotty moved from one group to another, quickly picking up the thread of each conversation and adding his own contribution to whatever piece of the technical puzzle each was trying to hammer out. "With subspace field tolerance at that level," he said to one of his junior engineers, "the system response time has to be much faster." He turned away then, and finally noticed Captain Kirk, who had been standing back, watching with admiration the way the man managed his team. "Captain. Sorry, I didn't see you there. It hasn't been an hour already, has it?"

"Not quite," Kirk reassured him, "but it seems you've really hit the ground running here."

"Aye, sir. My preliminary review of the *814*'s engine schematics looked promising, so Chief N'Mi and I bounced a few ideas off each other, came up with a basic plan. Now, we're seeing if it all holds together once we get down to the fine details."

"And the verdict?"

"There are still a few things I want to double- and triple-check," Scotty answered. "We would need to join the two ships together via a system of supports and run a pair of umbilical warp plasma lines from our engine to their nacelles. It'd put a serious physical strain on both vessels, and if anything goes wrong anywhere along the way, we could end up with two marooned ships instead of one."

"But . . . ?" Kirk prompted.

"But," Scotty continued, "if all works out, we could be at Wezonvu in about ten days. And from what N'Mi tells me, it sounds like the facility there could give the San Francisco Fleet Yards a run for their money."

The grin now pulling at the corners of the engineer's lips telegraphed the answer to the next question Kirk asked. "As of right now, your professional opinion about accepting the Domain's offer?"

Scotty's smile dimmed by a degree as he said, "Well, sir, I know there are other considerations ye have to take into account . . . but, ten days sure beats sixteen weeks."

"Yes, it does, doesn't it?" Kirk was forced to concede. "Get me your final, detailed recommendations as soon as possible." The captain turned and made his way back out of engineering.

There had been a part of him that had hoped Scotty would tell him the Liruq engineer's scheme was unworkable, and that he could simply refuse Laspas's offer on that basis. But the decision now remained his, and his alone, to make. Even discounting the possibility of more attacks in this unfamiliar star system, a grueling six-week schedule of EVA repair work was more of a risk than he cared to subject his crew to. But did that make entrusting his vulnerable ship to the mercies of these strangers a better course of action?

Kirk entered the open turbolift at the end of the corridor, took hold of the control throttle, and ordered it to his quarters. He absently watched the indicator lights slide across the pane of the motion indicator panel as his mind wandered. All through his career, the one thing that Kirk considered to be his most vital talent was his ability to read people. The Goeg commander did seem to be sincere with his entreaties of friendship, and Kirk had gotten the sense from the first that he and Laspas were very much of a kind—fellow ship's captains and leaders of men, fully embracing the adventure of space exploration.

Regardless, the thought of giving up control of his ship rankled him. It wasn't that long ago that the *Enterprise* had been seized by Rojan and his advance scouts from the Kelvan Empire, who had incapacitated the majority of the crew and taken the *Enterprise* out beyond the galactic barrier toward the distant Andromeda Galaxy, before he'd managed to wrest control back from them. And before that, the fugitive con man Harry Mudd had hijacked the ship and diverted it to his private planet.

But was Laspas another Mudd? Kirk actually laughed out loud in the privacy of the turbolift car at that thought—no, Harcourt Fenton Mudd was most certainly a one-of-a-kind individual. Nor did he believe that the Goeg Domain was another Kelvan Empire.

As soon as the car stopped and the doors opened, Kirk walked to his quarters and punched the comm button on his desktop. "Kirk to Uhura," he said as he slipped into the chair, "patch me through to Commander Laspas on the *814*."

Uhura acknowledged, and moments later, the alien captain's face appeared on his computer monitor. *"Yes, Captain Kirk?"*

"Commander Laspas," Kirk said, "I would like to accept your gracious offer of assistance."

Laspas gave Kirk an appraising look from the small screen. *"I imagine that couldn't have been an easy decision,"* he said. *"I know I would be hard-pressed to ask the help of a stranger."*

Kirk didn't deny that, but what he told the Goeg commander in reply was, "I'd prefer to think of it as the first joint venture between new allies."

A low, rumbling chuckle escaped Laspas's throat. *"Yes, that does sound preferable,"* he agreed. *"I will arrange for a briefing by Chief N'Mi for you and your key personnel."*

"Very good," Kirk answered.

Laspas reached below the frame, presumably to end the transmission, but paused before doing so. *"I have to admit, I'm glad our association is not ending here,"* he said, *"and that we will have this opportunity to build upon the foundation of friendship we've created here, James."*

"As am I, Laspas," Kirk answered, smiling. "As am I."

Four

The bridge of the *814* reminded Chekov of old twentieth-century photographs he had seen of the Baikonur Cosmodrome mission control center, during the early "space race." The crew stations were arranged in three tiered rows of six each, with a set of steps on either end leading down to a small open deck where Second Commander Satrav, the officer at the conn, paced back and forth. Rather than a single viewscreen mounted against the forward bulkhead, there was one large screen ringed by eighteen smaller screens, each showing the data or video feeds from each of the individual technicians' posts. On the dominant middle viewer right now, Chekov saw the gleaming white underside of the *Enterprise*'s engineering hull, growing slowly but perceptibly closer. Computer-generated overlays outlined in bright pink the ship's primary and secondary ventral airlocks, while all around him, Domain technicians were calling out figures and numerical coded instruction.

"Code 2-32, negative fifteen," Satrav ordered,

keeping his back to the rest of the crew as he focused on the numbers on the big screen. Chekov noticed the muscles of his broad shoulders tense under his plain gray uniform shirt as he directed the manual docking of the two ships.

"Copy, negative fifteen," replied the technician seated to the left of where Chekov stood in the second row of data stations, observing the operation of the Domain vessel. He would be spending a good deal of his on-duty time over the next week and a half aboard this ship, providing some small degree of oversight during the upcoming Starfleet-Domain joint mission, and would need to become as familiar with this ship as he could before getting under way.

"Status 2-12," reported another crew member in the forwardmost row of stations, where Sulu had been posted, taking his own crash course in Domain shipboard procedures.

"Code 2-30, oh-two-oh-seven mark nine-eight-nine-four."

"Copy, oh-two-oh-seven mark nine-eight-nine-four."

"Status 2-33, plus seven."

The ensign was feeling more than overwhelmed by the quick fire and overlapping exchange of shorthand being used to adjust the *814*'s velocity and relative orientation. A quick glance to Sulu told him that his fellow Starfleet officer was feeling the same way. He then stole a quick glance back over his shoulder to the third *Enterprise* officer assigned to study the operation of the Domain ship's command center. Contrary to the reactions he and Sulu had to what they'd been witnessing, Uhura's expression was one of obvious excitement and exhilaration. Rarely given the opportunity to get away from her regular post to take part in landing parties, Uhura was clearly relishing the chance to experience a new culture and its methods of communication.

"Code 2-30, oh-one-nine-two mark oh-oh-nine-oh."

"Copy, oh-one-nine-two mark oh-oh-nine-oh."

Chekov felt he was starting to pick up a little bit on what the numbers being tossed back and forth meant. The two four-digit figures, he assumed, were three-dimensional positional coordinates, just like the ones Starfleet used, though in fractions of degrees. "Code 2" was apparently a kind of prefix for a navigational command or status report, with negative and positive figures indicating a change in velocity. He supposed the abbreviated commands were intended to make things run more efficiently, though it seemed to him it was drawing the current docking process out longer than it really ought to have taken.

Sulu seemed to notice the same thing, and moved down his row to peer over the shoulder of the helm control operator, a male Liruq with a

patch of jet-black hair on the top of his head, between his ears. "Copy, negative six," the Liruq said
as he made the latest in a series of corrections to the
ship's velocity.

"It looks like thruster number two is about
half a second out of sync with the others," Sulu
observed, pointing to one of the readouts on the
monitor bank in front of him. The Liruq turned his
head slightly to look at the data Sulu was calling to
his attention, but gave no further acknowledgment.
"See, we're drifting out of alignment again," Sulu
said, this time pointing forward to the main viewscreen, where the bright colored ring that had been
positioned around the *Enterprise* exterior airlock
had drifted, and turned a dark, bruise-like shade of
purple. "You'll need to—"

"We know how to run our own ship, human!"
the Liruq hissed at Sulu.

"I wasn't saying you don't," Sulu answered
quickly, trying to placate his annoyed fellow helmsman. "I'm just pointing it out, so you could compensate."

The Domain officer twisted around in his seat
and fixed Sulu with a look of incredulity. "Are you
mad?"

Before Sulu could make any response, Second
Commander Satrav turned and fixed the two of
them with a fierce glare. "B'Gof!" he addressed
the technician. B'Gof snapped back around, facing

forward as Satrav moved toward him. "Is this human distracting you, Crewhand?" he asked.

"Yes, Second Commander," B'Gof answered, sitting up straight in his seat.

Satrav looked up at Sulu, an unreadable look on his face. Then he looked down again at B'Gof. "Code 10."

The Liruq gaped at his superior. "Sir?"

"We are now partners with the Federation humans," he told B'Gof, but speaking at a volume that was clearly meant to be heard by everyone in the command center. "If you are going to be distracted by them, you cannot properly perform your duties. Code 10."

A wounded expression flashed across B'Gof's face, which was quickly replaced by one of indignation as he vacated his chair. His shoulder clipped Sulu's, hard enough to send the smaller human back half a step, as he left his post. Chekov watched him stalk out the door, while his seat was immediately filled by one of the relief crew members who stood stationed by the bulkheads.

"And you."

Chekov turned back to see Satrav leaning against the long gunmetal-gray console and glaring at Sulu. Even though the workstation was slightly elevated from the forward deck, the Goeg still managed to loom over the lieutenant. "We are in the middle of a very delicate and complex maneuver," he said in a low rasp. "So unless you want us to put a big dent—or worse—in your pretty white ship, I suggest you make an effort to minimize your disruption of my crew." For this last, Satrav made eye contact with Chekov and Uhura as well, making sure he impressed upon them that he found each of them equal distractions.

Satrav then turned his back on them again, returning his attention to the master display wall and issuing orders again. The three humans exchanged silent looks, but said nothing, and continued to say nothing as they watched the docking maneuver proceed, the new helm officer struggling with the balky number two thruster.

It was one thing to look at the asteroid damage done to the exterior hull on a screen on the bridge. It was another thing entirely to stand on the ship and get to look at it up close.

It could have been worse, Scotty reminded himself as he walked carefully, step by magnetically aided step, around the patch of buckled and marred hull plating. As ugly as the damage was, the hull had not been breached, neither here nor elsewhere on the ship. No lives had been lost. That had been a blessing, no question. Still, it was with effort that Scotty had to turn his attention away from the impact site to the task that had brought him out here.

Several meters ahead, a thick beam of solid duranium rose up from the surface of the hull at an
angle—or, from another perspective, it extended
down and away from the *Enterprise*'s underbelly,
where Scotty now stood, reaching to the dorsal
hull of the *814*. This was one of six such struts that
formed the connections between the two ships, in
addition to the airlock and the warp plasma transfer conduits, and would ensure those connections
remained secure for the duration of their joint mission. As Scott reached the strut, he grabbed the tricorder secured to his thigh with a gloved hand and
scanned the welding seams, ensuring there were no
flaws or weaknesses in the molecular bond between
the hull plates and the struts.

"What is your judgment, Mister Scott?" came the
voice of Chief N'Mi over his helmet's internal communicator.

The engineer straightened up as he reached for
the suit's transmit control, positioned just over his
breastbone. As he did so, Scott could see, out the
high transparent top of his helmet, the figure in a
Domain EVA suit moving hand over hand along
the duranium beam, from the *814* to where he
was standing. "Everything looks good and secure,"
Scott answered his counterpart from the other
ship, "though I do wish your people had been a bit
neater."

From about three meters up (or down), Chief

N'Mi swung her legs down in a slow, weightless arc and planted her magnetized boot soles on the *Enterprise*. *"Neater?"* she asked.

"Right, look at this," Scotty said, pointing to the uneven lines of what looked like melted and cooled candle wax that marked the joining of support to ship. "I know we're under time constraints, and a molecular welder isn't the most precise tool there is, but they could have used a wee bit more care."

The visor of the Domain suit provided a more restricted view of the wearer's face than the Starfleet version did. Still, Scott could clearly see that N'Mi was not particularly sympathetic to his grievances. *"It's only a cosmetic matter,"* she told him. *"These hull plates will need to be repaired or replaced in any case, once we reach Wezonvu and detach the ships."*

"Aye, I know," Scott said, giving his shoulders a slight hitch underneath the silver-colored suit. "I just hate to see the old girl such a mess, is all."

"Who is 'the old girl'?" N'Mi asked.

Scotty chuckled. "The *Enterprise*. In our culture, we often refer to ships as 'she,' and assign feminine attributes to them." He shut the flap of his tricorder and refastened it to his suit, then began slowly walking back toward the secondary airlock.

Following alongside him, N'Mi asked, *"But you don't really think of it as a living being, do you?"*

"Not literally, no," Scotty said. "Though in a sense, the *Enterprise* really is one. She's got a beating heart in her warp engine . . . a mind in her computer banks . . . but her crew, they're what gives her a soul."

"*In the Goeg Domain, a ship is just a ship,*" N'Mi said. "*Its engines and computers are just machines, and its crew . . .*"

For a second, Scott was unsure if the comm link between them had been cut off or if the chief had cut herself off before finishing her thought.

"*Is just a crew,*" she finally added as they approached the airlock.

"Well, that's a shame," Scotty said, as he reached again for his suit communicator controls and signaled to have the airlock decompressed and opened. "As fond as I am of the *Enterprise* herself, it's the people I get to work with who make it worthwhile."

N'Mi had no reply to that, and as the hatch opened, he opted not to pursue the matter any further.

"Code 8-71," called out the Domain technician, a female Abesian named Fexil, to the mixed team of Starfleet and Domain engineers working in the cramped lowest level of the *Enterprise*'s engineering section.

Uhura, standing just behind her, consulted her data slate and translated, "That's a complete purge of the warp plasma conduit."

"Are you joking?" That question came from

Crewman Steven MacNeal, a young Centaurian who had just joined the *Enterprise* crew following their recent stop at Earth. "We just finished a code eight-whatever for a standard flush of the warp plasma conduit!"

"What reason would I have for joking?" Fexil asked, sounding exasperated by the experience of having to repeatedly explain her work methods to the Starfleet half of the detail. The Domain's system of command and status codes, Uhura had learned, had stemmed from the beginning of their efforts to integrate their Defense Corps, with the intention of bridging any language barriers and establishing standards of operation. It was somewhat ironic that the ship's senior communications officer was needed here in order to facilitate the use of those codes.

"What reason is there to have us do essentially the same procedure twice?" MacNeal protested.

"Code 8-71 is not the same as code 8-65," Fexil told him, struggling to maintain her professionalism. "There are trace contaminants in both ships' systems. They may not affect performance while that system is self-contained, but they could interact with other trace elements from the other vessel, and end up crippling both."

"I understand that, but why not have us do a full purge to begin with?" MacNeal persisted. "Or better yet, why couldn't we set up something to filter out those—"

"Mister MacNeal," Uhura cut off the young *Enterprise* engineer with a stern look. "You need only to understand what your orders are, not why you are given them."

MacLean looked as if he wanted to continue arguing his case, but muttered, "Yes, sir."

"Mister MacNeal," Uhura whispered into his ear, forcing him to turn back, "I don't expect there to be any more 'language barrier' issues between you and First Lieutenant Fexil, am I understood?"

"Aye, aye, sir," he said again. Uhura didn't get to exert her authority often, but she clearly had a knack for it, as MacNeal was suddenly in a rush to obey her orders. With the distraction over, the rest of the team went back to the task at hand.

Fexil made a low, croak-like sound that Uhura took as a sigh. "I don't understand how you manage to keep a ship of this size running with the way you do things."

"I have to apologize for Mister MacNeal," Uhura said. "I know Scotty made it clear to his entire team that they were to cooperate fully."

"I'm not talking about just him," Fexil told her. "Everything on this ship seems so uneconomical. Too many words, too much time to explain things to all these people," she said, gesturing to the accessway they were now walking down, past other work teams.

"I suppose this is a bit of a culture shock for

you," Uhura said as she followed alongside the Abesian.

"That's putting it mildly," Fexil answered. "Are all Starfleet ships like this?"

"No, the *Constitution*-class starships are actually the largest in service," Uhura told her. "The *Oberth* and *Miranda* classes are more comparable to your Class III as far as crew size is concerned, though you'll find the same operating methods on those ships."

Fexil shook her head, struggling to wrap her mind around such a thing. "It all seems *so* inefficient."

"Efficiency is measured by a combination of factors," Uhura said. "It may be quicker to issue a series of coded commands rather than to explain a process step-by-step, and I'm sure it works very well for routine operations. But we deal with so much that falls outside of the routine. In my experience, it's usually better to tell people the result you want, and let them use their particular knowledge and skill sets to achieve that result. For example, Mister MacNeal's idea for a warp plasma filter."

Fexil fixed Uhura with a strangely wounded look. "Then you think his insubordination was justifiable?"

"The way he voiced his idea was out of line," Uhura said quickly. "But the idea itself? You tell me."

"Tell you?" Fexil asked, confused.

"You're an engineer; what do you think?" Uhura asked. "Would a filter of some sort do the job of preventing any cross-contamination between the two ships' systems?"

Fexil was caught flatfooted by the query. "I . . . well, possibly, I suppose," she said tentatively, "if we had the time to consider it and design one . . ." She shook her head to dismiss the idea. "But we're under time constraints. . . ."

"Fair enough," Uhura said. "But in other circumstances, perhaps we could have been able to make the idea work." Fexil considered that, while also considering, Uhura suspected, the practicalities of a plasma filter. "And, if it did work, that would serve to make Mister MacNeal more positive about his contribution to the solution."

"And that's relevant?" Fexil asked. "Whether he's 'positive' while doing his duties?"

"Oh, yes," Uhura said. "Morale is vital, especially during extended missions like ours, far from familiar space for months or years at a time. We find morale goes hand-in-hand with efficiency."

Fexil gave her a look of skepticism. "Really?"

"Absolutely," Uhura told her, and gave her an appraising look. "What do you do with your off-duty time aboard your ship?"

Fexil shrugged. "Sleep. Eat. Study technical manuals and reports."

Uhura held back a small laugh, and wondered if that was a universal constant among all engineers. "Once we're done here and you're off duty, why not join me on the recreation deck? I get the feeling it would do you a world of good."

Blinking, Fexil hesitated, but then she smiled. "If you say it improves productivity, I suppose I should give it a try."

The name *Enterprise* had a long and proud history, going all the way back to the early eighteenth century. The last starship to bear the name was Earth Starfleet's NX-01, commanded by the legendary Jonathan Archer. Two centuries earlier, the ocean-going aircraft carrier *U.S.S. Enterprise* was the most honored ship in the United States Navy, and played a vital role in the Allies' victory over the Axis powers during World War II. The first space shuttle was named *Enterprise*, though it had never left Earth's atmosphere. As the prototype of Earth's first generation of reusable orbiter vehicles, it had been used as a testbed.

Kirk was reminded of that shuttle as he looked out the *Galileo*'s forward viewport at his ship, now attached to the *814*. For those early test flights, the space shuttle orbiter *Enterprise* would be carried atop an old-style jet aircraft, which would fly it to an altitude of some seven kilometers before releasing it and letting it glide, unpowered, back to earth. Here again, a nearly powerless *Enterprise* was secured to the top of another vessel, which they needed to rely on to convey them to their destination.

"Is something wrong, James?"

Kirk turned and looked up at Laspas, who was standing just behind him and Lieutenant Arex, the Triexian shuttle pilot. Lost in his reverie, Kirk had almost forgotten that his Domain counterpart had accompanied him in his visual survey of their conjoined vessels. The captain willed away his melancholia and answered, "No, no. Just . . . thinking." He turned back forward again as Arex guided the shuttle around underneath the navigational deflector dish, and the bow of the Domain Starvessel Class III/*814*. "You don't feel the same kind of connection to your ship I do, I suppose," he said. Scotty had related part of his conversation with Chief N'Mi to Kirk earlier.

"I take pride in my vessel just as you do," Laspas assured him. "I would be just as wounded if it were to be disabled, and my crew endangered, make no mistake."

"Oh, I'm sure, Commander," Kirk said, as Arex brought them in for another close pass underneath the *Enterprise* to examine the series of braces and tubes sticking out of her like some terminal hospital patient. "But . . . for me . . . for the *Enterprise* . . . it's a little more. Do all of the Defense Corps's ships go by numerical designations only?" he asked, turning back to the other man.

Laspas hesitated, and then answered, "Officially, yes. Our assignments to any one vessel rarely run longer than a cycle or two. I've commanded nine different starvessels since being promoted to commander rank. Giving proper names to inanimate objects, or forming any kind of attachment to them, is not something the Corps considers to be appropriate."

Kirk thought he picked up something more in that answer than what Laspas actually said. "But unofficially?" he asked.

"Unofficially?" A tiny whisper of a smile curled Laspas's lips. "When I was a boy, there was a popular series of historical novels about a fictional hero named Kawhye. He traveled the wilder regions of old Goega, riding his *gaat* named Windracer, fighting villains and saving the downtrodden." Laspas shrugged his shoulders and admitted, "I may have, once or twice, in an occasional flight of whimsy, employed a literary allusion during one of my missions commanding *814.*"

Kirk held back an amused smile. "But only once or twice."

"At the very most," Laspas insisted.

Lieutenant Arex chose then to interrupt, saying, "We've completed our circuit, sirs."

"Thank you, Mister Arex," Kirk said, and then asked Laspas, "What do you think?"

The Goeg dropped all hint of joviality, all business now. "Looks like all code zeros to me," he said, which Kirk understood as the equivalent of "green lights across the board."

Kirk nodded in agreement and said to Arex, "Take up position aft, Lieutenant." The shuttle pulled away from the ships, moving to a point several hundred meters off their sterns. As it did, Kirk reached for the comm control on the instrument panel. "*Galileo* to *Enterprise*."

"*Go ahead, Captain,*" Spock answered.

"Initiate transfer of full navigational control from *Enterprise* to the *814.*"

"*Acknowledged, Captain,*" Spock answered. Over the open channel, he heard orders and reports being relayed by his bridge crew, and after a minute, Spock's voice came back to inform him, "*Navigational transfer complete.*"

Laspas then tapped at his own communicator, hooked over his ear, and opened a channel to his own vessel. "*814*: standby codes 2-1, 2-2, and 2-3." He paused as his orders were acknowledged, then said, "Execute."

The impulse engines of both vessels began to glow, and as the *Galileo* maintained its station-keeping position, the dual starship began to pull away, heading out of orbit of Nystrom IV.

"*Velocity at point-one impulse,*" Spock reported. "*Engine synchronization optimal. Umbilicals and supports maintaining. Structural integrity holding steady within acceptable parameters."*

"Code 2-3, positive five," Laspas ordered, watching intently with Kirk through the forward ports.

"One-half impulse," Spock said. *"All systems nominal."*

As the two ships successfully carried out a series of tandem test maneuvers, Kirk found the dejection he had been feeling over the state of his ship lift. "Giddy-up, Windracer," he whispered as he watched the *Enterprise,* riding atop the *814,* gracefully complete its final operational drill.

Arex turned his long head to him. "'Giddy-up'?" But even though the archaic phrase was no more familiar to Laspas than to Arex, the Goeg picked up on Kirk's meaning and smiled broadly.

Kirk returned the smile as he tabbed the transmitter open again. *"Galileo* to *Enterprise.* Prepare the hangar deck for our return. Once we're secure, signal the *814:* we're ready to ride."

Five

In practically every civilization and culture ever encountered, this had been proven to be a universal constant: Rank has its privileges.

Laspas's personal cabin aboard the *814*, while far from luxurious by Federation standards, was a marked contrast from the austere nature of the rest of the starvessel. It was located near the ship's bow, with separate living and sleeping quarters, each with an exterior port affording a direct view of the stars slipping by at warp. A small corner kitchenette allowed for food storage and simple preparation, and Laspas occupied himself there by filling two heavy cups with steaming water and spooning a mixture of powdered bark and leaves into each. "*Heenye*," he said as he turned back around to Kirk, a mug in each hand, and offered one to his guest. "Highest quality, grown in the Bliss Mountains on Goega."

"Thank you." Kirk accepted the proffered cup and took a careful sip. It tasted like a strong black tea with cinnamon, steeped in salt water—not particularly pleasant, but not so terrible that he couldn't pretend to appreciate it. "Interesting," he said as he turned to survey the rest of the living area. His eye landed on a row of matched antique-looking leather-bound books on a shelf set into the bulkhead beside the cabin door. He ran his forefinger over the alien text stamped on the spines, and then pulled one from its slot. On the rear cover—or, if the Goeg read right to left, then the front cover—was an illustration of a Goeg atop some sort of four-legged riding animal. "This wouldn't be Kawhye and Windracer, would it?"

Laspas moved beside Kirk and gingerly removed the volume from his hands. "Yes. This was my father's collection," he said as he carefully replaced it on the shelf. "He's the one who first introduced me to the series."

"I'm sorry," Kirk said. "I didn't realize . . ."

Laspas quickly waved off his apology. "I shouldn't even have them aboard with me—too much risk of their being lost should anything happen. But it's nice to have this reminder of him. Besides which, I still enjoy the stories. Entertaining adventure tales with clear contrasts between hero and villain, good and bad."

"Unlike real life," Kirk commented.

"Yes, precisely," Laspas said as he gestured for Kirk to take a cushioned chair in the center of the room. "You were telling me earlier about that one mission of yours," Laspas continued, moving a second chair from his workdesk and sitting opposite the captain, "about the ancient computer that had enslaved an entire planet, that you convinced was acting against its own programming and caused its self-destruction?" Laspas shook his maned head in a gesture of awe. "That sounds like something straight out of a Kawhye story, if he had a spaceship instead of a *gaat*."

Kirk laughed at that. "Well, I certainly didn't feel like some hero riding in on his white horse at the time," he said.

"White horse?" Laspas asked.

"An allusion to a human genre of literature similar to your Kawhye tales," Kirk explained. "I technically violated Starfleet regulations by interfering with the society on Beta III. In a real sense, I destroyed that society."

"The way you described it," Laspas said, "it sounded like it needed to be destroyed."

Kirk nodded. "Yes, I know. Landru was standing in the way of any chance of advancement for the Betan civilization. But it's far easier to tear something down than to build up something new. I forced that responsibility on a people who weren't necessarily ready to tackle it. To this day, more than a year later, I still question whether I really did right by them." The captain paused to take a long draw of his *heenye*, and then said,

"I've never actually admitted that aloud." Kirk wasn't entirely sure why he was admitting it now to this alien, either. He couldn't have told McCoy, who had been "absorbed" by Landru. And though he considered Spock his closest friend, the Vulcan was also the one who had raised the question of the Prime Directive to him in the first place.

After a moment, Laspas commented, "When you command a starvessel, you don't have the luxury of doubting yourself, much less voicing those doubts to anyone." Kirk nodded in agreement, and the two men exchanged a look of mutual understanding. "For instance, there was one mission of mine, aboard my prior command . . ."

"Doctor," D'Abruzzo called out as he caught a glimpse of McCoy passing by the recovery ward doorway. "Hey, Doc!"

"Well, you're awake," McCoy said, sauntering into the room. "How are you feeling?"

"My arm itches like crazy," the lieutenant answered, his right arm across his chest, grasping his left arm and trying to knead through its tough, inflexible wrap.

"That's a good sign," McCoy said, looking up at the bio-readings displayed over the patient's head.

"Good for you, maybe," D'Abruzzo said, wincing.

"It feels like the itch goes all the way through to the bone."

"I don't doubt it," McCoy told him. "Your body is working overtime to heal the damage done." The readings from his electrosensor bandage showed the muscle density of his damaged arm and shoulder steadily increasing, and activity in his nerve receptors returning as well.

"Seriously, please give me something," the man pleaded, "before I end up gouging another hole in my shoulder with my fingernails."

McCoy gave him a long, wearied look. "How is it you security officers are so gung-ho to put yourselves in situations where you can get hurt," he asked, "and then, when you actually do get hurt, suddenly it's *my* fault you're in pain? Nurse?"

Christine Chapel stepped through the door from the lab. "Yes, Doctor?"

"Give Lieutenant D'Abruzzo ten cc's of hydrocortilene," he told her, then asked the patient, "How's your appetite?"

"I guess I'm kind of hungry," he said, though judging from the readings on his metabolism, it would probably be more than a guess once his mind was off his pain.

"I'll bring you lunch in just a minute," Chapel told him as she returned to the bedside with the loaded hypospray. McCoy left D'Abruzzo to the nurse's tender bedside manner. Leaving the ward, he ran straight into Doctor Deeshal, standing just outside the doorway. "Sorry, Doctor. Checking up, are you?"

"Weren't you a little harsh with Joe just now?" Deeshal asked.

McCoy bristled slightly at the other man's sharp, scolding tone, though he supposed he couldn't fault the alien for any misinterpretation of the scene he'd just witnessed. "He knows I was kidding with him," McCoy assured Deeshal. "The crew is used to my gruff yet lovable personality. If I were to start treating him with kid gloves, then he'd think I was covering up something that was wrong with him."

Deeshal arched one brush-like eyebrow at McCoy. "If you say so," he said, not fully convinced. He turned and looked into the ward as he added, "You know your people better than I do."

McCoy started for his office again, but stopped and turned back to see Deeshal was still standing where he was, and still staring, with an unreadable look on his face. "Is there something you aren't telling me?"

Deeshal started and turned, as if he had not realized the other doctor was still there. "What?"

"You keep looking into the ward with this odd look in your eyes," McCoy said as he moved back across the room to where Deeshal stood. "Is something wrong with D'Abruzzo? Is he not out of the woods yet?"

"Woods?" Deeshal repeated quizzically, but understanding lit behind his eyes almost as soon as he said it. "Oh, no. No, Lieutenant D'Abruzzo is recovering just as he should. It will still be some time before we know how fully his injury will heal, but for now, he seems to be doing well."

McCoy was relieved to hear that, though Deeshal's expression hadn't changed. "Well, then, what is it?"

"Your Nurse Chapel . . ." he said, and then appeared to struggle for words. "She seems . . . interesting. . . ."

"Interesting." McCoy tilted his head and folded his arms. "And what is it that interests you about her?" he asked.

Something in McCoy's demeanor or tone finally caused Deeshal's expression to shift. "I'm sorry. I didn't mean . . . I didn't realize that the two of you were . . ."

"What?" McCoy nearly shouted. "Christine and me? Of course not! I am a gentleman!"

Deeshal's eyes narrowed in confusion. "Yes? And Christine is a female."

"No," McCoy grunted, "I mean 'gentleman' in the sense that I would not use my professional position as her superior in such an untoward way."

"Ah, I see," Deeshal said. "Then, is there another man she has a relationship with?"

"I'm not sure how comfortable I am talking

about my nurse's private life behind her back," McCoy said, wishing he had simply continued on to his office and left the other doctor to silently moon after Christine. He could have told him about her not-so-secret crush on Spock in order to dissuade him, but that was a topic he honestly preferred never to even think about, let alone discuss at any length.

But before McCoy could say anything more, Deeshal jerked back away from the door, a stricken look on his face. "Oh, dear lord," McCoy muttered to himself, as he realized the adult physician before him had suddenly turned into a nervous teenage boy. A second later, Chapel walked in through the doorway. "Hello, Doctor Deeshal," she greeted him with her characteristic cheer.

"Hello, Nurse," he answered flatly, his professional mask firmly in place. "How is the patient?"

"He seems to be coming along very well, wouldn't you say so, Doctor McCoy?"

"Yes," McCoy nodded, "that's just what Deeshal and I were talking about, how good his prognosis looks."

"I was going over the literature on muscle regeneration from the Domain medical library," Chapel continued. Since getting under way from the Nystrom system three days earlier, both vessels had made the unclassified sections of their respective library computer banks open and accessible to the crews of the other. "There's some really revolutionary ideas in there, particularly about polyenzyme therapies."

"Really?" Deeshal asked. "You mean Izay's monographs? You read those, Nurse?"

"Don't let her job title fool you," McCoy said, something he'd had to tell more than a few people who had made the mistake of underestimating Chapel over the years. "Christine is an accomplished bioresearcher, and has a far better understanding of how to be a healer than half the doctors I know."

"I apologize for my shock," Deeshal told her.

"Not necessary," Chapel told him, her cheeks turning slightly pink in response to McCoy's praise.

"But, why would a person of such accomplishments opt to serve in this position?" Deeshal asked her.

"Oh," Chapel said, "mostly for the experience of serving on a starship, getting out of the laboratory and seeing the universe." Of course, that wasn't the only reason—Chapel had abandoned her bioresearch career years earlier following the disappearance of her fiancé, Doctor Roger Korby, and had accepted the position as nurse in the *Enterprise*'s medical department in hopes of finding him.

Chapel revealed none of this to Deeshal, and she had shot McCoy a quick sideways glance that communicated her hope that he wouldn't reveal any of it, either. McCoy was a bit confused by that look at first. Then he noticed that Christine was still blushing under Deeshal's gaze, and realized that it probably had nothing to do with his own earlier flattery.

"Well," McCoy said, suddenly quite uncomfortable. "Um . . . did you give D'Abruzzo his lunch, Miss Chapel?"

"Yes, Doctor, I did," she answered.

"Good. So then, um, why don't the two of you go get some as well?" he told them.

"The two of us?" Deeshal asked.

"Well, why not?" McCoy asked, covering his discomfort with irascibility. "The Goeg eat; I've learned that much about you over the past few days. Go on!"

Looking confused but not displeased, Chapel looked back to Deeshal and asked, "Shall we?" The Domain doctor shrugged by way of agreement, and followed as Chapel headed out of sickbay.

Once they had both disappeared behind the doors to the corridor, McCoy brought a hand to his face and pinched the bridge of his nose. "Well," he muttered to himself, "it can't be any worse than her and Spock."

Whatever else he may have thought about the Domain and the way they ran their ship, Sulu had to hand one thing to them: they knew how to eat.

He and Chekov shared a table in the officers'

mess aboard the *814*. They had just come off duty, which for the next week and a half would be aboard the Domain starvessel, serving as liaisons during the first duty shift. Rather than returning directly to the *Enterprise*, they had opted to try their luck and take their meal here. Like the rest of the ship, the mess was utterly spartan, with long rows of gray metal tables and low matching stools bolted to the deck. In contrast, the tray Sulu had set before him was filled with a colorful mix of chopped vegetables and noodles, in a slightly sweet sauce.

Across the table, his back to the bulkhead, Chekov took a look around the hall as he chewed a mouthful of his own food, a reddish-brown stew-like dish, then swallowed and said, "Do you think we should be sitting alone like this?"

Sulu froze, his utensil poised halfway to his open mouth. "What do you mean?" he asked.

"I mean apart from everyone else," Chekov explained. The mess was less than half full, and they had taken the open seats closest to the end of the serving line. The next closest diner was a large, intimidating-looking Rokean seated alone reading from a data slate. "The captain did say we were acting ambassadors."

That's true, Sulu reflected as he looked around the hall, and decided that they likely did seem a bit too standoffish to the Domain officers. "You're right," he told Chekov, standing up and picking up his tray. Chekov followed suit, and the two moved across the hall, past the bison-faced Rokean who, Sulu decided, looked very much like he wanted to be left alone with his reading. Instead, they approached a pair of Liruq engaged in casual conversation as they ate. "Hi," Sulu said to them, "mind if we join you?"

The two looked up at them, surprised. "No," said the one closest to Sulu.

"But, why?" asked the other one nervously.

"Just to be friendly," Chekov said, moving around the table and placing his tray down. "I'm Pavel," the ensign said as he sat, and stuck out his right hand. The Liruq looked from it to Chekov's face, having no idea why it, or he, was there.

"And I'm Hikaru," Sulu said as he took the stool opposite Chekov. "And you are . . . ?"

The man next to Sulu pulled himself up straight in his seat. "Rizil, Third Lieutenant, Environmental Control."

"Migor, Third Lieutenant, Environmental Control," the other Liruq announced in the same fashion.

"At ease, at ease," Sulu told them. "Like Chekov said, we're just trying to be friendly. We've been assigned as liaisons to this ship, and we just want to learn as much as we can about the Domain and the Defense Corps."

Sulu's attempt to ease the lieutenants' apprehension

had the opposite effect. Rizil's eyes shot all around the room, as if worried who was watching, while Migor suddenly became fascinated by the tray of food in front of him. "Or answer any questions you might have about the Federation, if you prefer," Chekov added quickly, trying to save the encounter.

"What is this about?"

All four men at the table jumped at the sound of Second Commander Satrav's voice cutting across the mess hall. The older Goeg stalked down the row of tables and stopped at Sulu's side. "Why are you interrogating my officers?" he demanded.

Sulu craned his neck back to look up at the senior officer, agog. "It's not an interrogation, Commander."

"We were only trying to have a conversation, sir," Chekov chipped in, "and be goodwill ambassadors."

Satrav scowled at the human, and then addressed his officers. "Third Lieutenants, were you aware that the captain of the Starfleet vessel has issued invitations to all Domain crew members to visit and make use of their recreational facilities during their off-duty time, at any time throughout our joint mission?"

"Yes, sir," the two Liruq answered in near unison.

"And it was your preference to remain aboard this vessel, rather than mixing with the outsiders?"

"Yes, sir," they repeated. A quick glance around the mess told Sulu that they were probably in the minority in that regard.

Satrav nodded approvingly. "Code 10," he told them mildly, and both Rizil and Migor grabbed their trays and moved to the far end of the dining hall. Satrav then turned his glare back to the two humans. "I understand that your intentions are innocent, Lieutenant Sulu, Ensign Chekov. But you are aboard this vessel only because you need to be, in order to facilitate the joint operation with NCC-1701. While I appreciate your desire to create goodwill, that is not your function while you are here."

The Goeg turned away, heading for the food service line. Sulu looked across the table to Chekov, who looked back silently for a moment, then shrugged and picked up his eating utensil again. "So much for making friends," he said before shoveling another bite into his mouth.

Spock stood off to the edge of the *Enterprise*'s Deck 6 recreation deck, passively observing the behavior of the large gathering. A significant majority of the *814*'s off-duty crew had congregated here, as had been the case over the previous nine shifts. They had been generally well-behaved guests, save for a single unfortunate incident two days earlier. One of the Liruq technicians had decided to try a cup of coffee from the food dispenser, unaware of the beverage's high levels of caffeine, a substance classified as a dangerous psychotropic drug in Liruq pharmacology. Though the technician's reaction was not life threatening, it did spark a minor panic, and necessitated additional protocols being programmed into the food synthesizers.

At the moment, though, there were no indications of any similar episodes in the offing. The first officer also noted that, whereas the Domain crew members had initially tended to keep to their own small cliques, they were increasingly interacting with members of the *Enterprise* crew. At present, he noted Lieutenants Uhura and M'Ress sharing a meal with a pair of Abesian officers, and Christine Chapel deep in conversation with Doctor Deeshal. Spock considered that particular pairing with an arched eyebrow. While it should not have been surprising that the two medical professionals would gravitate to one another, something struck him as odd about the quality of their social behavioral cues. . . .

"Mister Spock."

Spock turned toward the sound of his name, and saw that Chief N'Mi had just entered through the door behind him. "Chief," he greeted her with a dip of his head.

"I am surprised to find you here," she said. "I

hope the first officer's presence doesn't indicate any more troubles being caused by our crew," she said.

"No, you need not be concerned on that point," Spock told her, "though I am curious as to why my presence surprises you."

"You don't strike me as the type to engage in such frivolities," N'Mi answered, with a contemptuous gesture. "I assume that someone who has achieved as much as you would spend most, if not all, of his spare time and energies working toward advancing those achievements."

The Vulcan nodded slowly. "I will admit, your characterization of me is generally correct." From an early age, he had been determined to excel—a determination born of the need to earn Sarek's approval, and to exceed his expectations. "However, I would challenge your blanket characterization of all activities being undertaken here as frivolous." He gestured to a three-dimensional chess set, left with its pieces arranged in a checkmated game. "For instance, strategy games serve to improve the player's logical facilities." He sat behind the board, and began to reset it for the start of a new game. "There is a school of thought which posits that the more advanced a species and the more complex its mind, the greater the need for recreational play."

N'Mi looked skeptical as she took the seat opposite him. "Do you subscribe to this school of thought?"

"Not entirely," Spock allowed. "Although I have found, serving with humans for as long as I have, it does apply to them."

"Have you always served on vessels where the human crew was the majority?" N'Mi asked, watching him move the chess pieces from level to level.

"Yes," Spock said. "I've served aboard the *Enterprise* my entire career as an officer, first under its previous captain, Christopher Pike, and was offered the position of first officer when Captain Kirk assumed command."

"I can't imagine," N'Mi said. "To be the only one of your kind on a ship of this size, that must be terribly isolating for you. Why wouldn't you choose to serve on a Vulcan-crewed ship instead? You said there are such vessels in Starfleet, didn't you?"

The memory of the *Intrepid*—and specifically, of the death of its entire crew—came back to Spock unbidden. "Yes, I could have requested a posting on such a ship," he answered, forcing the recalled emotional shock back behind his mental barriers. "But I came to the decision, early in my Starfleet career, that by living and working alongside humans, that would better serve my efforts to be a Vulcan."

A look of confusion crossed the Liruq's face. "I don't understand. What effort does it take for you to be a Vulcan, and why would being among other Vulcans impede that?"

Spock sighed silently, then explained, "Because

I am not, in the strictest sense, a true Vulcan. My mother was human, and I am half human."

N'Mi's mouth gaped open. "You're a mongrel?" she said.

"'Mongrel,'" Spock repeated. "Vulcans generally refrain from overt expressions of distaste . . ." he said, even as he recalled the taunts of his childhood peers.

N'Mi's expression quickly shifted to one of mortified embarrassment. "I . . . I apologize, Commander Spock. I . . . you . . ." The engineer continued to stammer, standing up, nearly knocking her chair backward in her haste to leave. Spock considered giving her some sort of reassurance that he had not taken offense, telling her it was unnecessary to leave in such a state. Instead, he silently contemplated the board before him as N'Mi rushed off and out of the hall.

Just off the recreation deck was a small storage area, which housed a large array of entertainment items ranging from chess sets to jigsaw puzzles, and playing cards to portable computer games. In addition, it also served as a repository for an impressive collection of musical instruments. Many of the *Enterprise*'s more musically inclined crew members had their own personal instruments—Spock had his Vulcan lyre, and Scotty owned bagpipes—but most didn't. The transitory nature of a Starfleet officer's life precluded carrying extraneous possessions from one posting to the next. Therefore, a morale officer had established an assortment for the use of anyone who wished to play. Included were several styles of guitar, multiple woodwind and brass instruments, a Tiburonian wheel harp, a full set of Andorian percussion blocks, and the small stringed instrument Fexil currently held cradled in her hands.

"This looks almost like a *gelbartix*," the Abesian said, her entire face lighting up as she gently ran her fingers up the length of its wooden neck. "What did you call it?"

"A ukulele," Uhura said, smiling back. The Domain engineer's attention had been caught by the instrument collection immediately upon entering the small room, and the way she had been drawn to the ukulele was like watching the reunion of two long-lost best friends.

Fexil plucked at the four strings in sequence, then positioned her long elegant fingers on the frets and strummed a chord. "Almost sounds like a *gelbartix*, too," she said, giving her head a small shake of wonderment.

"Do you play?" Uhura asked.

"I haven't for years," Fexil answered as Uhura led her out of the storage room back into the recreation deck proper. "My mother played professionally, and she started teaching me as soon as I was big enough to hold one." She tried a few more experimental chords, and then was strumming out a melody.

"That's lovely," Uhura said after a few bars, thinking the melody sounded oddly familiar. Fexil smiled more widely, revealing a row of pink, gummy protrusions that served in place of teeth. As she continued to play, Uhura noticed the rec deck's background level noise falling and conversations halting as everyone's attention was drawn to the Abesian's impromptu performance. The alien melody started to repeat itself, and all of a sudden it dawned on Uhura why the song seemed so familiar. The rhythm was slightly different, and not all the notes matched, but it was close enough that Uhura found she couldn't refrain from adding old lyrics to the new song. . . .

"Beautiful dreamer, wake unto me,
Starlight and dewdrops are waiting for thee . . ."

Fexil's eyes bulged in surprise at first, but she didn't miss a beat as she segued into a closer harmony with Uhura's vocals.

"Sounds of the rude world heard in the day,
Lulled by the moonlight have all passed away . . ."

Instrument and voice flowed and melded together, complimenting one another like longtime musical collaborators, and ultimately rising to a final crescendo.

". . . Beautiful dreamer, awake unto me,
Beautiful dreamer, awake unto me!"

Fexil ended her rendition with an exuberant strumming flourish, and was rewarded by a round of enthusiastic applause, which took her aback. "Does that mean they liked it?" she whispered to Uhura, wide-eyed.

"Yes." Uhura laughed as she joined in the applause for her accompanist. "It means they liked it very much!" Fexil smiled shyly back at Uhura, and then to the audience.

"This is to indicate we liked the song?" Deeshal tentatively mimicked Chapel, clapping his hands rhythmically.

Chapel tried to hold back a smile at his confusion. "Yes, it is," she assured him. It was oddly charming how the alien doctor, who had exuded such poise and self-confidence in the operating room, was so tentative and reserved in this social setting. "Was that an Abesian melody she was playing?" she asked once the applause ended, and the alien woman began playing another soft song.

Deeshal nodded. "Yes, an old traditional song of theirs, called 'The Sailor's Romance.' The lyrics were something different, though."

"An old human song, written over four hundred years ago," Chapel said. "But the melodies were almost the same."

"By Erhokor, isn't that incredible?" Deeshal said,

shaking his head as he marveled at the connection. "Two completely different people, separated by almost a hundred light-years, the products of their own unique evolutionary and cultural developments, yet somehow, they both independently produce such remarkably similar pieces of music?"

"Yes," Chapel agreed. "It's something we see all the time, but still, I'm constantly amazed by it."

Deeshal looked dubiously at her. "All the time?" he asked.

"Well, we do encounter truly alien species, too," Chapel admitted. "But, there are still similarities and parallels. In almost all cases," she carefully qualified herself, "there is something that allows for a connection between us."

"That's really how you humans see others, isn't it?" Deeshal said, fixing her with an intent, thoughtful stare. "You look past the differences between yourselves and others, and focus on the similarities instead."

"Well, we try to," Chapel said. "Humans nearly destroyed themselves centuries ago because we refused to look past our differences and recognize that everyone is worthy of respect—even those we disagree with. It's a lesson we've taken to heart, and have applied to others as we've traveled out into the galaxy."

"So when you look at a Goeg like me," Deeshal asked, "your impression is . . . what?"

A corner of Chapel's mouth curled up as she tilted her head and considered the man across the table from her. "I see a brilliant, dedicated healer. A person who cares deeply about others, who is compassionate, kind, and generous."

Through the light coat of pale fur that covered his face, Chapel thought she saw Deeshal blush. "Actually, Nurse, I meant the Goeg in general; I wasn't soliciting compliments."

Now Chapel felt her own cheeks get warmer. "I'm sorry, I misunderstood," she said. "I hope you don't mind the compliments."

"Oh, not in the least," he told her, smiling widely. The rows of pointed teeth exposed in his lion-like muzzle might, at first glance, have appeared threatening. But Chapel could see in his eyes that his expression was one of enjoyment of their shared company . . . and perhaps admiration? Christine Chapel was certainly no stranger to the admiration of men; it was almost a monthly occurrence that some new crewman would land in sickbay and, at some point while under her care, express his deep (yet fleeting) romantic infatuation with her.

But it had been some time since she'd found herself the object of this more genuine sort of attention. It was something she had been hoping Spock might someday return to her, even though he'd never given any indication he would, even if he were to ever lower his Vulcan emotional shields.

"I have to admit, Nurse . . ." Deeshal said.

"Call me Christine."

Now there was definitely a pink tint beneath his light yellow facial fur. "It's a bit more of a challenge for me to look past our differences," Deeshal said, looking down at the table. "Like you, I try. I treat all my patients equally, of course. But even though it was obvious—while I was working on Lieutenant D'Abruzzo—how many similarities there were between Goeg and human, I found myself concentrating on the dissimilarities instead."

"Well, that's natural . . ." Chapel started to say.

"What I want to tell you, Christine," he said, clearly struggling with his thoughts, "is that right now, here, talking with you . . . those differences seem irrelevant. You are unique . . . and I realize that those two statements actually contradict each other." Deeshal finished with a small embarrassed laugh.

"That's okay," Chapel said, and slid her hand across the table to brush her fingertips against his. Their eyes met. "I think I know exactly what you mean."

Six

On the seventh day of their journey, the *Enterprise* experienced an inauspicious failure of one of its primary missions.

Spock sat in the captain's chair with his fingertips steepled in front of him. Though he had the conn, his command authority was severely reduced, with the *Enterprise*'s navigational control turned over to the Domain ship. As he watched the starfield on the forward viewscreen move and warped streaks of light slide past without effort, Spock reflected on how the current arrangement impacted the bridge's operational standards. While Lieutenants Arex and Kyle manned the forward astrogation panel, they were only monitoring their respective stations. The rest of the crew posted at the stations ringing the command well still had their own duties to perform, but turning control of the ship itself over to another crew had a marked negative effect on the crew's emotional state.

Spock found this somewhat troublesome. He recalled Chief N'Mi's query from days earlier, and considered that he would not need to concern himself with the crew's emotional state if they were Vulcans. But they were humans, and he needed to deal with them as humans. It was perhaps his greatest challenge as a Starfleet officer, and one of the reasons he had refused past offers to command his own ship.

As the Vulcan weighed the question of how to best address this pervasive emotional state, Ensign Frank turned in his seat at the science station and said, "Mister Spock, I think you should see this."

"See what, Mister Frank?" Spock asked, pivoting the chair in the junior officer's direction.

"I just picked this up on our long-range scans," Frank said, indicating the imaging hood on the console before him. "At first I thought it was a ship, but then I noticed some odd anomalous readings. I ran them through the data banks and found a correlation to the thing we encountered in the Gamma 7A system."

For a fraction of a second, Spock felt a jolt of emotions test his mental barriers. The "thing" Frank referred to was a giant spaceborne organism that had engulfed the Gamma 7A system, killing its four billion inhabitants and the crew of the *Intrepid*, and had also nearly killed Spock. The first officer made a concerted effort to maintain his emotionless bearing as he rose and moved to his regular station.

At first glance, Frank's comparison between his

discovery and the Gamma 7A organism appeared overstated. As the ensign had said, the object was twice the size of a *Constitution*-class ship, nowhere near the size of the other creature. And though smaller, it registered as a complex multicellular construct rather than a single-celled life-form. However, Frank was absolutely correct in noting the similarities between the biochemical signature and the genetic data Spock had collected during his probe of the Gamma 7A life-form.

"Fascinating," Spock said, as he pulled back from the scanner display. "I believe you are correct; this is a heretofore undiscovered form of space-borne life." He stepped back into the command well and resumed his seat. "It is unfortunate that we will not have the opportunity to study it fully." Spock disregarded the semi-articulate protest Frank voiced to that pronouncement and addressed the Triexian officer at the navigation station. "At our current trajectories, how long before this life-form is beyond scanner range?"

Lieutenant Arex keyed the variables into his console. "Just under fourteen minutes, sir."

"Couldn't we ask the *814* to adjust our heading?" Frank proposed. "Fourteen minutes of long-range scans isn't much."

"No, it is not," Spock agreed. "But deviating from our course to Wezonvu, and delaying our repairs, would not be in the *Enterprise*'s best interests." There was also his supposition that the Domain crew would not be favorably inclined to such an "inefficient" use of time, and further delaying the duties they were already putting aside in order to aid the *Enterprise*. "We shall simply have to make the most of our limited opportunity. Focus long-range sensor arrays two through five on the creature."

"Aye, sir," the ensign said. Though disappointment was unmistakable in his vocal inflection, this did not dampen the excitement of discovery manifested in his demeanor as he carried out his orders and studied the incoming data. Spock was gratified to note that—as he looked around the bridge and observed the rest of the crew following the conversation—they also shared in Mister Frank's enthusiasm.

Spock switched on the companel on the side of the captain's chair and said, "Bridge to sickbay."

"Sickbay. McCoy here."

"If you are not otherwise occupied, Doctor," Spock said, "I would ask you to report to the bridge."

"Why? Is there something wrong up there?" McCoy asked, concerned.

"If there were something wrong," Spock replied, "I would have required you to come, occupied or not."

"Dammit, you pointy-eared—" McCoy stopped in mid-outburst, then, after a curiously long pause,

said, "*Is it too much to ask for a simple answer to a simple question?*"

Spock raised an eyebrow in reaction. Since the dinner aboard the *814* back at Nystrom IV, McCoy had exercised an uncharacteristic degree of restraint during their exchanges. "There is no emergency, Doctor. We have made a scientific discovery, and I merely wished to solicit the input of a medical professional." He then added, "I will, however, settle for yours." Closing the channel, he cut off any retort the doctor may have offered.

As he did so, Spock heard a signal from the communications station behind him. "Mister Spock," Lieutenant Palmer, the officer manning that station, said, "we're being hailed by the Domain ship."

That struck Spock as curious. Most of the routine communications between the two ships were being handled by the liaisons aboard the *814*—currently, Lieutenant Sulu and Ensign Chekov—and the officers at the helm and navigation. There had proven little need for this more formal ship-to-ship protocol since getting under way from the Nystrom system. "Open channel, and put it on the main viewscreen," Spock said.

Moments later, the image of Second Commander Satrav, standing at the front of his command center, appeared. "*NCC-1701, code 5-58,*" he said. "*Your long-range scan arrays have gone out of their alignment,*" he then added gruffly, giving the impression that he was being put upon by having to explain his communication.

"We are conducting a scientific inquiry into an unusual spaceborne life-form," Spock explained to his Domain counterpart. "This is an unparalleled opportunity for us to gather data on a rare and—"

"Mister Spock," Satrav said, cutting him off, *"standard protocol is for all sensor arrays to remain in their standard configuration at all times, unless needed for a specific purpose."*

"There is a specific purpose now," Spock said. Behind him, he heard the turbolift doors open, and determined, without turning away from the Goeg on the viewer, that it was Doctor McCoy who had arrived. "Starfleet protocols place a high priority on scientific inquiry, and surely your vessel's own navigational sensors are more than sufficient for—"

"NCC-1701, execute code 5-59," Satrav ordered just before abruptly cutting the communication link.

"So what's code 5-59," McCoy asked from where he stood at the rail just in front of the turbolift, "and why are we executing it?"

"It is the order to bring the sensor arrays into alignment," Spock answered. "And we are not."

"No, sir?" Frank asked, turning in his seat with a look of concern.

"No, Ensign," Spock affirmed. "The Domain Defense Corps's operational standards are for their own ships; they do not apply to the *Enterprise*. Continue scans of the life-form."

"Life-form?" McCoy queried. "I assume that's what you called me up here to look at?"

"That is correct. Mister Frank, would you display your data again for Doctor McCoy?"

Frank keyed the command into the computer and slid aside for McCoy, who peered into the hooded viewer. "Hell, it looks like a giant jellyfish!" he said.

"Just the quality of insight I was hoping for from you, Doctor," Spock commented drily.

McCoy straightened up and spun around, some biting retort or another on his lips. But, rather than the expected eruption of emotional outrage, what the doctor said was, "How sure are you about the accuracy of these readings?"

"We're in the process of gathering what additional data we can in the available time frame," Spock answered, considering the doctor's use of restraint with interest, "but I have no cause to believe these readings are anything but accurate."

"Well, then, we have a pretty amazing find here," McCoy said, showing the same excitement Frank had earlier. "But what do you mean by 'available time frame'?"

"The subject will be beyond sensor range in approximately twelve minutes," Spock explained. "And given the nature of our current joint venture . . ."

". . . we can't change course to go after it," McCoy completed the statement, and sighed. "Damn, it's a hell of a missed opportunity."

Before Spock could agree with McCoy's sentiment, they were interrupted by Ensign Frank, reporting, "Sir! We just lost signals from sensor arrays two, three, four, and five."

Spock stepped up from the command well again and leaned over Frank's shoulder to check on those systems. Running a quick diagnostic, he discovered that the data feeds from those four arrays were being disrupted by a forced feedback loop.

"Those wouldn't be the same arrays our Goeg friend was so adamant about you realigning, would they?" McCoy asked.

"In fact, they would be." Spock moved back to the command chair and activated the companel again. "*Enterprise* to Sulu. Situation report, please."

"*Sulu here. Situation nominal, Mister Spock. Why?*"

"It appears that the Domain ship is interfering with our sensor systems."

"*What?*" Sulu reacted in shock. "*I saw the exchange between you and Satrav, but once he realized you weren't going to reset the sensors, he just gave the order to have that data filtered out from their navigation computers.*"

"I assume that was not the precise order he issued."

"Well, no, what he said was 'code 5-61.' If I had realized . . ."

"You are not to blame," Spock told him. That particular code, from Spock's understanding, should only have applied to the 814's own sensors. "Is Captain Kirk still aboard?"

"He and Commander Laspas were headed back to the Enterprise. That was about ten minutes ago," Sulu said, just as the turbolift opened again, revealing both the ship commanding officers, who were laughing at some shared private amusement.

"Thank you, Mister Sulu. Spock out." Spock closed the channel and moved around the command chair to intercept the pair as they stepped onto the bridge. "Captain, Commander Laspas. We appear to have a conflict between the two ships."

"A conflict?" Kirk was the first to ask. "What is it?"

"We had redirected four of our long-range sensor arrays for use in a scientific study. Second Commander Satrav protested this, and has now caused them to be disabled."

"What?" Laspas tapped his ear-mounted communication device. "814, code 8-0!" After a brief pause for the connection to be made, he said, "Second Commander, I am on the Enterprise bridge. First Officer Spock claims you had their sensor systems disabled. . . . Clarify."

Laspas listened for several seconds, during which

an expression of pronounced annoyance spread over his face. "And how often in your long career, Satrav, have you traversed this particular spaceway? . . . And in all those excursions, how many times have you ever encountered any navigational hazards or other spatial anomalies? Whatever risk there might be in allowing the *Enterprise* to use their own scanners for their own purposes would be negligible, wouldn't it?" Laspas paused to listen again, then raised his hand to his communicator and pressed what Spock assumed was a mute button. "Mister Spock, what is the status of your scanners now?"

Spock in turn looked to Ensign Frank, who checked and reported, "All affected arrays now operating normally."

Laspas nodded and pressed the same button again. "Code zero, Second Commander. Out." He touched another button on his earpiece, and then turned to the captain. "I apologize, James. The standardized protocols don't really apply in this current situation and . . . well, the Corps, by its nature, doesn't lend itself to easy adjustment to unique circumstances, I'm afraid."

"Not to worry; it was a simple enough matter to resolve," the captain told him, and turned expectantly to Spock.

The Vulcan did not mention how much valuable and fleeting time had been lost, or how much potential data. "Yes, simple enough," he replied.

Kirk nodded, pleased that the matter was closed. "Well, if there's nothing else, Mister Spock?"

"Nothing that should require your immediate attention, sir," he said.

"Very well. You have the bridge." He turned back to Laspas and gestured to the turbolift. "Are you ready for another go at three-dimensional chess?"

"Lead the way, James," the Goeg commander answered, and they both left the bridge.

"Is something wrong, Spock?"

Spock turned from the turbolift doors to face McCoy. "Why do you ask?"

McCoy fixed him with an intent, blue-eyed stare. "Because we've served together long enough that I can tell, even behind that cold stoic mask, that something isn't sitting right with you."

"Is that so, Doctor?" Spock asked, and turned away, calling up the long-range sensor readings at the auxiliary science station.

"Yes, that is so," McCoy said, standing as close as he could without making actual physical contact. "And I know there's something stuck in your craw, because you still haven't told me that there isn't anything wrong. You're worried about something more than the Domain ship futzing with our sensors, aren't you?"

"I would be negligent in my responsibilities as first officer if I did not concern myself about such matters," Spock replied, still not looking at the doctor.

"Have you talked to Jim about these concerns?" McCoy asked.

The spaceborne life-form was at the very edge of their sensors' range now, and more and more warp space noise was appearing in the data. Spock began to formulate a program to extrapolate whatever additional information they could to fill in the gaps. As he worked, he told McCoy, "There has been little opportunity for me to talk to the captain outside of Commander Laspas's company."

McCoy's eyes widened as he considered the first officer, and his lips twisted into a mocking grin. "Why, Spock, you're not *jealous*, are you?"

Spock finally turned his full attention to the doctor. "I see you have decided to resume your typical use of insult. Would you care to explain what twists of illogical reasoning led to that pronouncement?"

McCoy's smile dropped. "Spock, you don't honestly believe Jim's judgment is being impaired because of the friendship he and Laspas have struck up, do you?"

"If I did, I would have acted on that belief," Spock said.

"Then what's the problem?" McCoy asked. "From what I saw just now, it seems that friendship resolved a conflict before it got out of hand."

Spock considered that perspective, and then

allowed, "My concerns may, perhaps, be un-founded. Thank you, Doctor."

"You're welcome," McCoy said. "And . . . I'm sorry for that wisecrack about you being jealous."

"An apology is unnecessary," Spock said wearily. "You are, after all, an illogical human."

McCoy stared silently at Spock, blinked, and then answered, "Well, then, I retract my apology, you green-blooded hobgoblin."

Spock nodded and turned to head back to his place in the command chair, but still caught a glimpse of McCoy's wide, amused smile out of the corner of his vision.

Pavel Chekov's head jerked as the signal chime from his cabin door sounded, and he realized that he had nearly dozed off.

While standing upright.

In his sonic shower stall.

He muttered a Russian curse under his breath as he deactivated the cleansing head and rushed to the bedroom, where he'd laid out a fresh uniform. By the time Sulu signaled again, Chekov was hopping to the door on his right foot, tugging the left boot on at the same time. He cursed again as he tipped and fell against the doorframe, and righted himself just before the chime sounded for a third time. "Pavel, come on," Sulu said, as the door opened. "If we're late relieving Graham and Reynolds at the end of their double shift, we'll never hear the end of it."

"They're not the only ones working long shifts," Chekov said, sounding a bit more petulant than he would have liked. With the crew stretched as thin as it was with repairs, in addition to having observers assigned to the *814* bridge, a lot of the *Enterprise* crew were pushing themselves to their limits, and beyond. Today would be Chekov's third day in a row of working alpha shift aboard the *814*, then reporting to the *Enterprise* for a second shift, before dragging himself back to his cabin to collapse.

"I know," Sulu commiserated as they moved down the corridor to the turbolift. "But it's what needs to be done. And as senior bridge officers . . ."

". . . we're expected to set the example, yes, I know." The turbolift doors opened, and once the pair had boarded, Sulu took hold of the control throttle and ordered the car to Ventral Airlock 2. "It wouldn't be so bad if one of those two shifts wasn't aboard the other ship, though."

Sulu didn't argue with that sentiment. Nine days into their joint mission, it was becoming clear not only that the constant, high-pressure working conditions were the norm for the Domain ship, but that it was intentional on the part of their senior commanders. On the *Enterprise*, the Domain crew who were given liberty to visit and enjoy the larger ship's amenities had proven to be personable and pleasant. Earlier in the week, Chekov had been able to take a short meal break in the *Enterprise* mess, and had been treated to the sight of a quartet of Liruq engineers performing some sort of folk dance, while accompanied by science officer Rob D'Amato on violin. The exuberance they'd displayed there, Chekov now understood, was due to the fact that any behavior of that sort would have been unthinkable aboard their own ship.

It took several minutes for the turbolift to complete its course from the crew quarters in the saucer section, across to the engineering hull, and then down to the ship's lowermost deck. From there, Chekov and Sulu lowered themselves into the open airlock hatch, then climbed down the metal rungs that lined the short duranium tunnel that formed the primary link between the two vessels, into the Domain vessel, and through a set of heavy doors. On the other side, an annoyed-looking Abesian security guard wordlessly thrust a small data slate toward them, and they both in turn placed their thumbprints on its glasslike surface. The device gave two beeps, and the guard, still annoyed, gestured for them to keep moving. "Thank you, and you have a lovely day, also," Chekov told him as they moved out of the security area.

"Pavel . . ."

"What?" he asked Sulu innocently. "I'm only trying to be a goodwill ambassador."

The *814*'s command center was located near the core of the ship, and Chekov and Sulu had to climb down four levels of stairs, squeezing by other crew members going on or coming off duty, to reach their destination. Once there, Ensigns Graham and Reynolds relinquished their posts with grateful, exhausted nods, handing off the data slates they used for duty logs as they headed for the door at double-time pace.

Sulu sidled down the row of stations by the center's rear bulkhead, while Chekov moved to the first row and assumed the position behind the navigational sensor officer. The second lieutenant currently on duty, a Goeg woman named Asmar, looked back over her shoulder at Chekov and gave him a cold and wordless glare. "Good morning," he told her. She replied with a low subvocal growl before turning her attention back to her instruments. Chekov sighed and resigned himself to what looked to be another long, tense, and uneventful shift.

Just over two hours into that long shift, Chekov noticed Asmar stiffen in her seat as she monitored her screens. "Second Commander," she called out to Satrav, at his usual position standing before the array of viewers at the front of the room. "Code 4-77, oh-one-seven-five mark eight-oh-six-three."

"Code 4-10," Satrav answered, as Chekov punched a search command into his data slate. Meanwhile, Satrav spouted a series of numerical procedures, which registered only as a long string of seemingly random numbers in the ensign's consciousness. *How do these people keep all these damned numbers straight?* he wondered. After a moment, the meaning of code 4-77 displayed on Chekov's screen: *Apparent high-energy-yield event or events detected in or near primary space lane.* But what was a "high-energy-yield event"? Did that mean an exchange of weapons fire? A ship with a warp core breach? A subspace radiation burst? *Why can't they communicate in plain language?*

Chekov dropped the slate to his side, and refocused his attention on the computer screens Asmar was monitoring. Stepping in closer to get a better look, he placed a hand on the back of her seat as he loomed over her shoulder. She flinched only slightly at the invasion of her space, but maintained her own rapt attention on the information coming in from the ship's long-range navigational sensors. Chekov immediately spotted the "event" that had caught the Domain officer's attention; he studied the readings that scrolled up the screen. These numbers—representing measurable data—he had no trouble interpreting: it was a matter/antimatter explosion, about two light-years distant, just off their current course heading.

"Second Commander," came a voice from one of the stations behind Chekov. "Indications that Civil Transport Class I/*043* is in the vicinity of the 4-77."

"Or was," Chekov said just under his breath, prompting a look from Asmar that was equal parts annoyance and horror at the transport's apparent fate. It dawned on Chekov that his comment, as out of place as it was in this highly structured setting, could well have been taken as cold and compassionless. But Asmar had turned her face sharply away from him before he could apologize or offer any expression of sympathy.

Satrav turned to the display wall. Chekov noted that he was looking at one of the small perimeter screens, which was displaying the same feed as Asmar's station. He studied the data for several seconds, and when he turned back, Chekov was surprised to see that an unmistakable expression of sorrow had now washed over the man's normally gruff face. He looked to one of the rear stations and said, "Communications: 8-1." Chekov assumed, without referring to his slate, that this order was to attempt comm contact with the transport, though from Satrav's tone, he clearly expected this effort to be futile. Chekov looked at the data screen again, hoping he might find something there that could relieve the pessimistic mood now sweeping through the command center.

Then he saw it. "How large is a Class I transport?" Chekov asked Asmar.

She didn't immediately respond, and when the Goeg turned her head, she seemed confused by the idea that she was being asked a direct question. "How large?"

But Chekov had already raised his data slate and accessed the Domain's ship identification files. The Civil Transport Class I was slightly smaller than the Federation's *Whorfin*-class of ships, measuring 110 meters in length, with a mass of just under 150,000 metric tons. Chekov looked from his handheld device back to the readings on the navigator's screen. "They've ejected the warp core."

"Mister Chekov!" His head snapped up at the thunderclap-like voice of Satrav, who fixed him with a curious expression and said, "Clarify."

"The yield of the explosion is too low," he explained. "With a ship of that size, a containment breach within the ship's hull would have caused—"

"The energy output is greater than it would be for an isolated reactor detonation, though," Asmar said, though she did not sound too certain.

"But not that much greater," Sulu countered, as he joined Chekov behind Asmar's station and examined the data as well. "Look at this spike here, and the drop-off here," he said, pointing to the readouts. "If you boost sensor resolution, I'll bet you find out there were multiple explosions happening simultaneously: the warp core, ejected antimatter, and then one or more lesser secondary explosions."

"Negative result to code 8-1," the communications officer reported. The command center suddenly went quiet, and a dark dolor fell over its entire crew.

The silence was broken by Asmar, who said, "Second Commander, I believe the human may be right." From the looks that statement drew from Satrav, he was even more surprised to hear that opinion voiced than Chekov was. She continued, "The available evidence does indicate only partial damage to the transport. It could be the communications systems were damaged."

"Could there be survivors?" Satrav asked, his voice now dropping to an uncharacteristic whisper.

It wasn't until Asmar turned to look at Chekov that he realized the non-coded question had been directed at him. "It's possible, sir," he answered, "but there's no way of telling, not at this range." The Goeg officer took a moment to absorb that, his eyes going distant in thought. Chekov turned to look at Sulu, who shrugged back at him.

When Chekov looked at Satrav, he saw that the hope that had briefly sparked in his eyes had vanished. "Code 2-45," he said to the helmsman.

Chekov knew 2-45 was the order to resume their previous course. The sense of sad resignation that the rest of the Domain crew now exuded because of the executive officer's decision was palpable. "That's it?" Chekov demanded. "We're not even going to investigate?" The ensign knew the odds that there were survivors on the transport were slim, but he found it beyond belief that the Second Commander would simply disregard that possibility.

Satrav, who had begun to pace away, turned back. "You just told us that you didn't know if there were survivors or not."

"Yes," Chekov said, "but there is the chance—"

"And there is the chance your interpretation of the data is wrong, and they all died in an instant," Satrav cut him off. He scowled and shook his head as he said, "Our current mission is to convey your vessel to Wezonvu, as Commander Laspas agreed to do. That mission is not altered because of speculation and wishes."

Chekov turned to Sulu again, and saw that the lieutenant was just as stunned by the Goeg's reaction as he was. Sulu then said to Satrav, "Captain Kirk would certainly agree to the delay."

"Captain Kirk does not command this vessel," Satrav snapped back.

Chekov and Sulu exchanged another look. There was something surreal about the situation, trying to convince the Domain officer to undertake a rescue of his own people, and having him insist that his priority was to help the *Enterprise*, regardless of what the *Enterprise*'s officers suggested. Sulu gave him a small shrug, which Chekov took as a sign to drop the matter, and let Satrav do as he saw fit. Chekov realized there was little else they could do under the circumstances, but the idea of doing nothing rankled him.

"But if there are people left alive," Asmar interjected tentatively, "and they were to die because—"

"Code 10," Satrav snapped at her, and gestured to a pair of security guards who then moved from their posts at the sides of the room toward her. Asmar meekly rose from her seat, and Chekov gave her an apologetic look as he stepped back to make room for the approaching soldiers.

He was caught by surprise, though, when one of the guards, a big Rokean who stood at least half a meter taller than him, grabbed hold of the back of his collar. "Huh?" was all he could manage to say before he found himself elevated closer to the Rokean's height.

Sulu, being similarly manhandled by the other soldier, managed to be a bit more articulate. "What are you doing? You can't just put us off your bridge like this!" he shouted as the guards, preceded by a compliant Asmar, ushered them toward the exit.

"I cautioned you before about causing disruption of this vessel's orderly operation," Satrav said. He then turned away to face the main display wall again and tapped his ear-mounted communicator. "Laspas to Command Center," Chekov heard him say before they were taken out into the corridor and the door slid closed behind them.

The toes of Chekov's boots scraped along the

deck as the guard assisted him and Sulu back up the four deck levels to the airlock. "Our captain will hear about this," Sulu vowed the entire way back to the *Enterprise*. If the guards cared anything about this threat, they gave no indication. For his part, Chekov kept his mouth shut, wondering if it might have been better if he hadn't looked so closely at the sensor data. He wondered about a people who could heartlessly turn away from a helpless, stranded ship.

They reached the security checkpoint, where the same Abesian was still on duty. "What's happening?" he asked the guards when he saw them approaching with the Starfleet officers in tow.

"Code 10. Both of them," the Rokean said, sounding terribly amused, as he dropped Chekov back onto his feet.

"Is that why we're changing course?" the Abesian asked, as he held the thumbprint scanner out to Sulu.

"What?" Chekov blurted.

"We are?" asked the Rokean guard behind his back.

The Abesian nodded as he held his scanner to Chekov. "You don't feel it?"

Chekov paused, and tried to make himself aware of the feel of the Domain ship. On the *Enterprise*, he could usually detect the shift in ship's power that accompanied a change in direction or speed; apparently the same held true for the crew of this ship, too, because the Rokean was nodding now in agreement.

"Huh," Chekov's guard said, giving him an oddly impressed look.

"Guess you convinced Second Commander Satrav after all," Sulu's guard said, and then the guards pushed the Starfleet officers into the intership connecting tunnel.

"Changing course?"

Kirk stood up from his chair and stepped forward, leaning over Lieutenant Kyle's shoulder to check the astrogation board for himself. "Are you certain it's not just a course correction?" he asked.

"No, sir," Kyle answered as he reviewed the data coming through the helm station.

"Sensors aren't picking up anything that would require a correction," Lieutenant Arex added from his position to Kyle's right.

Kirk moved back to his chair again and hit the comm panel. "Kirk to Sulu: report." He got no answer. "Kirk to Chekov, come in."

Again there was no response, and Kirk looked to Uhura at her station. "Our signal is getting through," she told him, having already anticipated his question.

"Then why aren't they answering?" Kirk asked,

more to himself than to the communications officer. "Get me Commander Laspas."

Uhura nodded as she turned to her board, and
a moment later said, "Commander Laspas is responding, sir."

"Good. Open channel, and put him on the
main screen," Kirk said as he walked around in
front of the astrogation panel and faced the image
of his Domain counterpart. "What's going on over
there, Commander?" he asked before the other
man could say a word. "Where are you taking my
ship?"

Laspas's eyes went wide in shock. "*We've discovered a vessel in distress, and have initiated rescue
procedures,*" he told Kirk. "*Your officers told Satrav
you would be amenable to this.*"

That stopped Kirk cold. "A rescue mission?"

"*Yes, a civilian transport vessel that's suffered
a warp core breach,*" Laspas said. "*Under ordinary
circumstances, with a vessel of this class and size, we
would be severely limited in what we could do. But
with the* Enterprise *and its resources?*" The Goeg's
voice took on an unmistakably pleading tone.
"*James, there may be as many as two hundred and
fifty people aboard that vessel . . .*"

Kirk put up a hand and said, "Of course, we
don't object to undertaking a rescue mission. You
offered us your help when we needed it; we'd be
more than happy to do what we can for you now."

"*Thank you, James,*" Laspas said, a smile of relief crossing his face.

"Where are my officers, Laspas?" Kirk asked. He knew neither Sulu nor Chekov would have signed off on a course change, even for a crisis situation, without reporting it back to the *Enterprise.*

Laspas's smiling expression turned more serious. "*It seems that in advocating the change of mission, they incited at least one act of insubordination amongst my crew. Satrav had to have them removed before he could brief me on the situation.*"

"You had them removed?" Kirk asked, feeling his ire rise again. "We had agreed that we would have those liaisons aboard your ship as my observers and advocates at all times."

Laspas explained, "*From what Satrav tells me, they were quite impassioned, on the verge of inciting a mutiny.*"

"I . . . find that difficult to believe," Kirk answered, keeping his tone neutral.

Laspas shook his head slightly and said, "*I'm certain it was simply a case of misunderstanding, and your men's unfamiliarity with our protocols.*"

The captain appreciated that the commander was attempting to appease him without expressing any doubt in the motives of his officers. But he couldn't help but wonder exactly what the nature of this latest "miscommunication" was. "And where are Sulu and Chekov now?" he asked Laspas.

"They should be back aboard the Enterprise," Laspas answered. *"But now that the confusion has been resolved, they are welcome back aboard."*

Kirk weighed his next words carefully. "I think perhaps, for the duration of the rescue mission, it would be best if you and I were to communicate directly rather than through intermediaries. As to avoid any more miscommunication."

"That may be for the best," Laspas agreed. *"Though I do want you to know that we are immensely grateful to Mister Chekov for his invaluable insights. You have a fine young officer in that man, James."*

"Thank you," Kirk said neutrally as Laspas signed off. He remained where he stood, and wondered what Chekov had done to be singled out for such praise, so shortly after being ejected from the *814*. There was far too much miscommunication happening of late, and Kirk worried that he and Laspas were not as immune to it as either might have thought.

"Sir?"

Kirk shook off his reverie, and turned to the navigator. "Yes, Mister Arex?"

"I've received the coordinates of the crippled transport from the *814*," he answered. "I've calculated that our arrival at the Wezonvu Repair Facility will be delayed by approximately fifty-nine hours at minimum, not including the time required for the rescue operation itself."

"Thank you, Mister Arex," Kirk said as he

circled back around the astrogation station. "Uhura, intraship," he said as he settled back into his chair.

She nodded as she turned to her workstation, keyed in the proper sequence of commands, and then turned back. "Go ahead, sir."

Lifting his head toward the bridge audio receptors, Kirk said, "Attention, all personnel. This is the captain speaking. The *Enterprise* and the 814 have been temporarily diverted from our journey to the Goeg Domain's repair facility in order to assist our new allies in a humanitarian mission. This will mean at least three additional days of joint operation of our two ships. Your efforts thus far during this joint mission have been noted and are greatly appreciated, and I know I can rely on each of you to continue your exemplary performance as the *Enterprise* helps in this rescue mission. Kirk out."

The captain gestured to Uhura to close the channel, and as she acknowledged, Lieutenant Arex reported, "Course change completed, Captain. Now on an intercept course with the transport's coordinates at warp four."

"Thank you, Lieutenant," Kirk said, acknowledging the execution of an order he had not given, and watched the stars warp by, his ship out of his control.

Scotty felt a tap on the heel of his boot, and heard what he thought was someone saying his name. He switched off the sonic decoupler he was using and peered down to the lower opening of the Jefferies tube. "Hello?"

"Mister Scott?" he heard clearly now. "Chief N'Mi asked me to report to you."

"Ah, yes." Scotty climbed back down to the main engineering deck, where one of the *814*'s Abesian technicians was standing waiting for him. "Lieutenant Fexil, isn't it?"

"First Lieutenant Fexil, yes," she said.

"Right. I heard you the other night, playing with Uhura in the rec hall," Scotty said, giving her a smile and a wink. "Lovely performance."

Fexil dipped her head modestly and said, "Thank you, sir."

"So then, lass," Scotty said as he crossed to the worktable where he had laid his open toolkit. "I was talking with your chief, telling her that, seeing as we're going to be spending a few more days together than first planned, we could maybe get a few more of our repairs started before we lay in at your repair base."

"That would be an efficient use of time."

"My thinking precisely." Scotty put the decoupler back in its appropriate cutout in the kit, and then picked up the data slate he had laid on the table beside it. "I would really like to get some people up and inside our damaged warp nacelle pylon and see just how deep those microfractures go." He handed the slate to Fexil, and said, "I hope you don't mind that N'Mi volunteered you."

"Oh, no," she answered, unable to contain a small grin. "I'm actually thrilled to have the excuse to work on the *Enterprise*."

Scotty tilted his head, considering the woman and her reaction. "It's not going to be any day at the beach, you realize."

Fexil looked up at him, momentarily confused by his metaphor. "No, sir," she then assured him. "I understand this is work, and I will treat it as such."

"All right, good," Scotty said, then added, "Though if you wish to linger here a bit after the work is done, I won't deny you that." Fexil's smile returned on hearing that. "You know, lass," Scotty continued, "I get the impression . . . and I hope you don't take this the wrong way . . . but it seems the *814* isn't the most pleasant place."

Fexil reacted as if slapped. "Well, being an officer in the Defense Corps isn't meant to be pleasurable," she said. "It's one of the most important jobs in the entire Goeg Domain."

"Well, yes, of course it is," Scotty said in response. "But still, as hard and as serious as any job is, you've got to be able to take some pleasure in it."

The Abesian looked ready to dispute that, but instead said, "I'll review these requirements, and have a duty schedule prepared before the end of this shift, sir."

"Aye, thank you, lass," Scotty said, dismissing her, and shook his head sadly at her retreating form before grabbing another tool from his kit and climbing back into the Jefferies tube to continue his work.

"To ensure the record is clear as to the sequence of events," Spock said, leaning back in his chair and looking across the briefing room table to where Sulu and Chekov were seated, "when you initially pointed out the possibility of survivors to Second Commander Satrav, Mister Chekov, he opted not to investigate and to continue on to Wezonvu, is that correct?"

Ensign Chekov, sitting erect with his eyes straight ahead, responded, "Yes, sir."

Spock shifted his gaze then to take in both men. "And you questioned his decision?"

"He was using the *Enterprise* as an excuse for not investigating," Sulu said. "I felt that we had to make it clear to him that Starfleet would never prevent them from undertaking a rescue mission."

Captain Kirk leaned forward in his own chair beside Spock. "That's when Satrav told you, 'Captain Kirk does not command this vessel'?" he asked.

"Yes, sir," Sulu answered.

"At that point," Spock continued, "you say there was a single member of the *814* crew who spoke in support of a diversion, prompting Satrav to eject her and you from their command center."

"That's correct, sir," Sulu said. "And it wasn't until we were almost off the ship that we found out that Commander Laspas had reversed Satrav's decision."

Spock nodded, satisfied that this debriefing was now complete, if not entirely satisfied with the questions that still remained unresolved. The first officer turned to Kirk, who seemed momentarily lost in thought, but caught Spock's look and said, "Thank you, gentlemen. You're dismissed."

As Sulu and Chekov both stood to leave, Spock continued to observe the captain's face, trying to get a read on whatever thoughts were currently going through his mind. Spock was once again struck by how well the typically emotional human captain was able to repress any outward indications of his mental status. "Well, Spock," Kirk finally said once the doors had slid closed, "your thoughts?"

Spock tilted his head and said, "It would seem that Commander Laspas's claim that Misters Sulu and Chekov were in danger of inciting mutiny was an exaggeration, at best."

"Well, Satrav's claim, as related by Laspas," Kirk countered.

Spock inclined his head, acknowledging this distinction. "We've seen that the Domain Defense Corps is more strictly authoritarian than Starfleet. Clearly, Second Commander Satrav perceived a challenge to his authority where there was none."

Kirk nodded, and then sighed. "I suppose misunderstandings are almost inevitable early on in any association between two different cultures. We need to find a way to minimize these problems, especially now, as we head into what is potentially a dangerous situation."

Spock steepled his hands in front of his face as he considered his response. "Captain," he said at length, "I would suggest that the problem we currently face is not one of misunderstanding."

"No?" Kirk asked, raising one eyebrow.

"No, sir," Spock said as he turned to face the captain. "Satrav did not misunderstand Sulu and Chekov; he refused to listen to them, or to accept their input as valid. This incident, as well as others, illustrate the Domain's propensity for unilateral action, and a seeming unwillingness to engage in the type of cooperative effort we had agreed to."

"That's a rather broad condemnation, Spock," Kirk said. "Don't forget it was a Domain officer who offered us their help in the first place."

"My memory is intact," Spock assured the captain. "However, we have had several instances now where the Domain crew has shown they consider our interests to be secondary to their own."

"There are always conflicts of interest, Spock," Kirk said. "It's all but unavoidable. What's important is that we're able to resolve those conflicts peacefully and amicably."

"The interests of individual persons or groups will inevitably be in conflict with the interests of others," Spock allowed. "But actual conflicts can be avoided, if both parties are willing to do so."

"Are you suggesting the Domain is not as interested in avoiding these conflicts as the Federation is?" Kirk asked.

Spock nodded. "I believe the evidence to date supports that contention."

Kirk shook his head. "No, Spock. You're suggesting that these people will turn on us, that we were wrong to ever trust them. The Federation was built on trust. There would be no Federation if humans, Vulcans, Andorians, and Tellarites hadn't all learned to trust each other."

"This is true," Spock admitted. Indeed, there had been numerous times prior to the formation of the Federation when the trust among the founding members had been severely tested. "But as one of your countrymen once advised, 'Trusting too much to others' care is the ruin of many.' I am only advising that you not give them more trust than they have earned."

The captain did not immediately say anything in response, and Spock turned and left him to the privacy of his reflections, trusting he would make the proper judgment.

* * *

Deeshal had commented more than once about the size of the *Enterprise*'s sickbay, but it wasn't until McCoy visited the medical facilities aboard the *814* that he understood how drastic the difference was. "My freshman dormitory room at Old Miss was bigger than this," he joked as he got his first look at Deeshal's examination and emergency treatment room.

"Defense Corps efficiency," Deeshal said. McCoy had to admit, there didn't seem to be a wasted cubic centimeter in the tiny space. The walls were lined with cabinets, all meticulously labeled and color coded. On the deck, he noted the seams where a table could be raised if needed, and above, an array of lights and sensor pods. Deeshal pressed his hand to a panel by the door, which opened to reveal a library computer interface. "I've got the passenger and crew manifest lists of the *043*, finally." He started reading off the information. "There were seventy-one Goeg, twenty-two—"

"Are."

Deeshal turned. "What?"

"There *are* seventy-one Goeg," McCoy said firmly. "Don't write them off yet, Doctor. We need to keep a positive outlook, and keep hoping for the best."

Deeshal's head bobbed up and down as he said,

"You're right, you're absolutely right. There *are* seventy-one Goeg, twenty-two Luriq, seventeen Rokeans, eleven Abesians, nine Icorrs, and three Urpires." He typed in a sequence of instructions on the keyboard embedded on the inside of the panel doors. "All right, we'll want at least two hundred units of pelazine ready. . . ." He clicked another key to bring up a new screen on the computer monitor, and then scowled. "I have only seventy-seven units in inventory."

"Pelazine," McCoy said, referring to the Starfleet-issue data slate he carried. "Okay, this looks like a variation on cordrazine; our lab will have no trouble synthesizing all you need."

"Excellent," Deeshal said with a soft sigh of relief. "And your tri-ox is close enough to our oxygenation enhancer that we don't need to worry about that."

"Lucky, that," McCoy said, his thoughts turning to the patient who had proven that similarity. Lieutenant D'Abruzzo was almost fully recovered, though the healing of his arm had slowed down considerably in the last day or two. McCoy had resisted releasing him, but once their rescue got under way, they would need every bed they could get.

Deeshal continued, "We also should have a liter of diomotin on hand for the Urpires . . . for all the good it'll do us," he added under his breath.

"What does that mean?" McCoy asked.

"Urpires are notoriously fragile physically," Deeshal told him. "Plus, there are none in the Corps, and I've never had to treat one."

"Well, you never had to treat a human before last week, either," McCoy reminded him.

"That was luck, like you just said," Deeshal said with a sigh. "Giving D'Abruzzo that injection was no more than a calculated gamble on my part. If anyone deserves credit for saving that man, it's you and Christine."

McCoy scowled at the younger physician. "Doctor, again: you have to stay positive here. You don't have the luxury of doubt. I've never treated an Urpire before either, or a Goeg or a Liruq or any of the species on that transport. *I'm* relying on *your* help here. And Christine is relying on your help."

The mention of Chapel's name had the intended effect on Deeshal. "Right," he said, lifting his head and squaring his shoulders. "Right, so . . . if your lab can take care of the diomotin and the pelazine, I can have the rest transferred from our stores over to the *Enterprise*."

"Sounds like a plan," McCoy said, making notes on his slate, and also making a mental note to thank Christine.

By the time they reached it, the Goeg Domain Civil Transport Class I/043 was already dead.

Kirk had joined Laspas in the *814*'s command center, and as soon as they were in visual range, he knew it was too late. He, along with Laspas, Satrav, and the rest of the crew, stared in horrified silence at the image displayed on the central viewscreen. The transport's hull was still partially intact, thanks to whatever crew member had managed to eject the warp core and antimatter stores. But the secondary blast that had been detected, they now saw, was the ion-pulse impulse engines. The entire aft portion of the ship had been ripped away, opening large sections to vacuum. As Laspas issued a code command to scan for life signs, Kirk mentally reviewed the ship specs he had studied while they were in transit. Without warp or impulse engines, the vessel would have been left on emergency battery power only. And those batteries had a maximum life of only twenty hours, meaning any passengers that might have survived the explosion would have run out of breathable oxygen long before their arrival.

"Negative, code 4-9," said the Icorr officer at the main sensor station.

"Repeat code 4-9," Laspas ordered, without pulling his fixed glare away from the screen.

A funereal silence filled the crowded space. "Negative, code 4-9," the officer repeated.

"Kirk," Satrav said, also not turning his eyes from the screen, "while I don't believe your Starfleet sensors will detect anything different than ours will . . ."

Without letting him finish, Kirk pulled out his communicator and signaled the *Enterprise*. "Mister Spock, scan the transport for any evidence of life signs," he said. Given the advantage the Domain sensors had over their own in the Nystrom system, Kirk was just as doubtful as Satrav, but if there was the slightest chance . . .

"*Negative, Captain,*" Spock reported back after several seconds. "*We are detecting one hundred twenty-eight bodies in and around the vessel, all deceased.*"

"Acknowledged," Kirk said quietly as he folded his device shut and looked to Laspas. "I'm sorry."

"All for nothing." The words rattled in Satrav's throat before being forced through his clenched teeth. "This is what we all had our hopes raised for. To find . . . this . . ."

Laspas finally turned from the image of the transport and toward his exec. "Satrav . . ." he said in a muted, sympathetic tone, "code 10." Satrav nodded and marched for the command center exit, doing his best to maintain his dignified, commanding air. "His daughter and her family were lost in a similar accident," Laspas told Kirk in a low whisper as they watched the older man's shoulders sag as he disappeared behind the closing door.

Kirk didn't know what to say in response to that. What words were there at a time like this? How many people had he lost over the years? How many more had he failed to save? "I'm sorry there wasn't more we could do," he finally offered.

Laspas nodded. "As am I, James," he said, and then fell silent, standing with his back to the viewer, unable to bear the sight anymore.

The stillness that had taken the command center was then shattered. "Commander!" one of the Domain officers called from her station. "Code 1-7!"

Hearing that, Laspas instantly pushed his mournfulness aside and spun to the viewer again, as if expecting that some immediate threat had suddenly appeared there. When he saw the image was unchanged, he wheeled back on the crew member. "Clarify!" he practically roared at her.

"I executed a series three scan on the area of the breach, Commander," she said, "and I've detected residual evidence of weapons fire. The transport was defending itself against something at the time the reactor was ejected and detonated."

Laspas considered his junior officer with narrowed eyes. "First Hand Asmar, I don't recall issuing a code 4-70," he said.

"No, Commander. I . . ." She faltered for a second, then said, "It was when the Starfleet officer—Sulu?—looked deeper into the sensor data that we learned the transport vessel was still partially intact. I thought doing the same now, we might discover . . ."

"Code 4-71!" Laspas called out urgently. "The *Enterprise*, too, James! Scan for any subspace distortion trails leading away from this area!"

Kirk was momentarily caught off guard by the vehemence of that order, but gathered himself and withdrew his communicator again. "Spock, it looks like the transport may have been attacked by another ship. Scan for any sign of another warp vessel leaving the area."

"*We are currently on one of the Goeg Domain's primary space routes, Captain,*" Spock pointed out.

"Understood, Spock. Run the scan."

"Positive code 4-71!" called out a Liruq sensor technician. "Seven-five-one-two mark three-six-nine-eight, bearing four-five-one-two mark nine-nine-eight-five."

"Spock, did you copy that?" Kirk said into his communicator.

"*Affirmative, Captain,*" he answered. "*Scanning those coordinates. . . . Confirmed, sir. Detecting a recent subspace trail deviating from any established local space lanes.*"

"The Taarpi!" Laspas said. "Code 2-44!"

Kirk felt the deckplates under his boots vibrate, and saw the image of the dead transport slide below the bottom edge of the center viewscreen and disappear. He snapped his head to Laspas as the vibrations gained in intensity. "What is code 2-44?" he demanded.

"Pursuit course," Laspas told him, his lips curling up in something other than a smile. "We're going after the *pyurbs*, James!"

Seven

Laspas led Kirk out of the command center into a small ready room situated just on the other side of the forward bulkhead. Like the rest of the vessel, the commander's private retreat was small and efficiently laid out, with a narrow bunk, a workstation, and a head. It did boast a few personal touches, like the framed photograph on his desk that showed him as a younger man posing with an older couple Kirk assumed were his parents. On the small stand beside the bunk sat one of his Kawhye books, an illustration of a Geog *gaat* and rider embossed on its cover.

Once they were both inside, and the door shut behind them, Laspas moved close in the cramped space and pushed his muzzle toward Kirk's face. "James, we are going after them," he said in a tone that brooked no disagreement.

Kirk held perfectly steady, and met the other man's eyes with equal resolve. "I am still the captain of my own ship! The *Enterprise* is severely damaged; she's not fit for a hostile engagement. You do not have the authority . . ."

"I have all the authority I need!" Laspas roared. "They murdered over a hundred civilians! I have the duty to go after them, and make them answer for this atrocity!"

Kirk countered Laspas's rising frustration by keeping the tone of his own response calm and level. "You cannot unilaterally commandeer my ship and take it into an armed confrontation!"

"Then I'll have all the connectors cut, and set you and your damned ship adrift!"

Laspas's threat hit Kirk like a fist to the gut. "You wouldn't do that," he said, feeling none of the calm confidence he conveyed.

To his immense relief, he was right to call Laspas's bluff. "Damn it, James," the commander said, deflating. "These are the same *pyurbs* who attacked your ship back at Nystrom. Why in Erhokor's name are you opposing me on this?"

"We're both in this together, Laspas. I can't let you simply push me to one side and take this kind of action unilaterally, without any regard for my ship or my people," Kirk said.

"I have no less regard for your ship and crew than I do for my own," Laspas insisted, sounding slightly wounded.

And perhaps that's the problem, Kirk thought to himself, recalling the conversation he'd had with Spock earlier. He quickly dismissed that ungenerous estimation. He knew Laspas better than that.

Or he thought he did.

"I'm not a diplomat, James," Laspas continued, and tried to pace the tiny space. "It is not my intention to deny you what is yours. But I'm not one for negotiating. I'm a commander of the Defense Corps. When action needs to be taken, I act."

"Diplomacy is not exactly my strongest suit, either," Kirk told him. "We're very much alike, you and I, Laspas. So I know you can understand why it's so difficult for me to be in the position I'm in, and to have no control over my own command."

"I do understand," Laspas agreed, and Kirk could see in his eyes that he did in fact empathize with him. Then he fixed Kirk with his sharp, intense eyes. "But if you were in my position? If it were a hundred humans who had been murdered?"

"Of course I would want to go after their attackers," Kirk said, "humans or not." He'd done so time and again in the past, following attacks by the Romulans on the Neutral Zone listening stations, and by the Gorn on Cestus III. In such instances, if one of his officers had cautioned restraint, he had refused to let that stand in the way of doing what he felt was necessary.

"Well, then?" Laspas asked expectantly.

"*If* I were to agree to this," Kirk said slowly, "I would be making a tremendous show of faith in you, Laspas. The *Enterprise* is still recovering from our first encounter with the Taarpi . . ."

"But our combined abilities will give us a marked advantage over the vessel we're going after," Laspas told him.

Kirk waved that claim away, and stared directly into the Goeg's eyes, mustering all the persuasive power he could. "Understand this: I have pledged my life to keep my ship and my crew safe. If I'm to put the safety of my ship and the lives of my crew in your hands, then I need you to make that very same pledge."

"You have it, James," Laspas said, lifting his muzzle high, showing his exposed throat to Kirk as he said, "On my own life, I swear it."

Kirk drew a deep sigh, and then slowly nodded. "All right then," he said. "Let's go after them."

"*Code 2-5, five minutes,*" said the voice over the *Enterprise* bridge speakers.

From the Domain ship, Commander Laspas replied, "*Standby code 2-2.*"

"We're approaching the Nalaing system," Uhura interpreted for the benefit of Kirk and the rest of the bridge crew, "and preparing to drop out of warp."

Kirk nodded in silent acknowledgment as he paced a circle around the upper level of the bridge. His nerves were on a razor's edge, as they always were whenever heading into a potentially dangerous situation. When he was a cadet, he'd reprogrammed the *Kobayashi Maru* simulation test, doing away with some of the variables and allowing him to actually beat the test, a feat never achieved before. In the years since, he'd come to realize that he'd done himself a disservice. Out here, a captain didn't have the luxury of setting his own conditions, or picking and choosing the variables of any situation. And now, there were even fewer variables he had any power to control.

"Execute code 2-2," Laspas ordered his crew, and a moment later, Kirk felt the change in the vibration of the deck plates under his feet. On the main screen, the streaks of light shrank back to small points, the brightest of which was the star the Goeg Domain designated Star 12-982-09, and called Nalaing-Qo by the natives of the second planet. That planet, called Nalaing, was a major center of interstellar commerce, and also long suspected to be a safe haven for the Taarpi.

Kirk halted his circuit of the bridge beside Spock at the science station. "Any sign of the Taarpi ship on scans?" he asked.

"Negative," Spock answered. "The warp trail does indeed terminate here, but given the significant volume of sublight starship traffic in this system, it is impossible to determine where the vessel we have been pursuing may have gone from here."

"Captain," Sulu interjected, "the *814* is taking us on a heading toward Nalaing, half impulse speed."

Kirk stepped down into the command well and hit the transmit key on his armrest. "Kirk to Laspas. Have you identified the attacker?"

"Not yet," the Domain commander answered. *"We need to get into closer range."*

"Do we mean to engage the enemy in such close proximity to planetary orbit?" Kirk asked as he took a step forward and looked at the readouts on the astrogation panel. There were a number of ships in orbit, almost all of them civilian judging from their transponder signals, and many appeared to match the general profile of the ship they'd been pursuing.

"Don't worry, Captain Kirk," Laspas said, making a point of using his proper title during this stage of their operation. *"Once we manage to identify the Taarpi ship, they'll run. They can be vicious when preying on weaker vessels, but at heart they're cowards. We only need to flush them out, and then we'll have them."*

Spock looked up from his viewer then and said, "It appears the commander's prediction has come true. A ship matching our target's profile has made an abrupt break from planetary orbit."

"On-screen," Kirk ordered.

The image of the planet on the screen switched from that of a distant bright disk to a Class-M world colored in blues and whites, half shrouded in the darkness of night. Computer augmentation highlighted a single small speck of light in motion across the black semicircle.

"Captain," Chekov said, first studying his console and then turning to look at Kirk over his shoulder. "They are not running, sir."

"Confirmed," Spock reported. "They appear to be on an intercept course."

"Yellow Alert," Kirk called, at the same time Laspas, over the speakers, declared what he assumed to be the equivalent status code. Kirk opened the channel to the other ship again. "Kirk to Laspas. This is not quite what you planned, is it?"

Laspas answered with a sharp, *"Code 1-2,* Enterprise! *Code 1-2!"*

Uhura was about to offer a translation, but that was one of the directives Kirk had made sure he had memorized. "Red Alert!" Kirk ordered. "All hands to battle stations. Screens up, extended configuration."

Chekov punched two rows of buttons on his console. "Screens up, sir. Extended configuration stable." In their current joined configuration, the *814*'s dorsal shield emitters were being obstructed by the *Enterprise*, and likewise, the majority of the emitters on the engineering section's ventral hull were inoperative. The solution had been for the Starfleet ship, possessing the superior shield technology, to boost the power to the lateral defenses, and use those to shore up the Domain ship's defenses.

"Shield strength along the overlap?" Kirk asked,

referring to the zone where the two ships' defenses would be their weakest.

From the engineering station, Ensign Strassman reported, "Eighty-one percent." Kirk clenched and unclenched his jaw. They would just have to hope that would be enough.

"Enemy vessel at five thousand kilometers and closing," Chekov reported. On the viewscreen, the gray-green alien vessel was visibly drawing closer. It was of similar design to the *814*, except smaller and with significantly less power. That didn't make it any less of a threat, though, as the remains of the transport had attested.

Uhura, holding her audio receiver in place, announced, "The *814* is firing, sir." At the same time on the screen, Kirk witnessed an energy beam lancing out from below the *Enterprise* and streaking past the Taarpi vessel by what looked like mere meters. The Taarpi vessel then returned fire and, as the *Enterprise* offered a far larger profile, their beam scored a direct strike.

The lights dimmed marginally, but otherwise, the shields absorbed the brunt of the assault. "Shields are holding," Strassman called out.

A second later, the deck pitched. "What the hell was that?" Kirk demanded, gripping the arms of his chair.

It was Uhura who answered, "Commander Laspas has ordered the *814* to take evasive maneuvers," just as the deck then tipped in the opposite direction.

"Careful . . ." Kirk said in a low voice, addressing a crew who could not hear him, and who owed him no allegiance.

"Careful!" Scotty cried out as the *Enterprise* lurched again harder, throwing him against one of the orange webbed safety barriers at the edge of the main engineering section. "Ye can't jolt a ship of this size around like a beach ball!"

"*Your 'wee bairns' can handle a little rocking,*" Chief N'Mi snapped back at him over their open comm channel. "*More phaser hits like that last one, neither vessel can.*"

Scotty bit back his reply. The Domain engineer had made it clear that they had very different attitudes toward their respective ships, and that she considered him overly attached to and protective of his ship. Unfamiliar as he was with the Liruq and the idiosyncrasies of their language, he couldn't be certain if her jibe had been meant as humorous or if it was genuine mockery. Scotty had opted to assume it was the former, though there was nothing friendly in the woman's tone now. Not that he could blame her—both their ships were endangered, and both were being hampered by the other in their efforts to protect themselves.

The deck tilted again, and Scotty gripped the console before him as the lights and control panels flickered. "Blast it! These relays are still too sluggish!" Scotty hit a switch on his console companel. "Ogden, Farrell, we need that control circuit back on line now!"

"We've almost—"

"Not 'almost'—now!" Scotty cut Crewman Ogden off, then closed the channel as he noticed another alert signal blinking on his situation board. "Bloody hell. N'Mi, are you seeing this internal pressure spike in the starboard warp plasma umbilical?"

"Code 8-55 confirmed, Scott," she said, her tone reflecting Scott's concern. *"Attempting to counteract. Stand by for code 8-40."*

Emergency warp core shutdown, Scott translated silently as he started running for the main reactor control room. "Acknowledged," he shouted, and fought hard not to unleash any more caustic remarks. They'd known there would be a high risk, if forced into an armed confrontation, of overstressing the connections between the two ships. If the umbilical was compromised too soon after dropping out of warp, before the warp drive had completely cycled down, the results would be disastrous for both vessels. But a complete shutdown now would mean a long restart procedure once the crisis had passed, and until then, both of their ships would be in the same situation the *Enterprise* had started in: stuck in a hostile star system without their FTL drives.

Except not really—the *814* could simply cut the *Enterprise* free, engage their own warp engine, and be on their merry way alone.

Scott wasn't sure that was such a terrible possibility.

The engineer turned a corner, his boots almost slipping out from under him, and reached the reactor control room. Once inside, he immediately slapped his hand against the panel on the bulkhead, dropping the heavy containment hatch. A core shutdown wasn't a normally a dangerous procedure, but this wasn't a normal circumstance. If anything went wrong, the rest of the ship needed to be protected. As the hatch rumbled into place and sealed Scotty inside alone, he hoped to heaven nothing went wrong.

Turning away from the hatch, he went to the small chamber's situation panel and was both surprised and relieved to see that the plasma pressure reading was already dropping back toward normal. He reopened the channel to the Domain engine room and said, "Lass, you did it."

"Affirmative," N'Mi answered, her tone colored in relief. Then the deck shook again under Scotty's feet. *"But the danger is not yet over."*

"Aye," Scott said as he unsealed and reopened the hatch to return to main engineering. To himself, he wondered where the most serious danger to the *Enterprise* was coming from.

"Dammit!" Sulu swore as the Taarpi ship dodged another of his phaser shots.

"Steady, Lieutenant," Kirk said. "Don't let them rattle you." The ship shook again as the *814* initiated another maneuver. Strassman at engineering had managed to fine-tune the inertial dampers so as to minimize the worst effects of the jarring directional shifts, though not to cancel them out entirely.

"They're coming around for another pass," Chekov said, just as the ship shook again, this time under the enemy's weapons fire. As the *Enterprise* presented a larger target than the *814*, they had taken the brunt of the assault.

"I see them," Sulu said, sighting the Taarpi vessel through the extended stereoscopic viewer at his console. He triggered the phasers again, and on the main viewer, beams of blue phaser energy lanced out and struck home.

"Direct hit, amidships," Chekov reported.

"Weapons and engines only, Mister Sulu," Kirk reminded him of the orders he had given at the outset of this engagement. The plan he and Laspas had agreed upon was to disable the Taarpi shields and to use the *Enterprise*'s transporters to bring the Taarpi aboard for questioning, and eventually for trial.

"I'm trying, sir," Sulu said, frustrated. "But with our targeting systems disassociated from helm control, I'm being forced to compensate manually."

Kirk keyed open the channel to the *814* as the ship was shaken by another blast. "Kirk to Laspas. We need you to transfer helm control to us."

There was a slight hesitation from the Goeg commander before he responded. *"Clarify."*

The captain was caught short by that. Was he really being asked to explain a request to have control of his own ship given back to him? "Our weapons targeting is being hampered by the segregation of the two systems. We have the wider range of fire; it makes more sense for control to be given back to my bridge."

There was another wait for a response from the Domain vessel, and Kirk was about to ask Uhura if the link had been severed when Laspas finally said, *"Tie in all control stations with corresponding* Enterprise *bridge stations."*

Seconds later, posts that had been in near-silent standby mode for close to two weeks came back to life, and the familiar music of electronic tones and chirps filled the bridge again. "That's more like it," Chekov said as both he and Sulu conducted a quick review of their current status.

Kirk tried to put the frustration he was currently experiencing to one side to focus instead on the situation at hand. "Mister Sulu, fire at will."

"Yes, sir," the helmsman answered as the Taarpi ship made another swooping pass on the main viewscreen. Sulu fired weapons again, and this time his shot was far more accurate. "Direct hit on their impulse engine!" he shouted in triumph. "They're limping, sir. I think we have them."

Kirk struck the left arm of his chair with his fist, sharing in Sulu's jubilation, "Uhura," he said, "open a channel. Tell them to stand down and surrender their vessel."

Uhura turned to her console, then quickly turned back. "They're refusing our hails, sir."

"Captain," said Chekov, "I believe they are attempting to go to warp."

Kirk knew that he couldn't let that happen; he didn't want this pursuit to become an open-ended mission. "Sulu, move to intercept. Don't let them get away."

Sulu said, "Aye, sir," and an instant later, a photon torpedo was launched from the *Enterprise*, flew across the bow of the fleeing vessel, and exploded directly in its path.

Kirk leapt up from his chair. "Sulu! No!" he shouted. Using photon torpedoes against a vessel the size of this one would have been deemed overkill even before it had been disabled.

Sulu, though, had recoiled back in his chair, hands poised up and away from his control panel, as he watched aghast at the scene playing out on the viewer. The force of the blast had sent the Taarpi ship into a tumble, turning end over end as a series of smaller explosions, like a string of old-fashioned black powder firecrackers, flared along its outer hull. "I didn't do that, sir!" he said.

Before the captain could demand to know who did, he heard the whine and whoosh of another photon torpedo being propelled from its launch tube. Looking up to the screen again, he saw this one land a direct hit on the Taarpi ship, and watched in horror as the vessel was consumed in a white-hot fireball of matter/antimatter annihilation. Kirk grabbed hold of the back of Sulu's chair to steady himself, looking first at the horrified upturned face of the helmsman, then at his first officer. "Spock?"

The Vulcan turned in his chair away from his station. "The torpedo launches were not initiated by Mister Sulu." Kirk's follow-up question caught in his throat, and fury overtook his shock as he registered Spock's next words. "The triggering commands came from the *814*."

Eight

Spock stood as Kirk headed for the turbolift. Unbidden, Spock followed directly behind the captain, joining him just as the doors began to slide closed. Kirk pretended to ignore him as he ordered the car to the ventral airlock and squeezed the activation handle with far more force than necessary. They rode for several seconds in silence, Spock violating standard convention by remaining at the front of the car with his back to the door. Finally, Kirk met his first officer's passive stare and snapped, "Was there something you wanted, Mister Spock?"

Spock considered his commanding officer and friend for a moment longer before answering, "May I respectfully suggest that confronting Commander Laspas at this time would be unwise, given your present emotional state."

"Mister Spock, even you must recognize that my 'present emotional state' is completely justifiable," Kirk said testily.

Before Spock could elucidate on that point,

Sulu's voice sounded from the turbolift companel. *"Bridge to Captain."*

The captain reached over and replied, "Kirk here."

"Sir, we detected an escape pod from the Taarpi ship," Sulu reported. *"Three life-forms aboard."*

A small glimmer of hope broke through Kirk's dark expression. "Beam them aboard immediately, and alert McCoy."

"Already way ahead of you, Jim," the doctor's filtered voice interjected. *"We've got all three of them, and we're on our way to surgery."*

"Surgery?" Kirk asked, the light of his hope dimming. "How bad is it?"

"I wish I could tell you, Jim, but right now . . ." McCoy said, and trailed off uncertainly.

The captain sighed. "I know you'll do your best, Bones. Kirk out." He deactivated the comm unit's transmit button, and looked back to Spock. "You realize, if Bones can't save them, that's three more murders on my head."

"You cannot accept the moral responsibility for the actions of others," Spock told him.

"It was *my* ship that struck the killing blow," Kirk countered, pained. "I'm the one who agreed to cooperate with Laspas in this . . . vendetta. I believed him when he said what he wanted was justice, not revenge."

Spock paused to consider his response. "Might I

suggest the possibility, Captain, that the destruction of the Taarpi ship was not intentional? The first torpedo launched was fired across their bow."

"The first of two, Spock," Kirk reminded him.

The Vulcan acknowledged that point with a nod. "I would also note that the Domain does not possess photon weapons; the most powerful armaments in their arsenal are cobalt fusion torpedoes. It is likely they were unaware of our photon torpedoes' capabilities."

"Is that supposed to excuse them for co-opting our weapons systems?"

"No, sir," Spock said. "Although we had already agreed to assist the Domain against the Taarpi ship, and had already employed our weaponry against them."

Kirk shook his head at him, incredulous. "Spock, you're the one who took exception when they interfered with our scanners. Now you're defending their commandeering of our weapons?"

"No, sir," Spock said. "I am not defending what they've done, and I continue to be concerned by the seemingly cavalier treatment of this ship by Commander Laspas and his crew. However, we are in a position where continued cooperation with them is necessary if we are to reach their repair facilities. It is in our best interests to recognize that the Goeg Domain is not as similar to the Federation as we may have initially thought."

Kirk scowled. "That has become abundantly clear." The lift came to a halt, and the doors opened. The captain took a step forward, but Spock remained where he stood, blocking his path.

"Jim, I know from experience that it is pointless to recommend putting your emotions aside," Spock told him. "But I would advise you to take care where they are directed before acting on them."

Kirk finally allowed himself a small smile. "Mister Spock, never for a moment believe that your counsel is pointless." Spock acknowledged the sentiment with a nod as he stepped to one side, allowing the captain to disembark.

Damn Spock and his cold Vulcan logic, Kirk thought as he climbed down the connecting tunnel from the *Enterprise* to the *814.* For a man who claimed to be so unfamiliar with emotions, Spock had a strong understanding of their potentially destructive power. This shouldn't have been that surprising, given his own struggle to tame the human half of his nature.

But his friend also knew him well enough to have recognized there was more underlying his impulse to rush onto Laspas's ship. As much as he might have liked to deny it, Kirk understood Spock's subtle suggestion that beneath his anger at the Domain crew was anger at himself, for having placed so much confidence in Laspas.

Kirk's feet hit the deck of the *814*'s airlock entry chamber, and he willed himself to present the guard with, if not a friendly face, then one of a man in firm control of himself.

Once he had made his way down to the Domain ship's nerve center, he was greeted by an effusive Laspas. "James!" he said, crossing the deck toward him, wearing a broad smile. "We are victorious, thanks to you and your crew!"

"No, not thanks to us," Kirk answered adamantly.

Laspas chuckled at what he took to be modesty on Kirk's part. "Now, as much as I would like to claim the credit and the glory, it was your weapons that won the day."

The other man's exultant reaction to what had happened brought Kirk's tamped-down emotions to the surface again. "Yes, they were our photon torpedoes. But the responsibility for what was done with them is on your head, not mine."

Laspas stared at Kirk in open confusion, as did Satrav, who was drawn from his post into the exchange. "Captain Kirk, perhaps it's a problem with our universal translators, but it sounds as if you're displeased."

"Oh, I'm displeased," Kirk assured them. "I am highly displeased. I didn't give the order to fire those torpedoes. It was someone in your crew who hacked into our weapons control system."

"Weapons!" The Goeg commander crossed the deck in one long stride, to where a nervous-looking Liruq sat at one of the foremost stations. "Do you know anything about this?"

The young officer's eyes jumped from Laspas to Satrav and back as he stammered, "I . . . I saw the Taarpi were preparing to go to warp, Commander. They needed to be stopped."

"And so you used the Starfleet ship's weapons?"

"From our position beneath NCC-1701, we couldn't fire on them ourselves," the weapons officer explained. "It was our only option."

"Your only—?" Kirk started to say before restraining himself. It was not his place to reprimand the man while his commanding officer was standing right beside him.

Laspas turned to gauge Kirk's reaction, and then turned back to the Liruq. "Code 10," he told the junior officer, who immediately stood and vacated his station, seeming almost relieved to escape his commander's scrutiny.

"Another example of this 'initiative' you Starfleet officers are so fond of?" Satrav muttered. Kirk shot him an acid look, but the second commander had already turned away and resumed barking out his orders to the command center.

"James, join me," Laspas said, and led the way to the doorway tucked to the side of the forward viewer bank. Kirk followed him into his ready room, and waited as Laspas stood in silent thought for several seconds before turning around to face him.

"James, I can understand your objection to having your authority undermined and having a sensitive ship's system compromised. But . . . this battle was meant to be a cooperative effort. It's not really so important whether it was your crew or mine that struck the final winning blows, is it? We can both take pride in our victory."

Kirk blinked once in surprise. "You think that's what this is about? Bragging rights?" he asked. "Your crewman committed an act of mass murder! And he used my ship to do it!"

Now it was Laspas who expressed shock. "You call that murder? It was the animals aboard that ship who murdered over a hundred civilians!"

"You told me your intention was to apprehend them, question them, and bring them to justice," Kirk reminded him.

"Once you suggested it, yes," Laspas said. "Your idea of using your transporters was a good one, and if we had had the opportunity . . ."

"But your people didn't give us that opportunity!"

"They were about to slip away from us!" Laspas shot back, matching Kirk's irate tone. "Those animals would have happily destroyed you, just as their colleagues at Nystrom IV would have if we hadn't saved you."

Realizing they were both on the verge of boiling over, Kirk reined himself in and took a deep breath before continuing. "We do not take life unless absolutely necessary. One of the Federation's highest ideals is that all life, all living beings, are deserving of basic respect."

"Even when those beings do not share your unqualified respect for life? And who kill others with none of the same remorse?" Laspas asked.

Kirk nodded. "Even then, yes."

"Well, that is an . . . interesting philosophy," Laspas said coolly, considering Kirk as if for the first time. "It is regrettable that you have chosen to take offense at the way the Domain handles its own internal affairs." He turned to open the cabin door, and gestured to Kirk to walk out ahead of him.

Kirk stepped back out into the command center, with Laspas directly on his heels. "Satrav, report," the commander ordered.

"Standing by, code 2-45," the second commander answered.

"Captain Kirk." Kirk turned to Laspas, who stood so close behind him that he was forced to look up into his narrow slit eyes. "Would you have any objection if we were to resume our course to Wezonvu?" the commander asked.

"No," Kirk answered in the same neutral tone of voice. "No objection."

"Code 2-45," Laspas called out to the command

center, then looked back down his muzzle at the human. "Is there anything else, Captain?"

"No, nothing," Kirk replied as he turned to go, leaving the Goeg to his ship.

McCoy felt a sick sinking in his stomach as the three survivors materialized on the transporter platform, and Doctor Deeshal, standing at his side, uttered a single word: "Urpires."

They both rushed forward to examine their patients. Only two of the three were Urpires—insectoid beings, diminutive and frail-looking, even without considering their injured state. McCoy had only briefly reviewed the Domain's minimal basic information about the species ahead of their unsuc-cessful rescue mission. Now he loaded that data into his medical tricorder, and ran a scan of the two bodies lying crumpled in front of him. They were still alive, but judging from the ugly cracks in their chitinous exoskeletons, and the dark ichor seep-ing from those wounds and soaking their garishly colored clothing, they wouldn't be for much longer. The third survivor, an Abesian, appeared to be in slightly better shape, though her limbs were spasm-ing wildly, and she keened in obvious pain.

"I'll take this one first," Deeshal said, referring to the more seriously injured of the two Urpires. McCoy nodded and gestured to the first of the three two-person gurney teams standing by ready to get the injured to sickbay. As they carefully transferred the wounded alien onto the stretcher, McCoy heard Jim's voice from the transporter console, ordering the escape pod passengers to be beamed aboard. McCoy signaled to Ensign Houlihan to open the comm channel, and called out, "Already way ahead of you, Jim. We've got all three of them, and we're on our way to surgery."

"Surgery? How bad is it?"

"I wish I could tell you, Jim," he answered as Deeshal headed out the doors with his patient, and McCoy indicated for the second team to take the other Urpire, and the third the Abesian. "But right now . . ." He trailed off, his lips suddenly gone dry.

"I know you'll do your best, Bones," Kirk told him before signing off.

"Let's hope that's good enough," McCoy muttered, then called out to his orderlies, "All right, come on, time's a-wastin'!" They all rushed together to sickbay, McCoy continuing to scan both patients as he jogged alongside. The Abesian's injuries were minor—a broken femur, a possible concussion. The Urpire was much worse off, though McCoy couldn't say anything more specific than that.

When they reached sickbay, Deeshal was already in the surgical bay with his patient, assisted by Jabilo M'Benga. Christine Chapel stood just outside the doorway, prepped and ready to assist

McCoy with his procedure. McCoy directed her to take the second Urpire into surgery as well, and then filled in med tech Gannon, who started working on the Abesian.

After quickly finishing his own pre-surgery prep, McCoy entered the surgical bay, and stopped when he saw Deeshal, M'Benga, and Chapel all circled around the second Urpire. The first one lay alone on the other table, covered head to foot with a sheet, the surgical support frame over its mid-section deactivated and silent. "Dammit," McCoy whispered, and then said, "Tell me what's happening," as he started moving again toward the others.

"He was too far gone," Chapel told him, looking up briefly from her close monitoring of the still-living Urpire.

"And this one?" McCoy asked as he moved beside M'Benga. He was deftly manipulating the surgical frame controls as Deeshal issued urgent instructions and anxiously observed the effects.

"Extensive blunt-force trauma to the skull and thorax, with significant internal injuries and hemorrhaging," M'Benga answered without looking up or breaking his concentration. "I think we've stanched the worst of the bleeding."

"But we're not out of the woods yet," Deeshal added.

McCoy observed M'Benga as he continued working. Though nearly twenty years younger than

McCoy, M'Benga had far more interspecies medical experience, having interned on Vulcan and having served on a frontier starbase just prior to joining the *Enterprise*. If anyone was going to be able to treat such an unfamiliar patient, it would be him.

Though right now, that appeared to be a very big "if."

"Diastolic pressure dropping," Chapel called out urgently, at the same time as warning tones sounded from the diagnostic sensors.

"No," Deeshal growled. "We're missing something! What?" he demanded of no one in particular as he jabbed at buttons and twisted dials, running every scan the frame was capable of.

"We need to try something else," M'Benga said. "Something to slow down his autonomic systems until we can—"

"That won't work with an Urpire," Deeshal cut him off. "He'll crash, just like the other one."

"Brainwave activity becoming erratic," Chapel said.

Deeshal slammed the palms of his hands on top of the shell in frustration. Then he lifted his head and said, "2-0-1-9."

"What?" McCoy asked, silently biting back a caustic remark about the Goeg's damned obsession with numbers and codes.

"In the medical transfer case I brought over!" Deeshal shouted. "It's labeled two-oh-one-nine!"

McCoy crossed the surgery to the corner where the transport case from the *814* had been set, and quickly found the clearly labeled vial, arranged sequentially with all the rest. *Okay, the numbering system does come in handy sometimes,* he privately admitted as he grabbed a Domain-issue hypospray, inserted the drug cartridge, and crossed back to slap it into Deeshal's outstretched and waiting hand. The Goeg doctor wedged the nozzle of the hypo into the seam in the patient's carapace where his head met the thorax, and released the drug with a low hiss.

At first, the Urpire seemed to stabilize, but his life-sign readings remained uncomfortably weak. "Come on," Deeshal urged him in a low tone. "You know you don't want to die all the way out here, so far from Cravalco. Fight!"

Deeshal's exhortations weren't enough, though. "Brainwave readings faltering again," Chapel said, and the doctor's entire body sagged. McCoy looked from him to M'Benga, who wore a similar expression of defeat. The beeps and tones from the surgical arch abated, and then fell quiet, as did the four healers.

After several seconds of silence, Deeshal lifted his head. "Where is the third one?" he asked. "The Abesian?"

"Out in the main ward," McCoy said. "Her injuries were relatively minor."

Deeshal pushed himself away from the table and out the door of the surgical bay. McCoy followed him across the ward to where the third survivor lay, still unconscious, on her biobed. Deeshal considered the vital signs displayed on the overhead monitor, then the patient herself. He lightly ran his fingers along her leg, feeling for the fracture in the bone.

Then, when he found it, he pressed harder. Through her sedation, the woman began to wince in pain, and Deeshal reacted by squeezing harder still. "What are you doing?" McCoy asked, as the semiconscious woman's cries grew louder.

"Who were they?" Deeshal asked in a preternaturally calm voice as he continued his callous prodding. "What were they doing on that ship with you?"

McCoy had to physically grab the other man's arm and yank him away from the biobed. "What in the hell has gotten into you?" he demanded.

"There were Urpires on that vessel!" Deeshal said, still glowering at the patient as Chapel gave her another painkiller and sedative. "The Urpires are politically neutral, they take special pride in remaining above any kind of outside conflicts. There are no Urpires in the Taarpi."

"So?" McCoy asked. "What does that mean?"

Deeshal turned to face McCoy. "That means they weren't on her ship by choice. And that their injuries—their deaths—were most likely her doing."

As Kirk made his way to the 814's uppermost deck, back toward the airlock and his own ship, he passed a quartet of Starfleet engineers, led by a Liruq officer describing the repairs needed to the structures connecting the two ships in the wake of the recent battle. The captain put on a smile for them as they moved by, hiding his private concerns from them.

A fair amount of foot traffic was flowing through the hard dock connection, in both directions. In spite of everything, Kirk was proud of the way the two crews had managed to work together to keep things running as smoothly as they had. He also knew that many had formed friendships along the way. And he hated now having to worry about how trustworthy any of the Domain crew were.

After waiting for a pair of Domain crewmen—a Liruq and a Rokean—queued up ahead of him to log out with the guard and move through the airlock, Kirk climbed up after them to the *Enterprise*. As he stepped onto the deck of his own ship again, he found his chief engineer waiting for him. "Welcome back aboard, sir."

"It looks like we've got some more repair work under way," Kirk said, gesturing to the other crew members transferring between the two ships. "How bad is it?"

"Minimal, sir," Scotty answered, walking alongside the captain as he made his way to the nearest turbolift. "Our shields held up better than I hoped after the beating they took at Nystrom. The worst of it was from all the evasive maneuvering the *814* put us through. We're lucky we didn't end up ripping a chunk of our hull off."

Kirk's brow furrowed at hearing that. "Perhaps we should have a procedure in place for emergency separation," he said.

Scotty nodded. "Aye, that's something N'Mi and I had discussed from the get-go. Coordinating it would take quite a bit of doing—"

Kirk interrupted him. "I was thinking more along the lines of something that wouldn't necessarily require coordination with the *814*," he said, his voice lowered.

"Oh." Scotty's eyes widened as he realized what Kirk was talking about, and he dropped his voice as well. "Are we anticipating a genuine emergency situation?"

Kirk's lips pressed into a tight line of concern. "I just want to have options open to us," he said, as they reached the open and waiting turbolift.

"Well, I'll do what I can . . ." Scotty stated, shaking his head. "But without warp capacity of our own, we won't get very far."

"Understood, Scotty," Kirk said, clapping the engineer on the shoulder before boarding the turbolift. "We'll burn that bridge when we get to it."

Kirk ordered the lift to sickbay. As soon as he arrived and the doors opened, the captain heard a commotion coming from down the corridor. Bones's voice cut through the two others he heard. "I don't care who you are! This is my sickbay, and unless you're a lot less healthy than you look, you're not setting foot in here." Kirk picked up his pace, and saw the same Liruq and Rokean pairing who had come aboard ahead of him standing just outside the entry to main sickbay, being held at bay by Leonard McCoy.

"You are impeding the official business of the Goeg Domain," the larger Rokean said.

"And you're impeding my treatment of a patient!" McCoy snarled back. "Would you care to guess which I give more of a damn about?"

Before matters could escalate beyond mere words, Kirk wedged his way into the center of the group. "What is going on here?"

"What's going on, Captain Kirk," McCoy said, putting a stress on his name and rank for the benefit of the two soldiers, "is that these . . . gentlemen want to pull a seriously injured patient out of her bed and drag her off to some interrogation chamber."

"That patient is a dangerous terrorist," the

Rokean said, not seeming too impressed by the human captain. "She must be turned over to us."

"Oh, must she?" Kirk asked, not hiding his annoyance at having orders issued to him by interlopers on his ship.

"The Taarpi are the Goeg Domain's most inexorable threat. They have been responsible for—"

"I know what the Taarpi are responsible for," Kirk thundered at the guards. "They launched an unprovoked attack on the United Federation of Planets, nearly destroying my ship at the Nystrom system, and then tried to finish the job just minutes ago." Kirk stepped right up to the large Rokean soldier, nearly pressing his nose into his bovine face. "*We're* the ones who captured this woman, so *we're* the ones who will get first crack at questioning her. Then, once we reach Wezonvu and *I'm* through with her, maybe then we can discuss extradition to the Goeg Domain." Kirk took a step back then, and asked, "Do either of you have any problems with that?"

The Domain soldiers appeared to have been caught completely off guard. After McCoy's humanitarian appeals, they didn't expect the hard-line tack Kirk had taken. After a momentary show of uncertainty, the Rokean answered, "I will have to bring this to my superiors."

"Fine. You do that," Kirk said, pointing the pair toward the nearest turbolift. After another moment of awkward indecision, the Rokean cocked his head to his partner, and the two headed back the way they had come.

"Bravo, Jim," McCoy said once the duo were out of earshot.

"Never mind the accolades," Kirk said as he let his belligerent front slip away. "What's going on here, Bones? You said 'patient.' I thought there were three people in that escape pod."

The doctor's smile quickly evaporated. "There were. We couldn't save the other two."

Kirk took a moment, then asked, "And the one who made it, what kind of shape is she in? Will she be able to talk?"

"Give her a day or two to recover and yeah, she'll be fine. At least," he added, shooting a side-wise glare at Doctor Deeshal, "she will for as long as I have anything to say about it."

Kirk looked over at the Goeg physician as well, and it struck him that he had been standing there the entire time, oddly disengaged from the confrontation with the two soldiers and from the current discussion as well. As he noticed Kirk's look, he dropped his eyes to the deck, pointedly avoiding eye contact with anyone else in the sickbay.

The captain turned his back to the Goeg doctor, and whispered to McCoy, "Problem?"

"I'm not sure," McCoy answered, also trying to keep Deeshal from overhearing. "I hope not."

"All right," Kirk said, leaving it at that. "Keep me posted."

As he turned to go, McCoy stepped out into the corridor with him. "Jim . . . that was a pretty convincing show of anger you gave for those two guards. You all right?"

Kirk gave him a tight, humorless smile. "Nothing you need to worry about, Bones."

But McCoy caught him by the arm. "No one leaves my sickbay unless I say they're fit to leave." Kirk put up a token protest, but allowed the doctor to lead him into his private office, and then to plant him into one of the chairs in front of his workstation. "All right, Jim, let it out."

"Let what out, Bones?" Kirk asked.

McCoy took the seat opposite him. "We're getting a hell of a lot more than we bargained for when we first agreed to let these people 'help' us, aren't we?"

"You have a true gift for understatement, you know that, Doctor?"

"And I get the feeling that your little chat with Laspas went about as well as my last half-hour with Deeshal," McCoy continued.

"He didn't have the slightest compunction about destroying that ship!" Kirk nearly shouted, standing up out of his chair. "Or about using my ship to do so. The Goeg Domain is little more than an empire with a thin veneer of democracy covering it." His anger then suddenly spent, Kirk wrapped his fists around the back of his chair and said, "How could I have misjudged these people so badly?"

McCoy stood then, so that he and the captain were eye to eye. "It's hard enough to be a good judge of people you do know, let alone strangers. Hell, I was married to my ex-wife for over fifteen years, and I had no idea from one day to the next what she was capable of. You can hardly be blamed for not knowing what Laspas would do if we crossed paths with the Taarpi again."

"Maybe." Kirk shrugged. "But I assume your divorce didn't involve the threat of phaser fire, either."

McCoy chuckled at that, but before he could either confirm or deny Kirk's assertion, they were interrupted by the whistling of the intraship, and Uhura's voice saying, *"Bridge to Captain Kirk."*

Kirk tabbed the unit on McCoy's workstation. "Yes, Lieutenant?"

"Captain, there's a hail incoming from Commander Laspas, asking to speak with you."

Kirk and McCoy exchanged curious looks. "Pipe it down here to Doctor McCoy's office," he said as he slipped behind the desk and turned the monitor to face him.

"Captain Kirk," the Goeg commander said formally as soon as the connection was made. *"Why didn't you inform me that your ship had saved one of the Taarpi when you were aboard just now?"*

"Because I didn't know then," Kirk told him.

"We had tried to save all three, but two didn't make it, and the third is under the care of our doctor."

"You must hand this terrorist over to us," Laspas said. *"Even according to your own laws, you're not to interfere in the internal affairs of foreign worlds and governments. By holding this criminal, you are doing exactly that."*

Kirk almost had to laugh at the way Laspas had phrased his argument: *even according to your own laws.* As if the Prime Directive was a minor consideration in comparison to whatever legal or moral right he had as a member of the Domain. "I disagree," Kirk told him. "That vessel fired on the *Enterprise,* the *Enterprise* returned fire and forced the ejection of that lifepod, and it was the *Enterprise* who recovered it and its passengers. From where I stand, it's the Goeg Domain who wants to interfere in a Starfleet affair."

Laspas pressed his leonine face close to the monitor screen. *"By Erhokor, this is not a game!"*

"No, it is not," Kirk agreed, equaling the other man's intensity. "Your people intended to kill everyone on board. So you can understand why I might be hesitant to turn the sole survivor over to you and your tender mercies."

Laspas glared at him from the monitor for a silent moment. *"James,"* he then said, switching back to using his familiar name again, but not evincing any of his earlier camaraderie. *"I would like to settle this peacefully. But if forced to, I will employ other methods."*

Kirk's eyes flicked briefly to McCoy, whose expression was one of indignation mixed with worry. What "methods" was Laspas threatening? Sending armed soldiers onto the *Enterprise*? Or worse, using their control over the ship's warp engines and other systems to do them further damage?

The captain turned his attention back to the monitor and matched the Goeg's stare. "Laspas, I have gotten to know you rather well over these last several days. Not well enough, perhaps, but still, I feel my estimation of you as a good and honorable man was a correct one. So I believe you when you say you would like to settle this peacefully."

Laspas smiled. "*Thank you, James.*"

"But," Kirk continued, "this woman will not be turned over until my doctor is ready to discharge her. *Enterprise* out," he said, cutting the channel before Laspas could respond.

The captain leaned back in McCoy's chair and let out a long breath as he considered the now-blank screen before looking across to the doctor. "Well," McCoy said, "let's hope your estimation of Laspas is right."

"Amen to that," Kirk said.

Even though the mess hall was just as full and active as usual for the alpha to beta shift change, it felt oddly subdued now to Uhura, with so many of the

814 crew gone. She certainly couldn't fault Captain Kirk for the new restrictions, allowing only engineers and technicians who had legitimate work to do on the *Enterprise* aboard—he was merely adopting the same policy Commander Laspas had put in place on his ship. But it was terribly sad that what had started out as a way of exploring and celebrating new and exciting cultures had been cut short.

There were only three Goeg present, whom Uhura recognized as engineers. They were seated together at a single table, apart from the rest of the *Enterprise* crew, eating quickly and talking in low whispers among themselves. The lieutenant found herself repeatedly glancing their way as her dinner companions, all from the astrophysics lab, discussed their department's ongoing nystromite research. Their excited conversation about ionic lattice properties and electron band structure and other characteristics of the alien crystals for the most part sailed far over Uhura's head.

The near entrance to the mess opened, and Uhura looked over to see First Lieutenant Fexil entering. Their eyes met briefly, and Uhura offered her a smile. But though the Abesian engineer clearly noticed her, she made no gesture of recognition or greeting, and instead headed directly to the food slots. Uhura sighed silently, regretting that what had promised to be a rewarding cross-cultural learning experience had come to such a premature end. She continued to watch as Fexil collected her tray from the open food slot and carried it across the room to where her colleagues were seated. But as she took an empty seat, the other three abruptly stood and, without a single word, walked away and filed out of the room, leaving their half-eaten meals behind. Fexil behaved as if she hadn't even noticed, lowering her head and methodically shoveling her food into her mouth as fast as she safely could.

Uhura, shocked by what she'd just witnessed, excused herself from her tablemates and crossed the mess. "Mind if I join you?" she asked Fexil in a soft, sympathetic tone.

Fexil glanced up at her, then back down quickly to her food. "We're no longer allowed to fraternize with Starfleet crew any more than is necessary to perform our duties."

"Well," Uhura said, as she pulled out one of the recently abandoned chairs, "as one of the senior Starfleet officers aboard this ship, I think it necessary that we engage in a little fraternization." She sat, and faced the Abesian directly. "What just happened?"

Fexil kept her eyes down on the tray in front of her. "I don't know what you mean."

The lieutenant took one of the forks that had been left behind by the others, reached across the table to tap the edge of Fexil's plate, then lifted it, pulling the other woman's gaze up to her own face. "I'm pretty sure you do know what I mean."

"Nyota . . ." Fexil looked at her miserably. "I know you're trying to be a friend . . ."

"Oh, this isn't friendly," Uhura said, fixing her with her most serious look. "I'm a senior officer. If I witness something that I think may potentially put the ship at risk, such as an interpersonal rift that may compromise team performance, I am obligated to look into it, and report it if need be."

Fexil's eyes went wide, and the green coloration leached from her face. "Oh, please don't . . ."

Uhura put a reassuring hand on the other woman's forearm. "Then talk to me. What just happened?"

Fexil dropped her head again. "It's the Taarpi you took on board."

"What about her?" Uhura prompted.

"She's an Abesian."

Uhura nodded, and waited for Fexil to say more. "And?"

Fexil scowled at her. "Do I need to spell it out?"

Uhura's mouth fell open in disbelief. "You mean that because she's an Abesian, and you're an Abesian, your crew would treat you that way?"

"It's nothing I'm not used to," she muttered as she started poking at her food again. "Abesians aren't that well regarded by the Goeg to begin with."

"Why wouldn't they be?" Uhura asked.

Fexil shrugged. "It's just how things are. Abes was not technologically advanced when the Goeg first discovered our world, and there's still the general perception that Abesians are kind of backward, intellectually inferior . . ."

"That's terrible!" Uhura said. "But surely, you're living proof those kinds of stereotypes just aren't true: an intelligent and talented engineer serving as a first lieutenant on a Defense Corps starvessel."

"And then there are the malcontents like the one in your sickbay," Fexil answered, with a low hiss of frustration, "who instead of working and struggling to make a better life for themselves, think they deserve to have all that handed to them, and attack the Domain when they don't get it. It doesn't matter what any of the rest of us do; we all end up tainted by them."

Uhura was stunned by what she was hearing. Whatever else she might have thought of the Goeg Domain, she couldn't believe that an advanced interplanetary society could still harbor such prejudicial attitudes toward their fellow citizens. "I've seen you and your teams in action, though," she told Fexil. "Your people certainly seemed to respect you."

"They respect the rank, and they take the work seriously. But they have their more subtle ways, while we're on duty, of reminding me that I'm not as good as they are," the Abesian woman said pitifully.

"You can't believe that, though," Uhura told her vehemently. It was almost impossible to think that this accomplished young woman could actually accept the negative self-image forced on her by others. "If you weren't good enough, would Chief N'Mi have put you in charge of the integrated warp operations team?"

"But she's not Goeg, either," she answered ruefully.

"I don't understand."

Fexil finally looked up from her plate at Uhura and said, "No, I wouldn't expect you to." She then pushed away from the table, her food unfinished, and left Uhura to stare silently after her.

Pock-pock.

Chris Chapel closed her eyes and pressed the palm of her hand against their lowered lids.

Pock-pock.

The xenopharmacology text she was trying to read was difficult enough to plow through all on its own. The added distraction—

Pock-pock.

—only made matters that much worse. She really needed to get this down, if she had any hope of finishing the required academic work for her doctorate in any kind of reasonable timeframe.

Pock-pock.

She opened her eyes again and concentrated on the data slate lying on the desk in front of her. She just needed to focus and not to let—

Pock-pock.

Chapel bolted up out of her chair, marched from the anteroom into the near-empty main ward where Lieutenant Joe D'Abruzzo was still laid up, and snatched the hollow, palm-sized rubber ball he had been bouncing off the near bulkhead and deck for the last hour out of midair.

"Forgive me, Joe," she said when she saw the pitiful, disappointed look he gave her. "I know how bored you are, cooped up in here for so long . . ."

"I really don't think you do, Nurse," he said. "It's been over a week now. I'm this close to going completely buggy in here."

"Soon," she assured him. "Doctor McCoy still needs to monitor how your arm is healing."

"You mean how it isn't healing," he said, his head falling back onto his pillow.

Chapel stepped over beside him and placed a hand lightly on his wrapped left arm. "You took a lot of damage. You can't expect an injury like yours to heal overnight. You just have to stay positive."

"Please," D'Abruzzo said, staring at the biosensor array overhead. "With all of the sugar-coating you and McCoy have been feeding me, I think I'm getting cavities. If it was going to get any better than it has so far, you would have seen it by now, wouldn't you?" He waited for Chapel to answer, and when she didn't, he lifted his head and asked her directly, "Please just give it to me straight: I'm not going to get full use of my arm back, am I?"

"No, you won't."

Chapel whirled in her chair to see Deeshal standing in the doorway to the ward. "I had hoped we could save more of your muscle tissue before it necrotized, but I'm afraid I failed in that regard. But with the proper physical therapy regimen, there should be no reason you cannot regain some degree of functionality."

"Thank you, Doctor, for being honest with me," D'Abruzzo said, looking satisfied if not happy. He lay his head back down, and Chapel stood up to leave him alone with his thoughts, making sure to place the ball back in his open palm.

She then turned on Deeshal, and once they were back out of the ward and out of earshot of the patient, she told him, "Doctor McCoy is not going to appreciate your doing that."

"It seems to me I'm not likely to get any appreciation from anyone here, whatever I do," he answered.

"You're right about that," Chapel said as she brushed past him.

"Christine, wait," Deeshal said, trailing in her wake. "Can't we talk?"

"What would you like to talk about, Doctor?" Chapel asked as she took her seat at the desk again.

"I'd like to talk about why you've suddenly become so aloof toward me."

Chapel gave him an incredulous look. "Do you

really need to ask? After the way you treated that woman?"

"That woman is responsible for the deaths of over one hundred innocent people," Deeshal reminded her. "She should count herself lucky she's being treated at all."

"No thanks to you," said Chapel. "If you had your way, she'd have been dragged out of sickbay and thrown in a cell."

Deeshal looked affronted by that accusation. "She would have been brought to my medical bay, and taken care of there."

"Yes," Chapel said acidly, "I saw the way you would have treated her, Doctor."

"I forgot myself for a moment there," Deeshal said, dipping his muzzle in a fleeting look of shame. "But," he then continued, raising his head again, "I am also a member of the Goeg Domain Defense Corps. I also have a responsibility to help protect our citizens from those who would do them harm."

Chapel stood then to meet his eyes. "Then explain why you were willing to treat Lieutenant D'Abruzzo down on Nystrom IV, when only minutes earlier you were being fired on by the landing party."

"Well, that's different," Deeshal said. "Once we learned your people weren't Taarpi, I realized that the weapons exchange was just a terrible misunderstanding."

"But they were still actually firing at you," Chapel pressed him. "How could you be so sure of that?"

"I wasn't. But—"

Chapel preempted whatever qualification he was trying to make. "So you and your shipmates could still have been at risk, but you put your duty as a physician first," she said, just as she heard the approaching voices of Captain Kirk and Doctor McCoy. "That is what I'm asking of you here now."

McCoy led Kirk into sickbay, and tensed as he saw the Domain physician was present. "Doctor," he said to the other man, attempting a degree of civility. "Was there something you needed?"

"I came to check on Mister D'Abruzzo," Deeshal answered. "We spoke about his arm, and the progress of his recovery."

McCoy felt his good manners betray him. "And who authorized . . ." he began to harangue the alien doctor, but trailed off when he noticed Chapel putting up a placating hand and mouthing the words, *It's okay.* "Well," McCoy said, still scowling, "I suppose I did put it off longer than I should've . . ."

"I assume, Doctor," Kirk interrupted, stepping between the two and addressing Deeshal, "that you also had another reason for being here?"

Deeshal nodded. "It's been twenty-four hours. The Abesian can be questioned now."

"Yes," Kirk said, "and with respect, we would prefer that you not be here when we revive her."

"Hold on, Captain," Deeshal objected. "Your agreement with Commander Laspas says I have the right to be here."

"Yes, you do," Kirk said. The accord Kirk had reached with the Domain commander allowed the prisoner to remain in Federation custody—*protective* custody, McCoy mentally amended—for the remainder of their joint operations. However, it also permitted the Domain physician to attend to her and to be present during any formal questioning. "And we're not trying to keep any secrets from you—we'll have a comm link open, and you can listen from here."

Before Deeshal could protest, McCoy told him, "Listen, what do you think'll happen if we wake her, and one of the first things she sees is a Goeg in a Defense Corps uniform?"

"Yes, but . . ." Deeshal began to protest, but then stopped as his eyes flicked to the side and he apparently caught a glimpse of Chapel giving him an entreating look. "Very well. Perhaps it is best that the patient not be agitated any more than necessary."

"Thank you, Doctor," Kirk said, as he activated the comm unit on the wall and set it up to receive only.

And thank you, Christine, McCoy mouthed to his nurse before turning to follow after the captain into the private recovery room. The patient lay sleeping peacefully, the monitor above her head showing all vital signs in the middle green range. As a precaution, restraining straps had been fastened across her chest and her ankles. Her green skin was still slightly dry, though from what McCoy had learned about the amphibianoid race, that should reverse itself once her injuries were fully healed.

Kirk activated the comm unit by the bed, and then turned to the doctor. "Ready, Bones?"

"As ready as I'll get," McCoy said with a shrug. He pulled a hypospray loaded with the species-appropriate stimulant and pressed it to the patient's shoulder.

As soon as he pulled the device away, the Abesian rocked her head to the side and moaned softly. Her large, bulbous eyes opened slowly as she gradually came to consciousness. She stared blankly for several seconds, only gradually coming to the realization that she was not dreaming, and the two figures looming over her were of no species she'd ever seen before. She tried to jump off the biobed.

"Calm down, easy," McCoy said as the bands holding her in place were pulled taut. "We're not going to hurt you. You're safe. I promise."

The woman stopped thrashing, but was far from convinced she was safe. "Who are you? Where am I?"

The captain took a step closer and said, "My name is James Kirk, and this is Leonard McCoy.

You're aboard the *Starship Enterprise* from the United Federation of Planets."

"The . . . what?" Her head whipped back and forth from one to the other. "What are you?"

"Our species is called human," Kirk told her. "We're from a planet called Earth, over one hundred light-years from here."

Understanding crossed her face then. "You're from the supervessel."

"Supervessel?" Kirk asked.

"A gigantic white superstructure, with a large disk protruding from its bow," she said, "joined to a Class III starvessel."

Kirk nodded. "Yes. You're aboard that ship now."

McCoy noticed the woman's heart rate and respiration start to climb. "Where are the others with me?" she asked. "What have you done with them?"

Kirk lowered his head and told her, "I'm afraid they're both dead."

A look of pure hatred twisted her features. "You *pyurbs*," she spat at them.

"I am sorry."

The woman's head snapped to McCoy, and he continued, "We tried, but they were very badly injured, and we just weren't familiar enough with the Urpires to do anything to save either of them."

The woman considered McCoy, her eyes wide and suspicious. "But you know they were Urpires," she noted. "What do you know of the Urpires?"

"Almost nothing," McCoy admitted. "Your friends were the first we've ever actually encountered."

The woman considered McCoy a moment longer, then said, "Then I hope Erhokor forgives you." She then looked back to Kirk. "What do you plan to do with me, then?"

Instead of answering her, Kirk asked, "What is your name?"

The woman scowled at the evasion, but answered, "You can call me Ghalif."

"And you are a member of the Taarpi, Ghalif?"

"You seem to know a lot for someone from a hundred light-years away," Ghalif said, sneering. "How many Taarpi have you encountered?"

Kirk leaned in over the top of the biobed, making sure Ghalif received the full force of his glare as he told her, "Well, there were the ones who attacked my ship."

"Jim," McCoy said softly, as he noticed the woman's vital signs spiking again.

But Ghalif showed Kirk none of the anxiety her autonomic systems said she was feeling. "You allied yourself with the Goeg," she said defiantly. "We're entitled to defend ourselves."

"We only allied ourselves with them after your unprovoked attack on us in the Nystrom system," Kirk said, ignoring McCoy's caution.

"What were you doing in that system in the first place, if not helping the Goeg hunt our people down?" Ghalif asked.

"We're explorers," Kirk told her. "We were investigating the energy-absorbing crystals filling that system, and they were used as weapons against us."

"Explorers," Ghalif scoffed. "Why should I believe you're any more trustworthy than your Goeg friends?"

"How about the fact that you're here getting medical care, and not sitting in a Domain holding cell right now?" Kirk asked her. "Because I'm the only thing keeping you from facing charges for the deaths of over a hundred civilians on that transport vessel."

"Oh, the Goeg will blame us for that, no matter what," she said, the bravado gone from her attitude. "If I'm not the one jailed and beaten, it'll be someone else."

Kirk considered the shift in the woman's demeanor, and then lowered his face closer to hers. "Tell me what happened," he said. "If you weren't directly responsible for what your ship did to the transport, I will do whatever I can to ensure that you're treated—"

Ghalif started laughing. "You really are from the other end of the galaxy, if you think that's going to matter."

Kirk looked to McCoy, and they exchanged confused looks. "Why do you say that?" Kirk said, looking back to the Abesian.

She had stopped laughing, and simply shook her head instead. "If the Urpires were alive, maybe I'd be believed . . . but probably not."

"What are we supposed to believe?" Kirk asked.

Ghalif lifted her head and looked directly at Kirk. "It wasn't the Taarpi who destroyed that vessel; it was the Goeg. They murdered their own people, to discredit us."

McCoy entered sickbay deep in the night shift. Unable to sleep, he had decided to check on Ghalif and get a head start on some reports he'd been putting off. As he headed into his office, McCoy raised the lighting control to half-power. Caught in the shadows of his converted lab, someone was standing over his patient's bed. Not daring to call for security, McCoy grabbed the skull that stood on his shelf and headed to the lab where the Abesian woman was sleeping.

"Doctor, if you are trying to sneak up behind me, I suggest that you practice the skill," came the Vulcan's even tone.

"You and those damn ears," McCoy whispered, outraged. "Spock, what the hell are you doing in here?"

"Studying a Taarpi."

"You know, even for you, this is unusual." McCoy checked the readings; assured that his patient was progressing, the doctor turned and headed back into his office.

"Out with it," McCoy ordered.

"Doctor?" the Vulcan asked as he stepped into McCoy's office.

"You're here in the middle of the night, checking on a patient. Something that you could have done from your quarters."

McCoy sat in his desk chair and waited. With any other member of the crew, he would have placed his arm around the person, offering whatever comfort he could to get the troubled soul to open up. But McCoy knew that Vulcans did not like being touched. Spock prided himself on his self-reliance. No matter how much he wanted to speak, McCoy had to bite his tongue and wait. Proving how anxious he was, the Vulcan paced in front of the desk. Spock must have noticed McCoy's patient silence and realized what he was doing; the pacing stopped.

"I have served as Captain Kirk's first officer since he took command of the *Enterprise*. In those years, I have come to understand what you humans call his 'command style.' I have been able to anticipate his needs. This has not been"—for a moment Spock regarded McCoy—"easy." When the doctor did not rise to the bait, Spock continued. "But now I find his actions uncharacteristically subdued."

"He's not himself," McCoy offered.

Spock raised an eyebrow and considered the doctor's evaluation. "No, he is not."

"Spock, I haven't seen it."

"Doctor, I have." The Vulcan again regarded McCoy.

"Are you saying that he's unfit for command?"

"No," the Vulcan quickly countered. "I am concerned about his emotional well-being."

McCoy whistled low. "Damn. You're asking for my help."

"No, Doctor. I am asking you to help the captain." Spock headed out of the office, adding just before the doors closed on him, "Because I cannot help him."

Two hours before he would have reported to the bridge, the buzzer sounded outside Captain Kirk's quarters. Wondering what new calamity awaited him, he threw a uniform shirt on and unlocked the cabin door.

"'Bout time." McCoy stepped into his quarters. He was carrying a food tray with a covered dish, an urn, and two cups. Not standing on ceremony, the doctor shoved several books to the side of the desk, put the tray down, and ordered, "Eat."

Stunned, Kirk looked at the doctor, who had sat down in the guest chair and was pouring himself a cup of coffee out of the carafe. There were days when he wondered what he had been thinking when he offered this irascible Georgian, who had little respect for the dignity of the ship's captain, the position of chief medical officer. The coffee smelled good, better than the usual out of the mess. Knowing he was defeated, Kirk sat down. Taking the cover off the plate, he was surprised to see a stack of pancakes and sausages.

McCoy reached over and filled the second cup with coffee. "Kona. I've been hoarding them. Ground them myself. I've been checking your diet reports. You haven't been eating. Found that aside from throwing his captain, Lieutenant D'Abruzzo knows how to make buckwheat flapjacks."

"Bones."

"I can make it an order."

Not wanting to waste the extraordinary coffee, Kirk sipped some. "You know that the only thing I hate more than Spock managing me is when you try it."

"Me? I'm making sure that the captain is fit for command. You have to eat—just doing my duty as the *Enterprise*'s chief medical officer."

"Bones," Kirk warned.

"You know I thought that Scotty would need constant supervision once 'his bairns' were surrendered to another's control. I know that you—"

"Doctor McCoy, you are overstepping—"

"No, Jim, I'm not and you know it. Damn, I thought that Vulcan was a hard-headed mule. You've had to surrender control of your command to another man. The *Enterprise* is out of your control."

"Damn it, Bones!" Kirk slammed his hand down on his desk. "I don't need you shrinking me! *Enterprise* was disabled, so far out that it could have been months—hell, years—before we could get help. I made the best bargain that I could. I did what I could to save my crew, my ship—"

"And now you're wondering if you've made a bargain with the devil."

"I believe Laspas's intentions are good.

"Because you like him?" McCoy offered softly. "Hell, Jim, I know how lonely command is, and to share that burden with someone who truly understands what you are going through. . . . Jim, he's not you."

"What would you have me do, Doctor?"

"Admit how you feel, understand that you are not alone." McCoy took his cup and headed out of the cabin. "Eat," he ordered, "and trust your first officer."

Nine

Spock placed his thumbprint on the identity recorder the Rokean sentry at the *814*'s entry point held out to him. He started to pass, but the guard put up one large hand and pressed it against Spock's solar plexus. "Wait here, Starfleet," he growled.

Spock betrayed no surprise, nor any of the discomfort that came with the unwelcome physical contact. "To what purpose?" he asked.

"Code 6-59," the soldier answered. "All NCC-1701 personnel are to be accompanied by an escort while aboard this starvessel."

"Indeed." Spock took a half-step backward, showing that he was being compliant with the new regulation, and also breaking the low-level psionic link the Domain soldier had initiated. Even without the limited touch-telepathic connection, the distrust and antagonism the Rokean projected would be obvious to any non-Vulcan.

After only a few seconds' wait, another guard appeared from down the corridor and stepped right up beside Spock. The Goeg soldier stood at least

twenty centimeters taller than Spock, and looked
down with a silent, contemptuous glower. After several seconds of this ineffectual attempt at intimida-
tion, the guard jerked his chin, and Spock took that
as a cue to proceed about his business.

With his minder following on his heels, close
enough at times to feel his breath at the back of his
neck, Spock made his way to the auxiliary engineering section. As he'd determined earlier, Chief
N'Mi was there, along with two of her junior engineers, and the *Enterprise*'s Lieutenant Nakahara,
keeping a close eye on the cross-ship warp plasma
interchanges. All four turned at their arrival, N'Mi
treating both Spock and his guard with a look of
trepidation. "Mister Spock."

"Chief," Spock answered. "May I speak with
you?"

"You are speaking with me," she said curtly.

Spock inclined his head to acknowledge that lit-
eral truth, then said, "Then might we perhaps speak
someplace more private?"

"Mister Spock, I realize that things are run dif-
ferently on your Starfleet vessel," she said, her small
black eyes darting to the large Goeg behind him,
"but in the Domain Defense Corps, one does not
walk away from her duty post for a private conversation anytime she's asked."

Unmoved, Spock asked, "Would there be a more
opportune time?"

N'Mi shot a look at the guard again, and then told Spock, "Very well. My rest break is in thirty-four minutes. If you can wait, meet me at my cabin then."

Spock nodded his agreement to her, and then turned back down the corridor, the guard keeping pace behind him. When he reached the gangway that led back up to the airlock and security check, though, he started down instead.

"Where are you going?" the guard demanded. "You'll wait on NCC-1701."

Spock turned and gave the guard an arch glare. "Per the agreement Commander Laspas made with my captain, I am permitted, in my capacity as first officer, to observe and review all areas on this vessel which directly impact operations aboard the *Enterprise*. This would be a more efficient use of the intervening thirty-two and a half minutes, would you not agree?"

"For you, perhaps," the Goeg grumbled, and then remained silent as, for the next half hour, Spock walked a circuit of all the *814*'s primary and auxiliary engineering areas, with a brief stop at the command center. Second Commander Satrav gave Spock only the barest acknowledgment. Lieutenant Sulu watched him from his observational vantage spot in the rear, with his own Goeg guard close by his side. Per the new restrictions implemented by the Domain commander, only one Starfleet liaison officer was allowed in the command center at a time, and then solitude of the duty was apparently wearing on the helmsman. Spock offered a small nod of his head, calculating that it would be interpreted as a nonverbal message of support and encouragement. The smile Sulu returned indicated it was construed as intended.

At the end of the agreed-upon interval, Spock headed down to the *814*'s crew quarters deck, located N'Mi's cabin, and pressed the signaling button embedded in the doorframe. Seconds later, the door opened to reveal the engineering chief no longer in her uniform, but instead wrapped loosely in a brightly colored and highly translucent silken garment. "Hello, Mister Spock," she greeted him.

"Chief," Spock replied simply, choosing to assume that the obvious questions raised by the scenario presented to him here would be duly answered.

N'Mi stepped aside to allow Spock entry, and then looked to his escort. "Crewhand, I understand that 6-59 is in effect, but I hope you weren't planning to join us in here."

"No, Chief," the soldier said with a tone of distaste that Spock would have considered insubordinate from Starfleet personnel. He gave Spock one last disdainful glare before turning his back to him and taking up a defensive stance just outside the door.

The door slid closed, and the instant it did,

N'Mi's countenance turned from coquettish to furious. "What do you want?" she snarled at him, while grabbing a heavy robe from her bunk and covering herself. "Do you have any idea how much trouble you could be making for me by being here?"

"It was you who invited me," Spock answered.

"I mean aboard this vessel," she said. "If that guard knew the real reason I had invited you in here was to *talk* . . ." She trailed off, leaving the possible consequences of their surreptitious meeting unstated.

"Why did you agree to speak to me, then?" Spock asked.

The Liruq's anger dissipated. "Because I find you fascinating, Mister Spock. The fact that you have achieved what you have, in spite of your minority status and mixed parentage, but also the fact that while living among humans, you embrace your Vulcan nature."

"I assume that such is uncommon in Goeg society," Spock said. "I know you are the highest ranking Liruq in the Defense Corps; what is the highest rank achieved by any non-Goeg?"

"Why would you ask me something like that?" N'Mi asked, turning suspicious.

"Does the question bother you?" Spock asked.

The chief answered Spock's question indirectly by responding with one of her own. "Are you trying to get me to say something against the government

I am sworn to serve and protect?" N'Mi's cabin was quite small, as so much of the *814*'s interior was. Regardless, N'Mi had put as much distance between her and Spock as possible.

"I am trying to gain a better understanding of the relationship between the Goeg and the rest of the races within their Domain," Spock said, taking a cautious step closer. "I've learned recently that the Taarpi take their name from an animal native to the planet Lir, noted for being extremely fierce in the defense of its territory and its offspring. The name was initially used by a Liruq resistance group during the war against the Goeg thirty-four and a half years ago." Spock elected not to say what the source of that information was, and the Vulcan had resolved not to share the more inflammatory claims Ghalif had made to the captain.

"I see," N'Mi said flatly, arms crossed as she gave Spock a hard glare. "And because the Taarpi origi-nated on my homeworld, you assume I must feel some kind of kinship with them."

"Not at all," Spock said, noting the growing im-patience she was exhibiting toward him. "But as a native of that world, I imagine you are familiar with the sociopolitical conditions that led to the group's rise."

"I'm an engineer, not a sociologist."

"Chief," Spock said, "the *Enterprise* has been drawn inexorably into a conflict we do not fully understand, but need to. Your superiors have painted the Taarpi as mindless terrorists who hate irrationally and kill without motive. Such a simplistic characterization is at best unlikely."

"So you think, because I'm Liruq, I have this special insight you're looking for, is that it?" N'Mi asked, her dark eyes flashing. "Well, I am sorry to disappoint you, Mister Spock. I spent the early part of my life doing everything in my power to get away from Lir, and after that, to prove what I could do in spite of being born a Liruq." She stepped around Spock, moving to the cabin door as she told him, "I don't understand the Taarpi any better than you do, and what's more, I don't care to. Now, if there was nothing else you wanted . . ." She reached for the door control to excuse him.

"One more thing." When she gestured for him to go ahead, Spock said, "You expressed the opinion that, like me, you had accomplished all you have in spite of your race. I do not feel that is accurate."

N'Mi gave him a quizzical look, and Spock explained, "Rather, I would say that those accomplishments were in spite of others, who may have prejudicial attitudes toward you because of your race." Spock then reached out and put his hand on top of N'Mi's, pressing the control under her fingers and opening the door. "Thank you for inviting me in," he then told her, before turning back to the guard and, while ignoring his expression of disdain, led him back to the airlock.

When Chekov had first set foot in the *814*'s command center, he had been convinced that the purpose of the Defense Corps's coding system was to keep outsiders from knowing what they were doing. During those first few days, the ensign felt like he had no idea what was going on around him. He'd become used to the Domain crew considering him as some kind of slow-witted child for needing to think in complete sentences. But after two weeks of immersive learning, Chekov was surprised by how much he had absorbed. He had even begun to understand the logic behind the numbering system, and could hazard a pretty good guess at the meaning if a new one came up.

When he first heard the order for code 8-59, though, he was confused. Codes beginning with the prefix 8, he'd figured out, were related to communications—8-1 was "Scan subspace frequencies," code 8-2 was "Open hailing frequencies," and so on. Code 8-59 was unfamiliar, and as he scrolled down the list on his slate, he was surprised to learn that code 8-59 was "Communication silence."

Odd, Chekov thought, wondering what had prompted that order. He looked from his slate over to the Liruq officer at the communications station, on the far side of the command center. As he lifted his head, he saw a number of other crew members looking at him, or pretending not to be looking at him. Chekov froze, realizing that they were all expecting something to happen very shortly.

To him.

"Mister Chekov!" His head whipped around toward Commander Laspas, standing at the front of the room, the warp-streaked stars on the main screen seeming to radiate out from behind his head. "Code 10," the Goeg leader said, cueing a pair of guards to move from their posts and advance on him.

Chekov reached for his communicator, even as it now dawned on him why code 8-59 had been issued. Still, as he tried vainly to elude the soldiers, he flipped the grille open and shouted, "Chekov to *Enterprise*!" Unsurprisingly, the only response he got, before his wrist was grabbed and twisted back behind him, was static. "What is this about?" he demanded as both guards took hold of him and directed him roughly toward the command center exit. "You can't do this!"

Laspas turned his back and pointedly ignored Chekov. He was escorted out into the corridor and toward the gangway that led to the airlock. However, instead of heading up to the *Enterprise*, they started down, into the *814*'s lower levels.

Until now, Chekov had not been cooperative with his escorts, but he hadn't resisted his unexplained expulsion, either. Now, realizing that going along quietly could end badly for him, he let his step falter, trying to bring the soldiers off balance. As they reacted to the way his weight had shifted in their arms, he pulled with his shoulder, and broke the hold of the guard on his left-hand side. He twisted then, driving his right shoulder into his other captor's chest, while at the same time bringing his left leg up and driving his heel into the first soldier's knee.

Unfortunately, given the cramped confines of the Domain starvessel, the two-against-one odds, and the considerable size disparity between himself and his opponents, Chekov quickly found himself on the losing side of the fight. "So you want to play, do you, human?" the larger of the two said as he grabbed Chekov by the hair and threw him down the gangway, face-first into a bulkhead. Explosions of pain lit up the insides of his closed eyelids, and he tasted the blood that was flowing freely from both nostrils.

"Easy," the other one said, "you don't want to leave any marks."

The big one snorted dismissively. "If anyone asks, he tripped."

They half carried, half dragged Chekov the rest of the way down the gangway to the lowest deck, and then down the corridor to a small room, where they dropped him unceremoniously to the deck before leaving him and sealing the door behind them.

"Mister Chekov!" a voice said, and he looked up to see two other red-uniformed *Enterprise* officers, one moving across the deck to check on him, and the other lying in pain on the room's single narrow bunk, clutching her injured ankle. "Are you okay?"

Chekov looked up at the engineer, and then around at their small cell. "It doesn't look like it," he answered.

"Captain," Scotty reported from the bridge engineering station, "I've just lost contact with all of my engineering teams over on the *814*."

Kirk swiveled in his chair to face Scotty, and then Uhura to his left. "Lieutenant?"

Uhura's jaw tensed as she ran through a sequence of settings on her panel. "All communication with the *814* is being jammed, sir."

"Jammed? By what?"

"They're generating a low-level subspace inversion field," Uhura said as she continued to study and manipulate her board. "The hard connections are still intact, but personal communicators have been neutralized."

Kirk felt a ball of fury building up in his chest. He pushed himself up from his chair and ordered Uhura, "Get me Laspas."

"I've been trying, sir," Uhura answered. "They aren't responding."

"Can you punch through the jamming field?" he said, gripping the railing in front of her station.

Before she could answer, though, Arex interrupted, saying, "Captain, we're dropping out of warp."

Kirk spun back forward, and saw that the stars on the main viewscreen had indeed come to a standstill as the ship reentered relative space. At last estimate, they weren't due to reach Wezonvu for another fifteen hours. The hairs on the back of his neck were sticking out straight as he ordered, "Full sensor sweep. Location."

"Just under zero point nine light-years from our destination," Spock answered from the science station. "I am also detecting—"

"Sir!" Arex said, talking over the first officer. "Four ships approaching at full impulse, intercept course!"

"On the viewscreen, full magnification," Kirk nearly shouted. The starfield before him jumped, and the incoming vessels appeared, little more than slivers of reflected light at their current distance, but unmistakably growing closer.

Spock, peering into his hooded viewer, added, "The computer has identified them as Goeg Domain Defense Corps Short-Range Enforcement Vessels, Class I." Those, Kirk recalled from what he had studied of the Defense Corps over the past two weeks, were the Domain's top-of-the-line fighter ships. Highly agile and maneuverable, and each equipped with nearly three times as much firepower as any comparably sized Federation ship.

Spock then lifted his head away from his viewer and turned to face Kirk directly. "Their weapons systems are fully armed."

Ten

Through the blaring of the Red Alert klaxons, and the sound of his own pulse pounding madly in his ears, Kirk almost missed Uhura's report: "I've managed to get through the jamming field to the *814*, sir. No response."

Kirk silently vowed to make Laspas pay for this massive betrayal, assuming that they didn't get blown out of space before he had the chance. "Can we hail the incoming ships?"

"I haven't been able to get through the jamming," Uhura answered.

"Keep trying," he ordered, moving over to the engineering station. "Scotty," the captain said, leaning close and speaking in a low voice, "I think it may be time to burn some bridges."

"Aye," Scotty said, then added grimly, "The idea of abandoning our people over there, though . . ."

"I know," Kirk said. The fact that five men and two women were being held hostage was the only thing that gave him pause about breaking their connection to Laspas's ship. But there were 423 people aboard the *Enterprise.* "Transporters?" he asked Scotty.

The engineer shook his head. "Not as long as we're joined; it'd be the same as attempting intraship transport. I can have the transporter room ready to lock onto any human life signs once we're at least two hundred meters apart."

"Do it," Kirk said, even though he knew that they could be under attack by that point and might not have the time to drop shields and beam his crew back. The captain pushed those concerns aside and asked Scotty, "Are we ready to separate, then?"

"I've sealed off the umbilicals and the airlock, but we'll need another"—Scotty paused to check the chronometer on his console—"forty-seven seconds for the warp plasma levels to fall far enough. Otherwise we'll end up ripping sections of the hull off in the process."

Kirk nodded. "Carry on." The roster of those he was potentially leaving behind—Chekov, Cleveland, Farrell, Fradella, Kent, Nakahara, Strassman—ran through his mind. *I hope you all can forgive me.* "Mister Arex, ready shields and phasers."

"Standing ready, sir," the Triexian navigator acknowledged.

"Scotty?"

"Thirty seconds."

Kirk drew a breath, silently counting off the seconds. Just before he reached zero and gave Scotty his order, the tension on the bridge was broken by Uhura saying, "Captain, we're receiving an incoming hail from the lead fighter."

"Scotty, Arex, stand by," Kirk said, then stood up before saying to Uhura over his shoulder, "Open a channel, and put it on the main viewer."

The captain was not surprised to find himself looking at the image of another Goeg. This one did not wear the Domain Defense Corps uniform; instead, he wore a green suit of clothes, which Kirk took for Goeg civilian wear. His mane was a darker brown and cut shorter than that of Laspas and the rest of his crew. *"Captain James Kirk, I presume?"* he said, offering a small, tight smile.

"Yes, that's correct," Kirk answered. "And you are . . . ?"

"My name is Fallag, chargé d'affaires for the Goeg Domain," he introduced himself. *"On behalf of President Raltgel and the Executive Congress, allow me to welcome you to our space."*

"I appreciate the sentiment," Kirk told him, exchanging a quick look with Spock before continuing, "but sending out a squadron of Class I enforcers isn't exactly laying out the welcome mat."

Fallag's smile slipped then. *"The reason for this welcome, Captain Kirk, is due to the Abesian woman you are holding aboard your vessel. I know Laspas has tried to impress upon you the seriousness with which we take the Taarpi threat, but it was felt that we needed to ensure there were no additional 'miscommunications.'"*

Kirk felt the muscles in his jaw tense. "Commander Laspas and I have already come to an agreement, and he has given me his word that the *Enterprise* would be safely conducted to the repair base at Wezonvu."

"And it will be, unless you would like to carry through with the immediate decoupling you were preparing to initiate just now?" Fallag asked archly. Kirk gave nothing away, even as he heard Scotty mutter something indistinguishable behind him. *"Just be warned that if you do so,"* Fallag continued, *"it will be taken as a hostile act by the enforcer commanders."*

"Understood," Kirk said through his tightened jaw, then turned to Scotty. The engineer returned a look of resignation and started to reverse the steps that he had taken.

Fallag smiled again, saying, *"The enforcers will escort the* Enterprise *and Starvessel 814 for the remainder of your transit. And I should like to come aboard the* Enterprise, *with your permission."*

"Permission granted," Kirk said, idly wondering if refusing permission would make any difference.

"Excellent," Fallag said. *"I'm quite hopeful, Captain Kirk, that this meeting will mark the beginning of a long-lasting relationship between the Goeg Domain and the United Federation of Planets. Until then."* The envoy's transmission ended, and the four

alien ships appeared on the screen. They were in a diamond formation and close enough now that their deadly-looking profiles were clearly visible. The captain rubbed his hand across his eyes as a dull ache throbbed behind them.

"Sir?" Kirk turned to Lieutenant Uhura, who told him, "We're receiving a message from the *814*. All of our people are being put off their ship. They want us to unseal the airlock."

Scotty stepped up to the rail, saying, "We can still break away and try to make a fight of it, sir."

"No, Mister Scott," Kirk said. "Do we still have Domain engineering teams aboard?"

"Only for as long as it takes me to toss 'em out by the scruff of their necks," Scotty said.

Kirk nodded his approval. "Once you've done that, alert the shuttlebay to stand by. Mister Spock," he said, stepping out of the command well. "We have guests to greet."

"If there's one thing worse than a thug, it's a stupid thug," McCoy said as he held Chekov's chin and tilted it backward as he ran a tissue regenerator over his patient's nose. In addition to Chekov, four of the six engineers who had been held aboard the *814* had sustained minor injuries. In all cases, the official explanation from the *814* was that they had accidentally tripped and fallen. "If you're going to lie,"

McCoy grumbled as he repaired the damage done to the ensign's septum, "at least be creative about it."

"Yeah, that's the reason to be angry with them." The regenerator had the effect of making Chekov sound heavily congested when he spoke, though it did nothing to muffle the sarcastic undertone of his words.

McCoy deactivated his instrument and released his grip. "Sorry, Pavel. I don't mean to minimize what they did to you . . ."

"Don't worry about it, Doctor," Chekov said. "At least now they've shown their true colors, huh?"

"That they have," McCoy said, though that was of little consolation, as the *Enterprise* was still under the control of the Domain ship, and headed deeper into their territory. He lay the tissue regenerator aside, took up a hypospray, and gave Chekov a small dose of analgesic. "Go back to your cabin and get some rest. I've asked the captain to take you off duty for twenty-four hours."

"And I've approved that request." McCoy turned as Kirk, followed by Spock, entered sickbay. Both were in their full dress uniform, having just finished their initial meeting with the envoy from the Goeg Domain. From the look on the captain's face, that meeting hadn't gone well. Even Spock's expression seemed more dour than usual.

The captain exchanged a few words of sympathy and appreciation with Chekov before the ensign went on his way back to his cabin. Once the three of them were alone, McCoy asked, "How did things go with this Fallag fellow?"

Kirk answered by pressing his fingertips to the middle of his forehead and asking, "You wouldn't happen to have any of your special prescriptions on hand, would you, Bones?"

"That bad, huh?" McCoy said, and led them into his office. He unlocked a low cabinet where he kept his emergency supply of Kentucky bourbon, grabbing the bottle and three glasses. He set them on his desk and dispensed the amber elixir for the three of them. McCoy knew Spock would decline to drink, but his own upbringing wouldn't allow him not to make the offer.

True to form, Spock ignored his tumbler, while Kirk lifted his glass in a silent toast. The captain poured his drink back, then struggled to hide any reaction to the burning sensation as it ran down his throat. McCoy considered him with amusement as he savored his own drink, and once it looked as if the captain might be able to speak, he asked, "So, what happened?"

"Well," Kirk said, "the good news is, Mister Fallag has assured me that the *814* will be taking us the rest of the way to Wezonvu, that we will be able to have all our repair work completed there, and from there the *Enterprise* will be afforded free passage back to Federation space."

"Awful generous of them," McCoy cracked. "What's the bad news?"

Kirk stared into his drink and said, "The bad news is that, to get that guarantee, I had to threaten him with war."

McCoy had just brought his own glass to his lips, and nearly sloshed half of his bourbon down his front when he heard that. "Come again?"

"The captain is employing hyperbole," Spock interjected. "We merely informed Mister Fallag that if the *Enterprise* were to remain missing for an extended period of time, Starfleet Command would send out a ship looking for us." Spock paused before adding, "He may have given them the impression that Command would be sending several heavily armed *Constitution*-class vessels directly to Goega."

McCoy chortled. "All loaded with corbomite, I assume." McCoy appreciated how big a bluff that was. Given the nature of the *Enterprise*'s current mission, out beyond the farthest edge of Federation space and outside of reliable subspace radio contact, it could be a year before anyone back home came looking for them, if not longer.

"Not corbomite—photon torpedoes," Kirk told McCoy with a scowl, then explained, "Fallag was highly impressed by the way our weapons destroyed the Taarpi ship so easily and so completely. Turns out we owe Laspas's crew our thanks for providing such an effective demonstration of our strength for their leaders." Kirk tilted his head back and drained the rest of the bourbon in his glass in a single swallow.

The doctor winced at that bit of dark sarcasm from the captain. He hesitated and watched as Kirk refilled his glass before asking, "And what did he have to say about Ghalif?"

"Oh, he was exceedingly diplomatic and polite as we discussed the precepts of due process and the rights of the accused. He was even polite as he informed us that, under Domain law, Ghalif is entitled to absolutely none of it."

"Well, then, we won't be turning her over to them . . . right?" McCoy asked, even though he knew how tenuous their position was.

Kirk sighed. "Fallag agreed to an extradition hearing," he said, "though it's fairly obvious that he's looking at it as little more than a supervised interrogation, and that having us surrender her is a foregone conclusion."

"Jim—"

Spock cut the doctor off. "Mister Fallag was very clear that Ghalif's surrender was not negotiable. Even if there was an extradition treaty in effect between the Federation and the Domain, they would only need to demonstrate probable cause in order to have her remanded to their custody. Despite her claims of innocence, her presence on the vessel that destroyed the transport would satisfy that requirement."

"We don't have a treaty with them," McCoy snapped back at Spock, "nor would we sign one with a government that didn't believe in due process, or in decent treatment of their prisoners." McCoy turned back to Kirk. "You saw Chekov. I just had four other patients, all of whom became 'very clumsy,' all at the very same time that the *814* cut communications. What do you imagine they're going to do once they get their hands on Ghalif?"

Kirk slammed his glass down on the desk. "Doctor, I watched the summary execution of the rest of her people. I assure you that I have no illusions about what they may have in store for her."

After a moment of stunned silence in the office, Kirk slid his glass away and pressed the heels of both hands against his eyelids. The captain dropped his hands and looked up again. "I'm sorry, Bones."

"Don't worry about it," McCoy said softly. "I know you have your back against the wall." As helpless as he felt, the doctor knew that Jim was experiencing the same feeling for all of his crew.

As he reached for the bottle to refill his glass, McCoy heard his name, and turned to see Joe D'Abruzzo standing in the office doorway, back in his red security uniform. "Excuse me, sirs."

"Lieutenant," Kirk said, brightening. "It's good to see you on your feet and back to work."

"Thank you, sir," he said, returning the captain's smile.

"How's that arm doing?" McCoy asked. "That's not the reason you're here, I hope."

"It's . . . okay," he said, rotating his left shoulder and betraying only the slightest hint of discomfort. "I may not be able to throw you so easily anymore, Captain," he said, "but all things considered, I'm doing fine."

"Good to hear," McCoy said, then asked, "To what do we owe this visit?"

D'Abruzzo answered by stepping to one side, allowing another man to move into the doorway. "I'm afraid that I imposed upon Joe's good nature for this favor," Doctor Deeshal told the group.

"What in blazes?" McCoy growled as he pushed his chair back and jumped to his feet. "What do you think you're doing back on this ship?"

"Yes, I'd like to know that, too," Kirk added, looking irately from the Goeg to D'Abruzzo.

"Please, Captain, if you would hear me out, before ordering the lieutenant to throw me off your ship," Deeshal pleaded. "I've uncovered some information that I think you'll want to have." He paused, waiting for Kirk to decide whether he was going to listen or have him ejected forcibly.

"What sort of information?" Kirk said at last.

"The kind of information," Deeshal answered, "that I don't think my government would ever want to get out."

Fallag had a most disconcerting tic, in that he tended to flick the tip of his tongue out after every sentence or so and lick his upper lip. Taken with the Goeg's morphological similarity to Terran lions, it created the impression in Kirk's mind of a very hungry predator eyeing his prey. He could only imagine how Ghalif felt, as she was escorted in by Doctor McCoy, being the direct object of his seemingly ravenous attention.

The doctor held her gingerly by the elbow as he led her to the chair set in the center of the briefing room. The captain knew that she was recovered from her injuries and that McCoy was playing up his role as caregiver. Kirk wasn't sure that was such a wise strategy; most predators had no compunctions about attacking the weak and wounded.

Once the Abesian woman was seated and McCoy had taken a position directly behind her, Kirk said, "Computer, begin recording."

The machine positioned to his right came to life and said, "*Recording.*"

Kirk then struck the bell set on the table before him and said, "This hearing, for the purpose of considering the extradition of Ghalif, is hereby commenced. Present are Fallag on behalf of the government of the Goeg Domain, and Doctor Leonard McCoy, as defendant's advocate." Fallag considered Kirk's formalities with amusement, languidly running the tip of his tongue across his teeth. "You may begin your questioning, Mister Fallag," Kirk said, suppressing the impulse to punch him.

The Goeg envoy stood up from his seat beside Kirk and casually paced around to the front of the briefing room table, keeping his dark-eyed glare steady on the detainee. "Tell us, Ghalif, when did you first join the Taarpi?"

"Objection," McCoy said. "You haven't asked her if she is a member of the Taarpi yet."

Fallag stared at McCoy, and then back at Kirk, who pointed out, "He's right; you didn't."

The Goeg shook his head slowly, then turned back to Ghalif. "Are you a member of the Taarpi?"

"I am," she answered, proudly.

"And now that we have established that," Fallag said, "when did you first join the Taarpi?"

"Nine years ago."

"And in those nine years," Fallag demanded, pushing in closer to her, "how many deaths have you been responsible for?"

If Ghalif was at all frightened or shaken, she showed no sign of it. "I've never counted."

"Let's start with the first one, then. When was that?" Fallag asked.

"Objection," McCoy interrupted. "This is turning into a fishing expedition."

"A what?" Fallag asked him.

"What he means," Kirk said, "is that you're not making any specific allegations."

The envoy's previous amusement with Federation legal niceties appeared to be coming to an end. All the same, he turned back to Ghalif and continued, "Then let's start with your most recent atrocity. Tell us about how you destroyed Civil Transport Class I/*043*."

McCoy quickly retorted, "It hasn't been established how the transport was destroyed."

"You need to say 'objection,' Doctor," Kirk reminded him.

"I figured it was assumed," McCoy said with a shrug.

Fallag stalked over to the table, his patience finally at its end. "Captain Kirk, you told me that this hearing of yours was to establish the facts of this woman's actions, not the obfuscation of those facts."

"You're correct," Kirk told Fallag. "It is time we got to some facts here." He then turned to the Abesian at the center of everyone's attention and said, "Tell us about the other two people we recovered with you from the escape pod."

Ghalif shifted her eyes away from her questioner. "They're dead; what does it matter?"

"We're trying to establish facts," Kirk said. "It's

my understanding that there are no Urpires in the Taarpi. Why were they on your ship, and in your escape pod with you?"

"If I told you, you wouldn't believe me," Ghalif said.

Kirk looked sideways at Fallag, knowing that he would certainly mistrust anything she had to say, but hoping he might still be open to other evidence. "When we reached the wreckage of the transport and scanned it for survivors, only one of the one hundred twenty-eight bodies found was Urpire, even though there were three Urpires listed on the passenger manifest."

Fallag spun around, an almost comical look of shock on his face. "What?"

Kirk nodded, and slid the data slate he had in front of him to the other man. Fallag quickly reviewed the list displayed, and then snapped his head back toward Ghalif. "So you kidnapped them, and destroyed the transport to cover your tracks."

McCoy rolled his eyes. "Of course, because something like that draws so little attention."

"Why Urpires, though?" Kirk asked, the question directed as much to Fallag as to Ghalif. "The Urpires are neutral; the Taarpi have no dispute with them. Why them? Who were they?"

"Captain . . ." Ghalif began, betraying her apprehension for the first time. She knew exactly who they were, and she didn't want that information to come out here. Kirk thought he understood why, but it would do no good to let that knowledge die with her.

"Who were they?" Fallag demanded, momentarily forgetting the prisoner.

"According to the passenger list, they were just ordinary citizens of the Goeg Domain," Kirk said. Taking the slate from Fallag's hand, he then called up a new file. "But after checking a little further, it turned out that all three of the Urpires were traveling under assumed names. Genetic identifications were run on the two we recovered from the lifepod, and they showed that both were in fact officials with the Urpires' planetary government."

"Members of the Urpire Curia?" Fallag gaped. "Traveling secretly on a civilian transport?" Kirk held the slate out to him, and he immediately snatched it away and studied the file. The captain hoped the revelation would distract him from asking how Starfleet had tapped into the Domain's genetic identification database. Doctor Deeshal had shown extraordinary bravery bringing his findings to them, and he wanted to provide him cover.

With the thought of keeping Fallag off balance, Kirk pressed on. "There was one other thing we discovered. We compared our findings at the transport site against the passenger and crew manifests. It seems there was one additional Abesian passenger who also was traveling under a false identification, and was unaccounted for among the wreckage."

Fallag looked from Kirk to Ghalif, then back to Kirk again, genuinely confused. Ghalif—probably as much of an alias as the one she had used to book passage on the transport— appeared to be annoyed with Kirk for both discovering and then revealing all he had. "The Curia secretly reached out to the Taarpi several weeks ago and asked for a meeting," she began. "The Urpires are not blind to the injustices the Goeg Domain has perpetrated against their subject worlds. They're beginning to realize that they can't just stand idly by and allow Goeg despotism to—"

"This hearing is over," Fallag announced, tossing the data slate onto the table. "I'm not going to stand here and listen to the lunatic conspiracy theories of a murderous criminal."

"Oh," McCoy said, sounding disappointed, "but we didn't even get to the extra Goeg body yet."

In spite of himself, Fallag took the bait. "What?"

"There was one more Goeg body in the wreckage than was listed on the manifest," Kirk confirmed, tapping a finger on the slate. "There's no way of knowing who he or she was, of course . . ."

"His name was Neefrem," Ghalif volunteered, as Kirk had hoped she might. "He was from Corps Intelligence. He tracked me onto that transport, sabotaged the ship trying to stop our meeting, and—"

Fallag lunged across the briefing room, putting his muzzle within centimeters of the Abesian's face before either Kirk or McCoy could stop him. "You will be quiet now," he growled deep in his throat, then pulled away before McCoy could physically force him to do so. "This woman will be remanded to my custody as soon as we reach Wezonvu," he pronounced. Fallag marched out of the room, where one of the *Enterprise* security guards waited to escort him back to his ship in the shuttlebay.

"Now I know what you meant about him," McCoy told Kirk, before getting down on one knee beside the Abesian. "Are you all right?"

"Yes, fine," Ghalif said, then looked to Kirk. "I don't know what you thought you were going to accomplish. I could have told you he would never believe any of it."

"I hoped he would," Kirk admitted, moving out from behind the table toward her. "But I couldn't turn you over to them while keeping what I knew to myself. I'm sorry that it doesn't seem to have changed anything."

"Don't blame yourself," Ghalif told him. "Once a Goeg makes up his mind, a herd of wild *gaat*s won't make him change it."

"Now what?" McCoy asked Kirk.

It was Ghalif who answered. "Now, I wait until we reach Wezonvu, and I'll go with Fallag."

McCoy shook his head vehemently. "No. We can

protect you," he said, and looked to Kirk to back up that promise. The captain said nothing, unwilling to admit how few options he had.

"Who will protect you and your crippled ship if you do? No, even if you could face off against the whole Goeg Domain, I couldn't hide here on your ship like a coward. To do so would be an insult to everyone who has fought and sacrificed for the cause," Ghalif said.

Kirk could think of nothing to say to her. "Bones, do you want to escort her back to sickbay?"

McCoy looked to be on the verge of snapping off an impertinent answer, but instead bit his tongue, took his patient by the arm, and led her out of the room. Once they were gone, Kirk dropped into the chair Ghalif had just abandoned and sat there for several minutes more, alone with his thoughts and his guilt.

Eleven

Once the conjoined vessels dropped out of warp on the outskirts of the Wezonvu system, the engineering crew began the process of making the *Enterprise* an independent ship again. In the ship's labyrinthine lower levels, teams were working hard at the disassociation of the two drive systems, dismantling plasma transfer conduits and control systems. As Scott walked his inspection circuit, checking up on the progress being made, he reflected that what had been built in a cooperative effort by mixed teams a fortnight ago was being torn apart by Starfleet crew alone. Outside the ship, Chief N'Mi's crew took sole responsibility for physically detaching the two vessels from each other. As glad as he would be once the *Enterprise* was its own ship again, Scott couldn't help but feel a small twinge of regret for the way things were ending.

He returned to the main engineering control room and checked the master situation board, which had been reconfigured to monitor the workings of their jury-rigged dual system. Almost all of the indicator lights now glowed green, for those systems that had been fully transferred back to *Enterprise*, or had gone dark, for those that were now defunct. Once there was only one connection left, a voice came over the engineering intercom. *"Mister Scott,"* Chief N'Mi said, *"would you meet me at the connecting airlock for our final disengagement?"*

"Certainly, lass," Scotty said after only a momentary pause. He and his counterpart had had only the most perfunctory of exchanges since the engagement in the Nalaing system; Scotty was unsure why she had specifically asked for one last face-to-face before the two ships went their separate ways. But he took the turbolift down to the ship's lowest level, and there found the Liruq woman waiting inside the access tunnel, standing on the rungs at the midpoint between its two ends. "Chief," he said. "Is everything all set on your end?"

"Yes, Commander Scott, thank you for asking." Scotty cringed at the sarcastic undertone of her voice. She no doubt knew how close the *Enterprise* had come to forcibly separating the two ships, which would have done significant damage to her ship. But then N'Mi took a more conciliatory tone, saying, "It was quite a feat we pulled off together, making this journey. You and your people should take pride in the accomplishment."

Scotty gave her a grateful smile. "Thank ye, Chief. The same should be said for you and yours, especially since it was you who dreamed up this mad scheme in the first place."

"My people have a custom when guests take their leave," she said then, reaching into a pouch at her uniform belt and withdrawing a gray data card, "of presenting gifts for the journey ahead."

"Oh," Scotty said in surprise, and then silently scolded himself for not giving the woman enough credit to think she'd be willing to extend an olive branch as they parted company. He climbed down the rungs on the opposite side of the connecting tunnel, stopping directly across from her. "Well, that's awfully nice of you," he said as he accepted the offering and turned it over in his fingers, checking for any hint of what might have been encoded on it. N'Mi started on her way back down to the *814*, and Scotty called down, "I'm sorry I don't have anything to give in return."

"Don't be," she told him as her feet hit the deck below. "You people have already given us quite a bit." She placed her hand on the panel by the airlock hatch and said, "I wish you and your 'old girl' well," before the heavy door slid into place.

Scotty stared down curiously at the sealed panel, and then considered the data card in his hand. It wasn't until the warning lights began to flash above him, alerting him that the explosive bolts holding the connecting tunnel in place had been armed, that he scrambled back up into the *Enterprise* and sealed the other end of the tunnel.

"Decoupling complete, Captain," Scotty's voice reported over the comm, as on the main viewscreen, the bridge crew watched the *814* drop away from their keel. A sense of relief and liberty rippled through the bridge as they were at last under their own control again.

"And good riddance," Chekov added as the other ship slipped away. His physical injuries were completely healed, but Kirk knew the ensign had not recovered from his experience with the Domain.

"We are not free of them yet, Mister Chekov," Spock reminded him as he swiveled in his seat away from his station. "*814* is matching our course and speed, seven hundred meters off our stern." Laspas's ship would shadow the *Enterprise* for the rest of the way to the repair facility, and then put in for minor repairs and crew transfers.

"And let's not forget our friend, Fallag," Kirk added. The government envoy was aboard his ship in the hangar bay, waiting for the transfer of the Abesian prisoner to his custody that, per their agreement, was to take place once the *Enterprise* and the *814* had separated.

Lieutenant M'Ress turned in her seat at

communications and said, "Captain, Mister Fallag is hailing from his vessel. He wants to know—"

"Yes, Lieutenant, yes," Kirk sighed. "Let him know I will be there shortly," he said as he stood up and headed for the turbolift.

All the way down to sickbay, the captain tried to convince himself that he wasn't throwing Ghalif to the wolves because it was the most expedient course of action. Kirk reminded himself that, even if he were in a position to offer political asylum, she had already preemptively rejected the idea. With all the evidence Deeshal had brought them, there was still the very real possibility that it was Ghalif, and not Neefrem, who was responsible for sabotaging the transport.

The turbolift came to a halt, and when he entered sickbay, Kirk was surprised to find Doctor Deeshal there. Kirk looked questioningly from the Goeg to McCoy. The smile Bones gave him only raised more questions in the captain's mind. "Doctor Deeshal," Kirk said, turning back to him. "When did you come aboard?"

"Right after the ships decoupled," Deeshal answered. "I have to say, the more I experience your transporter, the more unsettling I find it. Being taken apart atom by atom and then projected through empty space . . ." he said, and shivered as he trailed off.

"Preaching to the choir here," McCoy said.

"Why are you here?" Kirk asked.

"I'm curious about that myself." Nurse Chapel stood in the doorway, leading Ghalif into the office. She stared at Deeshal, while the Abesian, dressed in an unadorned duty jumpsuit, considered the Goeg with an air of resignation.

Deeshal turned to Chapel, telling her, "Because the prisoner will still require someone to look after her. I've decided to take on that responsibility." He shrugged slightly, adding, "I felt it was my duty as a physician." A wide smile spread slowly across Chapel's face.

"That's a noble gesture, Doctor, but what happens when your ship leaves?" Kirk asked.

"It's not my ship anymore," Deeshal said with a shake of his head. "I requested that my assignment be suspended so I could do this."

Surprised, Kirk asked, "Laspas approved this? You told him about . . . ?"

"I didn't tell him everything," Deeshal admitted, dropping his voice again. "He's a lifelong Defense Corps man; he wouldn't have reacted to the things I discovered any better than Fallag did. But Commander Laspas and I have known each other for years, and he respects my judgment, even when he disagrees with it."

McCoy nodded and told Deeshal, "I think that shows some pretty good judgment on his part."

"Thank you, Leonard," Deeshal said, and then turned to Kirk. "I know you probably think pretty poorly of the Goeg people, Captain. Perhaps with good reason."

"I try not to judge entire people on the basis of a few," Kirk assured Deeshal. The doctor had definitely proven himself to be a perfect example for not making such sweeping judgments.

The doctor nodded in gratitude. "You should know that it wasn't easy for Laspas to call for support. He regrets the breakdown of the relationship you two had formed."

"Yes," Kirk sighed. "So do I."

Before Kirk could reflect too long on that revelation, the intraship whistled for attention. "Sickbay," McCoy said as he opened the channel.

M'Ress's voice answered. *"Mister Fallag has signaled again."*

Kirk moved to the wall-mounted comm unit. "Acknowledged, Lieutenant. Tell Fallag that his passengers will be there shortly," he said, putting an emphasis on the plural, and grinning to himself as he switched the unit off.

"I suppose we shouldn't keep him waiting," Ghalif said. She looked to Kirk and McCoy and said, "Thank you for trying to help." Her eyes flicked briefly Deeshal's way, but she couldn't quite bring herself to make eye contact with the Goeg.

"Yes," Deeshal added, nodding to both men before turning to Chapel. "And thank you, Christine . . . thank you, for everything."

Chapel moved over to where he stood, wrapped her arms around him in a hug, and placed a small kiss on the side of his face. "And thank you, Deeshal."

Under the power of its own impulse engines, the *Enterprise* entered orbit of the planet Wezonvu and approached its large repair facility. It consisted of cross-hatched latticework curved into a circular cylinder, with five smaller cylindrical slips positioned at regular intervals around its outer circumference. Spock had been impressed when he had reviewed the repair base's specifications: the facility was largely automated, utilizing robotic drones to perform almost all of the extravehicular repair work.

"*NCC-1701, code 2-32, negative twenty-one,*" the voice of the base's traffic controller ordered over the open comm channel.

"Copy, negative twenty-one," Sulu answered back unhesitatingly, and reduced their forward velocity by the proper percentage. Spock sat in the captain's chair, calmly observing their approach, while at the same time noting that the *814* had broken off and was now proceeding to one of the smaller docking slots.

As the docking procedure continued, Spock heard the rear turbolift doors hiss open, and turned to determine who had arrived. "Lieutenant Uhura," he said, "you're not due back on duty for another thirteen hours, eighteen minutes."

"I know, sir," she said, turning to him. "I came up here with this." She held up a plain gray data card. "Chief N'Mi gave it to Mister Scott just before we uncoupled from the *814*."

"What is it?" Spock asked, curious.

"Gifts," Uhura said, showing him a wide beaming smile. "Letters and other documents from the *814*'s belowdecks crew, to the friends they had made on the *Enterprise*." Spock heard a barely discernible epithet muttered by Ensign Chekov, but opted to ignore it. "Lieutenant Fexil sent several recordings of her mother's musical performances," Uhura said, as she turned back to M'Ress and handed the card to her. "I believe I also saw a file in there with your name, too, Mister Spock,"

"Yes, there is," the Caitian officer confirmed as she scanned the data card and the names indicated on the files. "Would you like it sent to your station, Commander?"

"Please do, Lieutenant," Spock said, standing and moving over to the science station. He found the transferred file and opened it on the monitor before him. It was a photographic image, showing Chief N'Mi with a young child seated on her knee. Judging from her appearance, the image had been taken approximately ten years earlier. The child, though he shared the characteristically prominent incisor teeth and high eyes of the Liruq race, also posed a prominently extended muzzle and a wispy gray-haired mane encircling his face. There was also linked to the picture a short piece of text: *"Spock: This is my son N'Lar. You are one of very few people I could ever let know about him. He will never reach high rank in the Defense Corps, but I do hope he can grow to be as confident in himself and his nature as you are."*

Spock considered the small half-Goeg child, and the life he must have lived within the Domain. Even having experienced the prejudices and animosity of others while growing up due to his mixed heritage, Spock still doubted that he could fully realize what this young boy would experience.

"Thirty seconds to full stop," Sulu announced from the helm, pulling Spock's full focus back to the present.

The Vulcan closed the file and returned to the captain's chair, sparing just a moment to reflect on how fortunate he was.

A swarm of robotic drones covered the *Enterprise*'s starboard pylon like picnic ants on a dropped piece of cake. Scott watched in quiet fascination through the panoramic transparent port that formed the front half of the repair slip's observational car. Gleaming metallic disks, each just over a meter in diameter, examined every square nanometer of the support structure's duranium skin. The globe-shaped compartment was one of four that could be maneuvered along the massive lattice-like frame that now encircled the *Enterprise*. From the car's control chair, where he was now seated, Scotty could monitor the activities of each one of a thousand small robots on a small screen to the right. To the left, another screen displayed a composite vid image meshed together from each of the robots' visual pickups. Scott watched as long, jagged, and highly magnified microfissures were targeted by the drones' re-fusion beams and repaired.

The engineer had to admit to being impressed by this facility, as he nudged the control lever at his right hand and guided the car down one of the vertical girders, down the length of the damaged pylon. Once below the level of the nacelles, he could see where the *814* was moored in a neighboring repair slot, just beyond the *Enterprise*. It appeared, from what he could see, that their repairs were close to finished and that they would soon be on their way. Now that their odyssey was nearly over, Scotty wished that he might have had more opportunity to interact with the Chief N'Mi, though with fewer complications. As part of her farewell gifts, she had included for him a Goeg technical journal. He'd only had the chance to skim through it briefly before they'd docked, but from what he had read, Scott imagined it would be his preferred bedside reading for most of their journey back home.

His thoughts were interrupted by the beeping of his communicator. He stopped the observation car and flipped the device open. "Scott here."

"Enterprise *here, Mister Scott,*" replied Uhura. "*Just checking in for your hourly progress report.*"

"Everything's continuing apace," Scotty told her, quickly referring to the screen to his right. "We're right on schedule, maybe a wee bit ahead."

"*How much is 'a wee bit'?*" she asked, and quickly added, "*Mister Spock is going to ask.*"

"Aye." Scotty looked at the numbers and decided they were on track to finishing about six hours ahead of his original estimate. "Tell him an hour to an hour and a half maybe," he told Uhura, secretly smiling to himself.

"*Sounds good,*" Uhura replied. "*Also, Sulu wanted me to mention to you, there seems to be some sort of intermittent glitch in the proximity detectors.*"

"What kind of glitch? Is he there?"

"*Right here, Scotty,*" Sulu answered. "*It was just a couple of times, from the sensor cluster at Deck Nine. An alarm was triggered, but shut off automatically in less than a second. Ensign Strassman ran a level-four diagnostic, but didn't find anything wrong.*"

"Odd. Tell her to go ahead and run a level three," Scotty said. "I'll see what I can see from out here." He pocketed the communicator and then pulled the control lever to the right, directing it onto an intersecting mag-track that would bring him toward the fore of the ship. There could be still undetected damage that had escaped the overwhelmed sensors. They would need a full inspection when they returned to a starbase, and no doubt a plethora of additional repairs. But there was no point in putting this one off now that it had been identified.

The car moved forward past the engineering hull and below the saucer section. Looking up through the transparency, Scott spotted one of the disk drones hovering near the sensor cluster in question. "Well, what are you doing out here?" he asked, and turned to the drone control panel. None of the drones he was working with had been deployed here.

He pulled out his communicator again. "Sulu, that proximity sensor you said had a glitch. What are you reading from it now?"

"*Right now, nothing, sir,*" Sulu said, as Scotty watched the small automaton hovering almost directly in front of the sensor cluster in question. "*Why?*"

Scotty heard a quiet alarm starting to sound at the back of his mind. "Are those sensors still modified to detect nystromite?"

"*No,*" Sulu said, "*we reset them after leaving the Nystrom system.*"

"Reset them for nystromite," Scott ordered. Then, realizing what else was in the vicinity of that sensor cluster, he said, "And send security to check on the lower torpedo launch tubes."

"*Sir?*"

"Now, Sulu." Scott set the communicator aside and hit the control button to deploy another drone from the cache carried by the observation car, and manually targeted it to intercept the rogue. It didn't detect the other drone until Scotty finished keying the nystromite detection protocol into its sensor programming. Then it was able to detect not only the drone, but the photon warhead it had smuggled out through the *Enterprise*'s opened torpedo launch tube.

"You rutting bastards," Scotty spat, forgetting for a moment that he still had an open comm channel to the bridge. "You seeing this now, Sulu?"

"*I see it!*" Sulu shouted excitedly. "*I've alerted security.*"

"*The board is still showing the torpedo tubes closed and sealed,*" Chekov chimed in.

"They must've installed a backdoor program when they took control of the launcher the first time." *I should have looked for that after the incident at the Nalaing system,* Scott berated himself, but he pushed such recriminations aside. Right now, he had to stop the other drone, and hope that doing so wouldn't detonate the photon warhead. If that happened this close to the hull . . .

Whoever was controlling the rogue drone detected Scott's on an intercept course. The torpedo-laden robot attempted to run away from the

Enterprise—toward the *814*. "Oh, no, you don't," Scotty growled as he pushed his drone to maximum acceleration. The gap between the two closed quickly, as the mass of the warhead kept the thief from gaining velocity. Then, unexpectedly, the other drone changed course and headed for the underside of the saucer. It then adjusted its course again to avoid collision, but at the same time, released its hold on the photon warhead, which continued on a straight line toward the hull.

"Oh, bloody hell," Scotty cursed. "*Enterprise*! Incoming!"

Seconds before striking, small shimmering circles of light rippled out and away from the tumbling weapon, as if it had just hit the surface of a lake. The deflectors arrested its momentum and brought it gently to a standstill, mere centimeters before contact.

"Well done, Sulu," Scotty said as he returned his focus to the fleeing drone. With new determination, he rammed his own drone into the little thief, causing a brilliant explosion of sparks. Scotty engaged the manipulating servos and made sure the propulsion systems of the captured drone were well and truly disabled. He executed a maneuver to bring it around back toward the ship. "*Enterprise*, prepare the shuttlebay," he said as he programmed his drone to bring the damaged one in. The engineer took hold of the car's control lever to bring it back around to the hard docking connection to the ship. The rest of the repairs would wait.

"Because you had them."

Captain Kirk stared agog at Fallag, who in turn looked down haughtily at him from the viewscreen. "I beg your pardon?" He had just accused the Domain envoy of illegally violating his ship and stealing three of their photon torpedo warheads, and Fallag had reacted as if the concept of "sovereign territory" was completely irrelevant to him.

"You have these photon torpedoes," Fallag said, *"these advanced, dangerous weapons, more powerful by an order of magnitude than our own most formidable defenses. Did you think the Goeg Domain could simply sit back and let a rival power have a monopoly on such dangerous, destructive devices?"*

"So you view the Federation as a potential enemy now?" Kirk asked.

"Is that even in question, given your support of the Taarpi?" Fallag countered. *"Not to mention your theft and falsification of Domain data records."*

Kirk was tempted to ask how Fallag could simultaneously accuse him of taking data from the *814* and questioning the veracity of that data, but resolved not to be sidetracked. "And that gives you the right to engage in this sort of espionage?"

"We're entitled to defend ourselves, our people,

in any way necessary. Now your Starfleet will think twice before launching any sort of incursion—"

Kirk turned away from the screen and signaled to Uhura to cut the other man off in mid-screed. At the same moment, Scotty stepped off the turbolift, carrying a data slate and looking deeply troubled. "Sir, I tapped into the memory of our little Artful Dodger," he said. "Just as you thought: the other two photon warheads it pilfered from us were brought straight to the *814*."

"Where's the *814* now?" Kirk barked, no longer willing or able to contain his outrage. Just hours before, he was beginning to think that perhaps he could understand and excuse Laspas's actions, and then this.

After consulting his computer, Spock answered, "We recorded them leaving their repair slip and exiting the system six-point-three minutes ago."

Immediately after we realized what they were up to, Kirk thought, disgusted. "Heading?"

"The Nalaing system," Spock said.

"Mister Scott," Kirk said, spinning back to the engineer, "your last report said our repairs were ahead of schedule. Are they far enough along that we could have warp drive?"

"Sir," Scott said, deep lines furrowing his brow, "the damaged pylon is still far from one hundred percent—"

"That's not what I asked," Kirk shot back.

Scotty looked dismayed, but answered, "We can do warp four for a few hours, sir. But all it would take is one undetected subspace pocket, anything out of the ordinary that could knock our warp field—"

"Understood, Mister Scott," Kirk said, looking the chief engineer straight in the eye, silently reassuring him that he wasn't being needlessly reckless, and was as concerned about the ship as he was.

Scotty nodded, and sat at the engineering station. "Standing by to initiate an emergency separation from the repair dock," he said.

Kirk couldn't help but smile. "Always prepared, Scotty?"

Scott shrugged. "Aye. Compared to breaking away from a moving ship, this is a walk in the park."

"Let's hope so. Scotty, cast off."

The entire ship vibrated around them, and Kirk could hear the straining of the mooring clamps resonating through the hull. "*Warning,*" sounded the base's automated system through the comm, "*shut down all drive systems immediately.*"

"Turn that thing off, Uhura," Kirk ordered, and moments after the voice subsided, so did the resistance applied to the outside of the ship.

"We're clear of the station," Sulu reported.

"Then set course for Nalaing," Kirk ordered. "Best speed."

The captain hoped their best would be good enough.

Twelve

There had been a field of unusual subspace activity about four light-years out from Wezonvu, which Chekov had noted during the journey in. They hadn't been able to get detailed readings of its size or extent, but he made sure the *Enterprise*'s course back to Nalaing veered clear of the potential hazard, without adding an undue amount of transit time. Once they had passed its coordinates, and he felt the rest of their plotted course safe, he stood up from his station and moved to the side of Kirk's chair. "Captain," he said, straightening to full attention, "I hereby present myself for disciplinary action, sir."

Kirk raised one eyebrow as he looked at him. "Ensign?"

"Yes, sir," Chekov said. "I was on duty when the torpedoes were smuggled off the ship."

The captain considered him seriously for a long several seconds. "And you feel you were lax in your duties?"

"I regret that I was, sir."

"What, specifically, did you fail to do, Mister Chekov?"

"I did not anticipate the security breach while we were in hostile territory," he answered. "I did not ensure that our weapons were secure."

"I see," Kirk said, his left elbow on the arm of his chair, regarding the earnest young ensign. "You feel that you should have had guards stationed at the photon torpedo tubes, in case stealth drones were able to open them from the outside without tripping any alarms, sneak inside, and steal the warheads."

Slowly, it occurred to Chekov that the captain was gently mocking him. "Sir . . ."

"Resume your post, Mister Chekov," Kirk ordered him.

"Aye, aye, sir," Chekov said, and slid quickly back into his seat.

"Good," Kirk said. "Now that that's settled, how long until we intercept the *814*?"

Chekov referred to his console and answered, "One hour, sixteen minutes at current velocity."

"Sir," Spock said from his station, "by my calculations, the *814* will reach the Nalaing system in forty-six point eight minutes."

The captain opened the comm on the side of the command chair. "Bridge to engineering. How is that pylon holding up, Scotty?"

"*Still holding steady, sir*," Scotty answered, his voice tinged with relief, and a hint of disbelief.

"We're going to warp five," Kirk declared.

Both Chekov and Sulu pivoted in their seats as Kirk waited for a response from the engine room. Finally, Scotty said, *"That wasn't a question, was it, sir?"*

"It was not, Mister Scott," Kirk affirmed.

After another significant pause from the chief engineer, he said, *"I'll redirect as much extra power as I can to the structural integrity field. That should give us a little extra to work with."*

"Excellent, Scotty." The captain closed the channel, leaned forward on the edge of his chair, ordering, "Sulu, increase speed to warp five. Bring her up by increments of point-one."

They were able to push the *Enterprise* to warp four point seven, cutting significantly into the *814*'s lead. Though not quite enough. "The *814* has just dropped out of warp," Spock reported from his station, "and is now entering the Nalaing system."

"Time to intercept?" Kirk asked, sitting forward in his command chair, both hands balled into fists.

Sulu answered, "Four minutes, twelve seconds."

Kirk clenched his jaw, biting back the impulse to demand more. He had already pushed his overstressed starship to its limits, and then beyond. He had to discover what precisely Laspas was planning to do with his two stolen warheads. At this point, all he could do was hope four minutes would be enough time to stop him . . . and that the *Enterprise* would still be up to that task.

As the seconds on the astrogation console's chronometer rolled forward at a painfully slow pace, Kirk noticed McCoy had arrived on the bridge and was now standing unobtrusively in the alcove in front of the turbolift. He said nothing in reply to Kirk's questioning look, but just gave him a simple nod that said he was just there for whatever moral support his presence might offer.

"Captain." Uhura turned in her seat, pressing her receiver to her ear. "The *814* is broadcasting to the planet."

"On speaker," Kirk ordered.

Uhura complied, and Laspas's voice filled the bridge. *"Nalaing! This is the Goeg Domain Defense Corps Starvessel Class III/814. It has been long suspected that the leadership of the terrorist organization Taarpi has been given refuge and material support on your world. We now have evidence proving the native government of Nalaing has been knowingly sheltering these enemies. . . ."*

"Evidence they probably tortured out of that poor woman," McCoy said angrily.

Kirk was inclined to believe that, just as he was inclined to disbelieve whatever "evidence" Ghalif might have surrendered. "Hail them, Uhura," he said, as Laspas paused in his broadcast.

Uhura had already turned back and started manipulating her console. "Starvessel *814*, this is the *U.S.S. Enter—*" she said, before a loud crackling blast of static sounded over the comm. Uhura winced in pain as she quickly yanked the remote receiver out of her ear.

"What was that?" Kirk asked. "What happened?"

"That," Spock answered from the science station, "was the detonation of a photon weapon, in high orbit above Nalaing."

"This was a demonstration of the power that will be brought to bear should the native government refuse to surrender the Taarpi criminals," Laspas then continued, *"and those who have acted to shield them from justice, to us immediately."*

"Damn!" McCoy said. "Did he just threaten to use a photon torpedo on a populated planet?"

"Open a channel!" Kirk told Uhura, grabbing the back of her chair and leaning over her station. Once he saw that she had established a connection to the other ship, he shouted, "Laspas! Commander Laspas, this is James Kirk. Respond!"

"They are receiving, sir," Uhura told him after several seconds without a response.

Kirk leaned in even closer to the audio pickup on Uhura's console. "Laspas, hold your fire! You can't detonate a photon torpedo inside a planetary atmosphere! If you do, you will kill every living thing on that planet!"

Kirk and Uhura both watched the controls that would indicate a hail being received. After what seemed like an interminable pause, it finally illuminated. Uhura punched the control, and Kirk turned to the image of the *814* command center that now filled the main viewscreen. Laspas and Satrav stood front and center. Just behind Laspas, Kirk noticed Chief N'Mi looking on, her expression serious and agitated. "Laspas!" Kirk said, marching to the front of the bridge.

But the Goeg commander was pointedly not looking at the captain. Rather, he looked past him, toward the starboard side of the bridge. *"Mister Spock,"* he said, *"Chief N'Mi informs me that you Vulcans do not lie. Is this so?"*

Spock stood up from his seat and answered, "Yes, Commander."

"And what Kirk just said about using photon weapons on a planet's surface? Was that true?"

Spock looked almost as surprised to be called upon as the arbiter of scientific truth as Kirk felt. "Yes, it is," he told Laspas. "Unlike the strikes you have previously witnessed, against a relatively small ship in the vacuum of space, a photonic detonation inside the matter-rich environment of a planetary atmosphere would result in an uncontrolled matter/ antimatter chain reaction—"

"Of course he's going to support his superior's claims," Satrav interrupted. *"How can we believe that a man who says, 'I am not lying,' is not a liar?"*

"*Because he is saying the same thing I told—*"

"*Chief!*" Laspas snapped irritably at N'Mi. The Liruq engineer dropped her chin to her chest and fell silent, though from the way her jaw and neck muscles tensed, it was taking a significant effort on her part to keep her tongue still. Laspas, however, noticed none of this as he turned away from her and back to Kirk. "*Why tell us this now?*" he asked. "*This seems like the kind of information you should have shared when you offered these weapons to us.*"

Kirk was sure that the universal translator had suddenly malfunctioned, and turned, mouth agape, toward Uhura. "Those weapons were stolen off my ship," Kirk said as he turned back, making sure he spoke each individual word as clearly as possible. "They were never offered."

Then it was Laspas who looked to have been shocked by what he was hearing. But before he could say anything, Satrav snarled, "*This is outrageous! Now you regret the deal you struck with Fallag to ensure the repair of your ship, and so you make this accusation against us to try and save your Taarpi confederates!*"

Laspas looked from Kirk to his executive officer, the expression of shock on his face shifting as it slowly dawned on him that it hadn't been the Federation strangers who were lying to him. Before he could express his thoughts aloud, the voice of an unseen third party joined in.

"*Defense Corps Starvessel: this is highly unusual. Nalaingers have long been partners to our Domain allies, and have always done all, within reason, to cooperate with you. We would be willing, as always, to enter into negotiations to consider your grievances and—*"

"*Code 8-9!*" Satrav called out to his communications technician, and the voice of the Nalaing spokesperson was cut off midsentence. The second commander pointed then to another of the crew members arrayed behind him. "*Weapons! Standby code 3-1.*"

"*Bozhe moi,*" Chekov said. "There are seven billion people on that planet!"

"Commander Laspas," Kirk shouted, drawing the Goeg's attention back to him. "You remember the conversation we had after the first time you used our photon torpedoes against the Taarpi. Surely you must realize that I never would have agreed to just hand those weapons over."

"*How we got them is irrelevant,*" Satrav sneered at Kirk, and then turned to Laspas, meeting his look of disillusion and disappointment with defiance. "*We have the means to eradicate the Taarpi now.*"

"Along with all seven billion sentient beings on that planet," Kirk reminded him, "the vast majority of whom have absolutely nothing to do with the Taarpi! Laspas, whatever disputes we have, whatever the differences between us, I know what we share is the importance we place on what we do, the decisions we make. We agonize over our choices before we act, and long after. Think about what you're about to do, and about how you're going to live with it for the rest of your life."

Laspas stared at Kirk, his expression unreadable. Then he turned away, and called out to his crew, *"Weapons, counter code 3-1. Communications, code 8-11."*

The muscles all up and down Kirk's back and neck released their tension at once. Behind him, he thought he heard more than one sigh of relief. He turned to Uhura to confirm that code 8-11 was an order to reestablish communications with the Nalaingers on the planet.

"Commander Laspas, code 10!"

On hearing Satrav give the order relieving Laspas of duty, Kirk turned back to the viewer to see the second commander now holding a handheld weapon on his superior. *"Satrav,"* Laspas growled in disbelief, *"what do you think—"*

"You've let yourself be swayed by these . . . aliens," Satrav told him. *"I have no other choice. Code 10, Commander."*

Laspas clenched and unclenched his fist as he stared daggers at his mutinous executive officer. *"All this time we've served together, Satrav, I never would have thought you capable of something like this."*

"I cannot allow a compromised leader to continue

to lead. We have our orders, and we will carry them out."

As the confrontation played out on the viewscreen, Kirk felt the shift in the vibration of the deck under his feet and the telltale signals that the ship was dropping out of warp. He leaned over Sulu's station to take a quick look at the readout. They had finally reached the Nalaing system and were on approach to the planet at full impulse. "Sulu," he said in a rushed whisper, "once we reach orbit, put us between them and the planet, and raise shields." Sulu nodded quickly and initiated the maneuver.

But they were too late. "*Code 3-1,*" Satrav ordered his weapons officer.

"*Don't!*" said another voice, and when Kirk turned back to the viewer, he saw Chief N'Mi at the weapons station, grabbing the wrist of the Rokean stationed there. The weapons officer looked from her to the two opposing Goeg, at a complete loss as to what to do and whose orders to follow.

"*You are way out of line, Chief,*" Satrav told her, baring his teeth at her while at the same time keeping one eye—and his weapon—on Laspas. The commander continued to clench and unclench his hands, clearly frustrated by the powerlessness he was feeling.

"*You're holding a pistol on the vessel commander,*" she shot back fearlessly. "*I'm not the one who's out of line.*"

"*Keep your Liruq mouth shut,* pyurb, *unless you—*"

Suddenly, the communications link was severed, and the viewscreen switched to an image of the *814* above Nalaing, growing closer as Sulu brought them into defensive position. Kirk pivoted toward the communications officer. "Uhura, what happened?"

"I cut them off, sir." Before Kirk could ask why, she answered, saying, "I believe Laspas was trying to send us a message, the way he was flexing his fist. He was flashing three fingers, one finger, then a fist, same pattern repeated."

Kirk cast his mind back, and realized that, yes, he had noticed the variation in his hand movements. *3-1. The same code Satrav had issued to the weapons officer: launch weapons.* That couldn't have been what Laspas was trying to communicate, though. Why would he order the *Enterprise . . .* ?

"Sulu, are we in place yet?" Kirk asked.

The helmsman nodded as he manipulated the impulse drive controls on his board. "Now positioned directly below the *814,* sir," he confirmed.

Kirk turned to Chekov and ordered, "Target their main power generators and fire phasers."

Without hesitation, the ensign powered the phaser banks and announced, "Firing," as he launched a salvo against the *814.* On the viewer, phasers shot out from the *Enterprise* emitters and struck the Domain vessel amidships. A section of new hull plating—one of the hastily applied patches that covered one of the points where the vessel had been physically connected to the *Enterprise*—went spinning away, burning a bright streak in the planet's upper atmosphere.

"The *814* is returning fire," Spock reported, and in the same instant a small flash of light blinked from the *814*'s bow.

"Yes!" Kirk exclaimed, drawing curious looks from around the bridge. Their provocation had momentarily distracted the *814* from the nonthreatening planet below, and triggered an automatic retaliatory response with the weapon they had at the ready. "All hands, brace for impact," Kirk ordered, his eyes glued forward as the stolen photon warhead was returned to them.

The Domain missile flew in a spiraling pattern, no doubt to confuse any attempt at evasive maneuvers by its target. The *Enterprise* held steady, though, and took the full brunt of its impact and explosion on her forward shields. The deck rocked under Kirk's feet, and the bridge lights flickered briefly, but otherwise, the defensive systems had protected the ship from the worst of it, and more importantly, had protected the planet below. Kirk let out the breath he was only dimly aware that he'd been holding.

His relief, it turned out, was premature. "They're launching another volley!" Chekov shouted.

"Not more photon weapons?" Kirk asked. As focused as he had been on the two stolen warheads, he hadn't stopped to reason that, for a society on the technological level of the Goeg, it would have been reasonably simple, once they had the advanced weapon in their possession, to reverse engineer and manufacture their own.

"Negative," Spock answered. "They are armed with standard cobalt fusion warheads."

"Oh, what a relief," Bones cracked from where he stood in the back of the bridge.

"And we are no longer their primary target," Spock added.

Kirk saw Spock was right: the missile volley was spread in such a way that three of the four incoming weapons would miss the ship on their way down to the planet. "Phasers, Mister Chekov. Knock them down before they get past us." The lower-yield weapons would not do as much harm to the planet as the photon warheads would, but they could still obliterate major cities and trigger a nuclear winter— a slow planetary death as opposed to a quick one.

Phaser beams lanced out from the *Enterprise*. Chekov's expertise destroyed all three of the warheads intended for Nalaing. The fourth and last one, though, he could not target in time before it hit the ship's defensive screen and exploded. The force of the blast, though a fraction of a typical photonic detonation, was enough to knock out the closest shield emitter and trigger a string of failures throughout the ship's overtaxed systems. The bridge went dark, and Kirk felt the hold of artificial gravity momentarily slip before the emergency power kicked in and he could plant his feet back firmly on the deck. "Report," he called out as he took his seat again.

"Captain," Spock was the first to respond, "our shields are gone."

Kirk did not like the tone of finality he heard in his first officer's voice. "Gone?"

Spock nodded. "Our power generation and distribution systems had been stressed to their limits. The loss of the single shield generator was enough to effect a total subsystem failure." He paused, and then added, "We may need to withdraw, sir."

Kirk knew that was the logical course of action. They'd accomplished their objective of preventing the use of their photon weapons against Nalaing. If Satrav was still intent on bombarding the planet, they wouldn't be able to prevent it for very long without any defenses of their own. But could he in good conscience fall back and let that happen?

As the captain was weighing his choices, it occurred to him that the *814* had not fired any further salvos, either at Nalaing or the *Enterprise*. He watched the Domain ship hanging still against the backdrop of the galaxy, giving no sign of the hostile posture adopted only minutes earlier. The rest of the bridge crew also watched and waited in tense silence. "Spock," Kirk whispered, careful not to break the stillness that had fallen over the bridge, "what's going on over there?"

"Unknown, sir," Spock answered. "All their systems are operational. Our strike against them caused only minor damage, which cannot explain this current state of inactivity."

Kirk turned from his right to his left. "Uhura, hail them."

"Aye, sir," she answered, and then a moment later, "They're responding."

"On-screen," Kirk said, turning forward again.

The *814* command center reappeared on the forward viewscreen, though this time both Laspas and Satrav were absent, and N'Mi stood alone before the banks of operations stations. *"Hold your fire,* Enterprise. *We request a truce."*

"A truce," Kirk immediately agreed. "What's happened over there?"

"There was an attempted mutiny against Commander Laspas. It has been put down, but the commander was injured in the ensuing struggle," N'Mi told them.

"Seriously?" Kirk asked with genuine concern.

"I cannot say," the chief answered, also looking highly fretful. *"As I believe you're aware, our physician transferred off this vessel shortly after arriving at Wezonvu."*

Kirk pivoted in his chair. "Bones . . ."

"On my way," McCoy said over his shoulder, already stepping into the open turbolift car, headed for the transporter room.

Kirk turned back to N'Mi. "Doctor McCoy will be there shortly. What about Second Commander Satrav?"

"He has been placed under arrest," N'Mi said, betraying the slightest hint of a grin on her serious face. *"It would seem that he and several others on our crew had led the conspiracy to steal photon torpedoes from your ship while at Wezonvu, and falsified the Defense Corps orders to strike Nalaing. I assume you will want him transferred to your custody to face charges?"*

"That's not something we need to worry about just now," Kirk said. Another extradition battle was about the last thing he was looking forward to at the moment. "Am I to take it you are in command of the *814* now, Chief?"

"No," N'Mi said, as if bewildered by such an improbable assumption. *"The vessel is still Commander Laspas's. No non-Goeg has ever commanded a Defense Corps starvessel."*

"Yet," Spock said, stepping down into the command well and addressing the Liruq woman on the screen.

N'Mi answered Spock with a nod and just the slightest hint of a smile. "Yet."

Thirteen

The civilian spacedock and repair facility in orbit of Nalaing was much smaller and less technologically advanced than the one at Wezonvu. Designed to service small freighters and other commercial space vessels, it consisted of eight wharf-like platforms branching off at right angles from the main perpendicular habitat and support module. It was barely big enough to accommodate a Goeg Class III starvessel, and it was dwarfed by the *Enterprise*.

The Nalaingers insisted the Starfleet ship make port there, and further insisted on doing all they could to assist the crew that had saved their world. Being in no position to turn down the offer, Kirk had accepted. It took some creative navigation, but they were able to position the ship in such a way that the overtaxed starboard pylon was parallel to the longest platform, upside-down and at an angle relative to the station's orientation. Of course, it made no difference to anyone aboard the *Enterprise*, who enjoyed the same up and down provided by the ship's artificial gravity that they always did.

But looking out at his ship from one of the facility's observation decks, Captain Kirk was put in mind of a man being held by his ankle, dangling over the planet below.

Kirk chuckled at himself and shook his head as he turned away from the wide transparent port and toward the set of doors he heard sliding open on the opposite end of the room. Two individuals entered, the first one a Nalainger he had met previously, named Altoing. The short, compactly built humanoid had the blue complexion of an Andorian, without the antennae, and a tuft of wiry violet hair sprouting up from the top of his head. He wore the brightly colored vestments of his office, which the universal translator had given as undersecretary of interplanetary affairs, though the captain had quickly ascertained in their prior conversations that he was no mere midlevel bureaucrat. The person accompanying the undersecretary was a tall insectoid, and though he had never seen a living one before now, Kirk recognized this alien as an Urpire.

"Salutations, Captain James T. Kirk," Altoing said in his surprisingly sonorous voice. "I would like to introduce you to Kikkikizz, Emissary of the Urpire Curia."

"It is a pleasure to meet you, James T. Kirk," Kikkikizz said, swaying back and forth in what Kirk assumed was their analog to a nod or a hand wave. "On behalf of the Curia, I wish to express our appreciation for your efforts to save the lives of our fellows."

"Thank you, Emissary," Kirk said. "I only wish those efforts had been more successful."

"As do we all. But we cannot change what has come before, only what is yet to come," the emissary said. "We also thank you for helping uncover the truth of what happened to Civil Transport *043*."

"I assume, by your presence here, Emissary, that Ghalif's claims about negotiations between the Taarpi and the Urpire Curia were correct?" Kirk asked, and found himself wondering what had ultimately become of the Abesian woman.

"Yes. 'Taarpi' is a name that's been adopted by a vast number of people across the Goeg Domain," Kikkikizz explained. "It is a code word for those who oppose the imperialist rule of the Goeg."

"Most express that opposition in words only, or through nonviolent acts of defiance," Altoing added. "There is a minority who use violence and bloodshed. It's that minority who are the most visible, though, and who give the Domain justification for going after any and all political dissidents."

"Ghalif and her group of Taarpi approached the Curia some time ago to request our help," Kikkikizz said. "The Urpires are isolationists, and we are dispassionate about the outside universe. We've watched the growing conflict within the Domain for many years, but we had resolved not to become involved. It was Ghalif who presented us with the argument that our neutrality was tacit approval of Goega's continued oppression, that the only way to end the continuing cycle of attacks and reprisals— which has been so detrimental to all our worlds— was to end our silence."

"Your government is not coming out in support of the Taarpi?" Kirk asked.

"We support peace and stability," the Urpire said.

"The Domain will never share that goal," Altoing opined. "Nalaing has been under constant harassment from the Goeg for decades, because we refuse to take the same draconian measures they do against suspected Taarpi members. It's only because we are a vital center for commerce that they haven't threatened to bombard the planet before now."

"But now something's changed," Kirk observed.

A scratchy, sigh-like noise emitted from the Urpire's mouth. "I fear that change is their discovery of the Curia's willingness to become involved. In trying to bring peace, we've instead instigated the murder of a hundred innocents on transport *043*, and nearly brought about the destruction of this planet." Despite how physiologically different the Urpire was, and his near lack of facial expression, it was exceedingly clear how saddened he was, and how guilty he felt.

Altoing added, "If they're truly willing to go to

such lengths, then it will take far more than words from the Curia to sway them. If only the Federation weren't so distant . . ."

Altoing trailed off, but Kirk could see where he was going with his thought: *If only the Federation weren't so distant, they could bring their huge starships and powerful weapons to bear against their oppressors.*

"Imposing a change like the one you're hoping for from the outside is rarely the best option," Kirk opined. "Lasting change always comes from within. You shouldn't give up so easily. I see parallels between the Goeg Domain and other empires throughout galactic history, which have eventually been forced to bend to the will of their peoples. Change can be slow, but I believe it will eventually come."

"I wish I could believe you, Kirk," Altoing said, scowling. "But with respect, you don't know the Goeg. They are arrogant, stubborn, utterly convinced of their place above all other races. I don't see them ever willingly loosening their grip on the rest of us."

"I've noticed those tendencies, too," Kirk admitted. "But, just like the Taarpi, the Goeg are not a homogeneous race, but a collection of individuals. I have to believe that not all of them are as intransigent as you think they are." Kirk turned to Kikkikizz, adding, "Emissary, a wise woman from my planet once said, 'Never doubt that a small group of thoughtful, committed citizens can change the world. Indeed, it is the only thing that ever has.'"

"An interesting observation," Kikkikizz said, sounding thoughtful. "Though I would counter that much would depend on the character of those citizens, and their ability to bring increasing numbers into their group."

"A fair point," Kirk said, nodding. "So the key is to cultivate such individuals."

"Are you speaking of someone in particular?" the Emissary asked.

Kirk risked a small smile. "In fact, I am."

Laspas threw an arm over his face as the door to his sleeping quarters opened, guarding his eyes from the harsh light being cast into the gloomy interior. "For Erhokor's love, go away, McCoy!" he snarled.

"It's not McCoy," Kirk said as he stepped into the commander's private sanctum. The door closed behind him, and he kept his back pressed against it, waiting for his eyes to adjust to the depressing darkness.

Another annoyed growl rumbled from Laspas. "What do *you* want?" he asked, rolling away from Kirk.

"Bones has been rough on you, has he?" Kirk asked.

Laspas sighed, and turned onto his back again, but kept his eyes on the overhead rather than facing his visitor. "He means well," he allowed grudgingly, "but he has shown little of the deference due to the commander of a starvessel."

Kirk chuckled softly and said, "Don't take it personally; he's the exact same way with me." As his eyes adjusted, Kirk noticed the disarray in the room. Clothing had been dropped carelessly about the deck, a half-eaten tray of food sat on the bedside table. No self-respecting Starfleet officer would allow his quarters to fall into such a state, and Kirk was sure the same held for a Defense Corps commander. Kirk took a step closer to the bed and asked, "How are you feeling?"

"I'm healing," Laspas said, declining to elaborate further.

Kirk knew what it felt like to be incapacitated and rendered unable to carry out his duties. He couldn't imagine, though, having those injuries come at the hand of a long-trusted fellow officer. "I wanted to tell you that it took courage for you to do what you did. Not only to act on your own convictions and defy your orders, but to trust me enough to send that covert message."

"So, I have the admiration of the man I invited to attack my ship. At last, I can sleep easy again," Laspas said, his upper lip curled in a self-effacing sneer. "I suppose I should also acknowledge your restraint in firing only once at my vessel," he added after a brief hesitation, finally turning his head Kirk's way.

"You're welcome." Kirk pulled a low stool to the side of the bed and sat, bringing himself closer to eye level with Laspas. "What happens to Satrav now?" he asked.

Laspas turned away again and closed his eyes. "The question you should be asking is, what happens to me, once word of what happened here gets back to Goega?" he said. "I'm the one who defied orders, after all. Worse, I was aided by N'Mi in defying those orders."

"Worse, because she's not Goeg?" Kirk asked.

Laspas nodded. "The best to be hoped for is that, once I return home and am brought before a Corps tribunal, I will be stripped of my rank and given a nice cool stockade cell."

"And what of Chief N'Mi, and the other crew members who backed you?" Kirk asked.

Laspas shook his head wordlessly, and then turned to look at Kirk again. "Just between you and me, James? I hope that, once I've recovered and resumed full command, she deserts."

"What? You hope she deserts?" Kirk asked.

"I hope she has enough sense to save her own hide," Laspas elaborated. "She's a brilliant and dedicated engineer, and she does not deserve to be executed for the mistake of coming to my defense."

Kirk was appalled to hear that the Liruq woman could face the death penalty for putting down a mutiny. "Do you really think that was a mistake?" he asked Laspas. "You don't think she should have supported you?"

Laspas shook his head in self-pity. "What I think hardly matters."

"Laspas," Kirk said, demanding the other man's attention. "Do you believe it was a mistake to refuse orders to commit genocide?"

"No," he answered. "The only mistake I made was being so credulous about how we got your warheads, and to believe you had so little integrity. Refusing to destroy an entire planet? No, I have no regrets about that."

"If you go back and fall on your sword, Laspas, what's to keep your superiors from attempting the same thing again?" Kirk asked. "If you allow yourself to be removed from command of this ship, and someone like Satrav is put in charge . . ."

"I'm hardly in a position to allow or disallow anything," Laspas said, shaking his head.

Kirk stood up from his stool, moved back to the door, and pressed the interior illumination control. Laspas roared in pain as the light struck his eyes, and Kirk raised his voice above the other man's to be heard. "You are still a decorated commander in the Domain Defense Corps," Kirk reminded Laspas as he peered through his slitted eyelids. "You still have your ship, and you still hold a position of power and respect, if you're willing to use it."

"Use it how? Against the Corps?" Laspas's eyes adjusted to the light, and when he could see Kirk's face again, realization hit him. "You're suggesting I become part of the Taarpi," he said.

"I'm suggesting you take a stand for your principles," Kirk told him. "I know that it's easy for me, an outsider, to stand here and tell you what to do. You've dedicated your life to the Domain and the Corps, just as I have to the Federation and Starfleet. I've never been put in the kind of position you're in now, and I can't honestly say what I would do if I were." Though Kirk had butted heads with the admiralty and various Federation officials in the past, he'd never been in a situation where he believed his superiors had evil intentions and needed to be actively opposed. The captain shuddered to think anything that even came close to the Domain scenario would be possible in the Federation. But Kirk wasn't naïve enough to believe the people who held power in the Federation were infallible.

"You just told me you had no regrets about defying your superiors and averting an atrocity," Kirk continued. "What you need to ask yourself now is, whatever you decide to do next, what kind of regrets *will* you have?"

Laspas said nothing, and turned away once

more. Realizing that there was nothing more he could add, Kirk turned to go. As he did, he noticed one of Laspas's father's books lying open, spine up, on the deck, as if it had been thrown across the cabin. Kirk picked it up and carefully unfolded the creased interior pages. "And if that fails," he said as he closed the book and placed it on the bedside table, "ask yourself what Kawhye would do."

Pavel Chekov watched dispassionately as the gold-colored ball rolled across the table, bounced off one of the stubby lighted posts positioned in a seemingly random pattern on the low-friction surface, and then drop through a hole into a pocket below. "That's two hundred credits you owe me," Sulu said with a wide, gloating smile.

"How did you get so good at this game so fast?" Chekov asked. Neither of them had even heard of dom-jot prior to coming aboard the Nalaing station, and now Sulu was hustling him as if he'd been playing the game for his entire life.

"I used to play a lot of billiards as a kid," Sulu said. "I think it's what first got me interested in physics."

"I've played billiards, too," Chekov said. "But this really isn't all that close." While the object of both games was to use a cue stick to sink the balls placed on the table, dom-jot also involved negotiating the obstacles arranged around the irregularly shaped table and activating the lights in random patterns controlled by the table's circuitry. As far as Chekov was concerned, it was all too complex for what should have been a simple diversionary pastime.

Sulu shrugged and started pulling the balls out from the channel underneath and placing them back on the tabletop. "Close enough so if you understand all the differences, you can make adjustments. Double or nothing again?"

"I think I'll just head back to the ship," Chekov said as he laid his cue on the table.

"Come on," Sulu cajoled. "I'll spot you two points this time."

Chekov shook his head. "I'll see you on the bridge next shift." The ensign hadn't been comfortable leaving the ship and coming aboard the station. After the security breach, he had been in a heightened state of concern—or paranoia, according to Sulu. It had taken several minutes of relentless cajoling from him before Chekov agreed to a short visit. All during their dinner and the drinks during their dom-jot match, his mind had been fixed on what was going on back on the ship, and whether Lieutenant Arex was keeping close enough tabs on any potential security violations.

Outside the recreation hall, Chekov stepped onto a moving walkway, which ran the full length of the station and would take him back to the dock where the *Enterprise* was now moored. The broad concourse he was carried along was lined on both sides by restaurants and shops, all doing a steady business, catering to a variety of unfamiliar aliens.

And one familiar one. Several meters ahead, walking down the center of the second walkway, which ran in the opposite direction across the station, Chekov spotted one of the big Rokean guards who had ejected him from the *814* command center. The ensign froze in place, even as he told himself that there was no reason to be worried—he wasn't coming for him.

Except he was. The other walkway riders gave the uniformed soldier a wide berth as he made a beeline for the Starfleet officer. Chekov tensed as the Rokean quickly closed the distance between them and then stepped over the low divide between the two conveyors without losing balance or showing any other sign of unsteadiness. "Mister Sulu," he said as they now stood face-to-face.

"It's Chekov," he corrected him, holding himself steady.

The guard shrugged, as if the distinction was unimportant, but then surprised Chekov by saying, "I hoped to find you here. I wanted to offer an apology to you."

"You do?" Chekov asked in disbelief.

"You humans are strange, but you're not as dangerous as Second Commander Satrav said you were. We should not have beaten you."

Chekov's hand subconsciously moved up to touch his nose, and he willed it to fall back to his side as he told the soldier, "Thank you. I appreciate that."

"And even though there was no one left alive on that transport," the Rokean continued, "it was good that you saw that it wasn't just an accident." From the darkening of his expression, Chekov guessed that word was getting out about the Domain's culpability for the loss of the transport. It had occurred to him earlier that, had he not found a reason for the *814* to divert from their original course, he could have spared himself a good deal of pain. Knowing his actions had helped to uncover an atrocity made him feel a little better about it.

The Rokean then gave Chekov a big, stubby-toothed smile, and squeezed both of his shoulders in his large hands. "You are a credit to your race, Chekov."

"Thank you." Chekov winced. "You too."

With the press of a single button, the low steady thrum of the giant matter/antimatter reactor was joined by two higher alternating notes, creating a steady rhythm that, judging from the smile Scotty wore as he turned from the situation console, was music to his ears. "Isn't that the most beautiful sound ye ever heard, sir?"

Kirk shared the engineer's smile. "Definitely among the top three," he agreed. The warp plasma relays had been restored and realigned, and the mellifluous sounds emitting from the engines confirmed this. "Anything else left outstanding, Scotty?"

"Only a few minor touch-up repairs," he answered. "Considering the fact that the Nalaingers have never seen anything like the *Enterprise* before, they did a hell of a job. There are some things only we can do, but nothing that should prove any trouble."

Kirk crossed his arms and tilted his head at the engineer. "If I'm hearing you right, Scotty . . . there's really no reason for us to head straight back to Starbase 43. Is that right?"

Scotty's smile slipped slightly, but he answered, "Aye." Then the engineer shrugged his shoulders and added, "She's spent enough time in dock; I suppose it's high time she got back to doing what she was meant to do."

Kirk gave the chief engineer a broad smile and clapped him on the shoulder. "Plan to get under way as soon as possible."

"Ready anytime you are, sir."

The captain headed to the closest turbolift, and minutes later, the doors opened onto the bridge. Stepping off, he saw the image on the main viewscreen of the repair station, along with the planet

Nalaing slowly rotating behind it. "Why, Mister Spock," Kirk said as he moved down into the command well, where his first officer was in conversation with Doctor McCoy. "I hadn't realized that hanging upside down from their repair dock bothered you as much as it did me."

Spock stood up from the command chair. "Even if I were capable of such a trivial emotional reaction, Captain," he said, "there would have been nothing to prompt it since we were never upside down."

"Funny," McCoy interjected, "once we were clear of the station, you wasted no time in giving the order to reorient the ship to match the station."

The first officer raised an eyebrow at him. "I was following standard procedure, Doctor."

McCoy scoffed, and Kirk watched for any slight reaction from Spock. When he decided none was forthcoming, he broke eye contact and settled into his chair. "Mister Chekov, we should still be within twenty light-years of the Frattare 85 quasar?" That stellar phenomenon had been their next mission objective.

"Eighteen point three, to be precise," Chekov answered. "Shall I lay in a course?"

Before Kirk could answer in the affirmative, Uhura interrupted. "Captain? I'm picking up a general hail from an incoming Domain vessel."

The captain went into full alert mode, and he noticed like reactions from Sulu and Chekov, seated at their stations in front of him. "Let's hear it, Lieutenant," he told Uhura.

"*Starvessel Class III/814, code 8-22 from Short-Range Enforcement Vessel Class I/7704. Codes 8-0, 7-87, and 7-89.*"

Kirk recognized the voice of Fallag, and the call number of the vessel that had been docked in their hangar bay days earlier, but beyond that, he understood none of the rest of the message. "Uhura?" he asked, turning to the communications officer.

"He's saying the *814* hasn't reported back," she translated, "and is asking for an explanation and status update."

Spock stepped up to his station and reviewed his readouts. "Long-range sensors are showing four enforcement vessels, including Fallag's ship, escorting a Goeg Domain Class I starvessel, approaching Nalaing at warp four. Estimated arrival in sixteen minutes, eleven seconds."

"A Class I," Kirk echoed. Those were the Goeg Domain Defense Corps's largest and most powerful ships, he recalled. That the Domain was sending one to check up on the *814* was not good news.

"Jim . . ." McCoy said, recognizing the conflict now playing across his friend's face. "We can't stay here. These people aren't our responsibility." Kirk knew he was right, of course, but the idea of leaving now . . .

Kirk's thoughts were interrupted by another,

familiar voice. *"This is Commander Laspas respond-ing. The orders which had been issued to this vessel were both illegal and immoral. This officer and his crew have declined to follow."*

Kirk wanted to cheer out loud. The 814 had broken orbit a day earlier, without any notice to the *Enterprise* or to the authorities on Nalaing. He had regretted not knowing what decision the com-mander had come to. He was heartened to know that decision now.

"Laspas, code 9-109," said a third unseen party.

"That was from the Class I vessel," Uhura said. "They just demanded Laspas's surrender."

"This officer and his crew also decline to face a tribunal run by those who issued the illegal and im-moral orders. This officer has evidence that his supe-riors have acted to intimidate our allies in the Urpire Curia, have violated the sovereign rights of an alien government, the United Federation of Planets—"

Fallag's voice cut in, trying to drown out Las-pas's. *"Code 9-109! Code 9-109!"*

But the Goeg commander, refusing to be cowed, raised his own voice. *"—and have committed nu-merous other crimes against citizens of the Goeg Do-main. This evidence is currently being transmitted."*

"Code 8-59!" Fallag shouted, and the transmis-sion from his ship cut off with an audible pop.

"Comm silence," Chekov interpreted, turning around in his seat and flashing an amused smile. "They're trying to shut him up."

Kirk nodded. "Afraid to hear the truth." He wondered if any of Laspas's data transmission had gotten through before the code 8-59 was issued.

That unvoiced question was answered moments later, when Spock reported, "It appears that the Class I starvessel has dropped out of warp, beyond this system."

"Engine problems?" Kirk inquired.

"Negative," Spock said, lifting his face from his viewer. "They've just stopped."

"I'll be damned," McCoy said. "He got through to them."

Kirk shared the doctor's incredulity. "Uhura, can you raise the *814*?" The lieutenant acknowledged affirmatively, and a moment later, Laspas appeared on the main viewscreen, no longer wearing his Corps uniform. Behind him, Kirk saw N'Mi pacing the foredeck of the command center, issuing orders. "Laspas, that was quite a speech you gave," Kirk told him. "It seems to have stopped your fellow starvessel commander dead in his tracks."

"*Yes, it would seem so,*" Laspas said, the corners of his mouth stretched as far back as they could go. "*Though I think they were probably more shocked by my refusal of the 9-109. That's the sort of thing that only happens in bad military fiction.*"

Kirk returned the Goeg's smile. "But it seems, at least, they are willing to listen to you."

"*Well, if they are,*" Laspas said, "*I'm willing to talk.*"

"*But if not,*" N'Mi interjected, moving forward to the commander's side, "*we should avoid letting Nalaing become a target.*"

"*Yes.*" Laspas nodded, and then turned to his crew and ordered, "*Standby code 2-43.*" He then turned back and said, "*I suspect our paths will not cross again, James.*"

"Never say never," Kirk told him. "I wish you luck."

Laspas dipped his head low and said, "*Thank you, my friend. Windracer out.*"

"Windracer?" McCoy repeated. "What's Windracer?"

Kirk looked to McCoy and told him, with a glint of amusement in his eye, "*Windracer,* Doctor, is a good name for a starship. Chekov," he then called to the navigator, "course laid in?"

"Laid in, sir," the ensign answered.

"Then let's be on our way."

The *Enterprise* broke free of the station, and the planet fell away behind them.

"Godspeed, Kawhye," Kirk offered quietly, as the *Enterprise* jumped to warp.

ACKNOWLEDGMENTS

My thanks go out to the following:

To the folks at Pocket Books and CBS for giving me the opportunity to tell this story.

To the fans who create invaluable online resources, particularly those behind Memory Alpha (http://en.memory-alpha.org/wiki/) and The Star Trek LCARS Blueprint Database (http://www .cygnus-x1.net/links/lcars/blueprints-main2.php).

To the numerous local coffee shops where I camped out over the course of writing this book, for use of the space and for free refills.

To A.M., D.B., and M.R., for their friendship and encouragements.

To fellow *Trek* authors and friends Kevin Dilmore, David R. George III, Robert Greenberger, David Mack, and Dayton Ward for their camaraderie, and especially to Scott Pearson, for allowing me to occasionally be a terrible person.

ABOUT THE AUTHOR

WILLIAM LEISNER began his professional writing career with three winning stories in the late, lamented *Star Trek: Strange New Worlds* competition. His *Star Trek: The Next Generation* novel *Losing the Peace* was chosen as one of the top media tie-in novels of 2009 by Unreality-SF.net and by SciFiChick.com. He has also written for the shared-world fantasy series *ReDeus*. His original fiction has appeared in *Lissette's Tales of Imagination* and the 2013 anthology *A Quiet Shelter There*. He is currently at work on a historical fantasy novel set in the American West, and maybe a few other ideas. A native of Rochester, New York, he currently lives in Minneapolis.